For Rae ♡
See you soon!
Anne

The Spanish Mask

Anne Cleeland

ARTEMIS
—PRESS—

Other Regency books by Anne Cleeland:

Tainted Angel

Daughter of the God-King

The Bengal Bridegift

The Barbary Mark

The True Pretender

A Death in Sheffield

Chapter 1

Elena watched the plume of smoke, rising black and ominous in the distance, and judged that it originated somewhere in the southern valley near the Convent—although it was difficult to see, through all the tall pine. *It seems I chose the wrong day to humor Maria Lucia*, she thought; *my luck*.

She stood with Eduardo on the balcony of the Castillo, a small fortress strategically situated on a hill overlooking the valley. Below them, she could hear the anxious murmuring of the servants who'd come out onto the terrace to observe the smoke. The faint sound of men's voices, shouting in alarm, could be heard drifting upward from the valley on the breeze, the words undistinguishable.

"Is it the French? Do the soldiers come again?" asked the boy in a thready voice. He was seven, and small for his age.

Absently, Elena replied, "I don't know, Tomás."

"Eduardo," he corrected apologetically.

She looked down at him and smiled. "Your pardon, Eduardo—shall we go out the back? *Rapido*, now."

Taking his hand, she led him quickly down the servants' stairs and then—after pausing to listen carefully—through the doors that led into the kitchen, where the servants should have been busy preparing the midday meal but which was instead deserted, the roast left hanging on the spit with its juices dripping onto the hearth.

As she pulled the small boy toward the scullery door, Elena whisked a large bread basket from the work table. "You must stay close beside me, Eduardo."

"Perhaps it is not the French; perhaps it is *El Halcon.*" The boy's hushed voice held a measure of hope as he hurried beside her.

"Perhaps." Elena paused on the back stoop, and made a rapid assessment. Several of the household guards were trotting through the side yard, slinging their weapons over their shoulders with a sense of grim urgency. Unfortunately, most of the guards had traveled to Madrid with the Castillo's Señor, hoping to gain assurances that the Castillo would remain under its current ownership. In Spain, nowadays, nothing was certain.

After thinking for a moment, Elena placed the basket on the ground, and loosened her black Postulant's habit, untying the strings in the back so that it billowed out over her slim figure. "You must hold onto the side of my skirts, Eduardo, so that no one sees that you are with me. We will go into the woods."

The boy nodded, his pinched face pale as he gripped the coarse fabric in his fists and matched his steps to hers.

Resting the basket on her hip, Elena moved purposefully across the courtyard at a steady pace, shifting the basket to shield the boy, depending upon which side someone approached.

No one impeded their progress—indeed, they invoked little curiosity, what with the dire events unfolding—and they slipped through the wrought iron gate at the back, past the herb gardens, and then into the woods that lined the hillside. Once within the shelter of the pines, she took the boy's hand, threading her way through the trees as they climbed up the hill. "Do you know these woods? Is there a good hiding place?"

"No," he panted. "I am not allowed to play here."

Elena paused to catch her breath, assessing the trees overhead with a practiced eye. "It is too sparse to hide in the branches—we will have to go to ground."

"There?" The boy pointed to a fallen trunk, rotting along the forest floor.

"Yes—very good." Dropping to her knees, she began to scoop out leaves and vegetation from beneath the decaying trunk. "Help me, Eduardo."

Hesitating, he knelt beside her and tentatively pawed at the earth under the trunk.

"It is a shame we do not have a weapon for you," she remarked, digging steadily.

He turned to stare at her. "*Qué?*"

Still digging apace, she glanced up at him. "You are the *caballero*. If the soldiers come, you must protect me from them."

Astonished, he continued to stare at her, but she did not return his regard and instead continued with her endeavors, reaching in up to her elbows to clear out the leaves beneath the fallen tree. After a moment, the boy rose, and stepped back. "I will find a stick."

"Good." She bent her head to peer into the cavity she was creating. "Something sharp."

After rummaging in the underbrush for a moment, he returned to her side, clutching a likely stick. Winding her skirts around her legs, Elena lay on the ground and wriggled into the narrow space beneath the trunk, her cheek pressed against the dirt. Shrill screams and crashing sounds drifted up from the grounds of the Castillo, just down the hill. "Come along."

Copying her movements, the small boy lay on his stomach, facing her, and wriggled under the trunk.

He then gasped and recoiled from the sight of a rabbit's carcass, rotting in the recesses of the lair, its eyes eaten out by maggots.

"I beg your pardon, Señor Conejo," Elena whispered in a solemn voice. "We stay only for a little while."

After a moment, Eduardo cautioned the dead beast, "You must stay quiet, Señor."

From her hiding place, Elena reached out to rake some of the displaced leaves back along the crevice between the ground and the trunk, so that their burrow was obscured, then faced the boy in the dimness with her chin resting on her hands. "We wait."

"*Si,*" the boy agreed as he clutched his stick, his knuckles showing white. "We wait."

Breathing in the scent of damp earth and decomposition, Elena gazed into the boy's soft eyes, and wondered how Maria Lucia and the other Sisters did. One would think the French would not harm the nuns, but one never knew in this war; the two allies had already turned on each other in the blink of an eye, so perhaps a shared religion meant little.

She and Maria Lucia were Postulants at the Convent, and the other girl had asked Elena to switch duties with her today so that she could arrange for a clandestine meeting with her latest beau. Normally, Elena stayed close to home and tended the Convent's orchards whilst Maria Lucia came to the Castillo to teach Eduardo his lessons, but the other girl had pleaded for the switch in assignments because the orchards provided a better opportunity to slip away unnoticed.

"Please, Elena," the girl had begged. "You must be tired of staying so close, day after day. Go up to the Castillo—the food is a hundred times better, and he is a sweet little boy."

"You are mad." Elena had shaken her head in amusement. "You will be caught, and sent away in disgrace."

"Fah; what would they do—send me home? You know they dare not. And in any event, my *bello* Roberto is worth any amount of disgrace."

Laughing, Elena had finally agreed; they were so similar in appearance that their black habits and white scarf headdresses made them interchangeable, and besides, no one would think the girls had been so bold as to flout their Abbess' directives.

And it had been indeed a welcome change—to venture out away from the Convent, to have a look around the beautiful Andalusian hills as she walked up the road to the Castillo, and to remember her country as it had been before the long and miserable war against Napoleon. But of all days for the enemy—or at least she assumed it was the enemy—to come storming into this obscure and war-weary village, it had to be this one. And in a twist of fate, Elena found herself responsible for the boy—the neglected ward of the local Señor, currently away from home. *I must decide what is to be done,* she thought, holding Eduardo's gaze and trying to convey calm reassurance. *I dare not return to the Castillo.*

The voices of men could be heard—close by, perhaps even as close as the base of the hillside. French—not that there had been much doubt. Elena met Eduardo's gaze, and placed a single finger to her lips. He nodded, and they lay—frozen—whilst the alarming sounds of frightened women and tromping boots could be heard faintly in the distance.

The breeze carried snatches of the soldiers' conversation to them, and it appeared they were discussing the situation—although it was difficult to make out any words, as Elena's French was nearly non-existent.

She judged from the tenor of the discussion that they were trying to decide if it was worth a search, or if it was a hopeless cause. Suddenly a Frenchman's voice shouted out in rudimentary Spanish, "*Princesa*, if you are here, you must come out—we will not hurt you."

Startled, Eduardo's gaze met hers, and she shook her head, frowning a warning at him. The voices were silent for a few moments, waiting for a response, and Elena was actually heartened; it seemed to her that the shouted message was relayed without any real conviction—*they think we are long gone,* she thought; *or at least, I hope they do.*

After another discussion, the soldiers could be heard thrashing about in the underbrush, coming closer and closer to their location. Eduardo's hand crept over to take hers as they waited, straining to listen in the tense atmosphere. Fortunately, the footsteps never came very close, and in a short time, the voices could be heard retreating back to the grounds of the Castillo.

Elena whispered, "We will wait; they may be trying to trick us—to draw us out."

Her companion nodded, and she could see that his hand no longer clutched his stick as tightly. "They think you are a princess," he whispered in wonder.

"They are fools," she pronounced, and the boy pressed his mouth into his hand to stifle a giggle.

Now that the immediate danger seemed to have passed, she rested her cheek on the cool dirt, and took a deep breath. What to do? Could she return to the Convent?

It seemed ill-advised—although perhaps she and the boy could circle around to the back where the orchards were, and reconnoiter.

If nothing else, she could tie some apples in her apron so as to have something to take with them to eat—she was hungry, not having had a chance to sample the Castillo's fine food before the crisis. If it seemed too dangerous to show themselves, then they would have to make their way on foot toward the east—no easy thing, with such a small boy, but there was no question of leaving him behind.

After she'd gauged that enough time had passed to safely leave their hiding place, they wriggled out, brushing off the dirt, and stepping carefully so as to avoid breaking any branches. A group of horses were tethered in the stable yard of the Castillo, and after observing them, Elena circled in a wide arc along the tree line to the bottom of the hill, avoiding the road.

They walked in silence for a while amongst the trees, Elena grateful the route was downhill. Whenever they spotted another traveler, they retreated into the trees until any potential danger had passed, so in this manner the journey was often interrupted.

"Should we go hide in one of the houses?" asked Eduardo with a hint of hope.

Elena felt a twinge of pity for the boy; he had not complained, even though he was undoubtedly tired and hungry—she certainly was. "No—we should not trust anyone. Instead, we will go to find help."

Thankfully the boy didn't ask for further elaboration, but only nodded, as he used his stick to prod the ground as they walked along. "Are you a princess?"

"No," she replied with a small smile. "I think they were having a joke."

At long last, they made a cautious approach to the

back orchards of the Convent just as dusk began to fall. Elena could see no lights shining from the windows—not a good sign, but at least the building was still standing. The place was eerily silent—the Holy Sisters must have left at the first alarm, which was a relief. It also meant she could steal a few apples without fear of detection. "Keep watch," she whispered, and then quickly began pulling apples from low-hanging branches, so as to deposit them into her tied-up apron. "Here." She turned to toss one at her companion, so that he could eat whilst he waited.

"*Gracias*," said a man's voice.

Whirling, she confronted the man who stood a few feet behind her—not a soldier, but she didn't stay to discover more; dropping her apron, she picked up her skirts and ran toward the outbuildings, away from Eduardo.

She didn't get far; an arm came around her waist and lifted her easily off her feet whilst a broad hand covered her mouth. "Quiet—they wait for you within," he whispered into her ear.

Elena reconsidered her impulse to bite down on his hand as he swiftly retreated back into the orchard, carrying her without comment.

Whilst she debated whether she should start struggling in earnest, the decision was taken out of her hands.

"Put her down." Eduardo confronted the man, his stick held before him like a sword, even though it trembled a bit.

"I surrender," her captor said immediately, and set Elena down, although she noted that he still hung onto the fabric at the back of her habit.

In a constrained voice, Elena explained, "This—this gentleman says it is a trap, Eduardo—that the soldiers wait for us within." *Ingles*, she thought in surprise—he was English, although he spoke Spanish. It did not bode well.

"You should go home," suggested the man to the boy, not unkindly.

Elena protested, "No—no, he has no one to go to; he comes with me."

Ducking his chin for a moment, the man considered. "Very well, Your Excellency."

Eduardo and Elena stared at him. "I believe," Elena offered, "that there had been some sort of mistake."

"We shall see," the man replied easily, and indicated they were to retreat into the woods.

Chapter 2

With cautious optimism, Elena trudged behind their escort as he threaded his way through the trees and over the crest of the hill, their pathway illuminated by the new-risen moon. He had not identified himself, and for some perverse reason, she refused to ask him who he was, or what he intended. *He cannot mean to harm us*, she assured herself; after all, he'd swung Eduardo onto his back and now carried him, which didn't seem the act of a ruthless brigand.

For his part, Eduardo was tired, his head bobbing with the movement of the man's steps. As she walked behind them, Elena noted that the man was tall and broad-shouldered, although the light was too dim to make out his features. His dark hair and beard were long and unkempt; indeed, he was dark enough to pass for a Spaniard—until he spoke, of course. She wondered why an Englishman would be here in the Sierra Moreno Mountains, searching her out so as to thwart French soldiers who were also searching her out, and didn't much like the conclusions she drew. Although to the good, he'd saved them from the French ambush, which was very much appreciated—unless his own intentions were worse, of course.

Whilst she pondered these events, the man raised his head and issued a soft whistle. Elena looked warily around them, expecting a response, but there was none; instead, they continued their hike until they came to a small clearing.

The Englishman deposited the now-sleeping Eduardo onto a pile of pine needles, and, stifling a sigh of relief, Elena sank down to the ground herself, tired to her bones after the exertions of the past few hours, and aware that the day was probably far from over.

Without comment, the man tossed the apple she'd given him onto her lap.

"*Gracias.*" She took it up, but glanced at Eduardo.

"Eat—he will be fed."

With a nod, she crunched on the apple—refusing to look at him, even though she could feel his scrutiny as he crouched down on his haunches across from her. Despite everything, she found herself wishing that she weren't quite so disheveled.

"The boy—he is yours?"

This caught her amused attention, as she was nineteen, and the boy was seven. "No, *Ingles,*" she responded gravely. "He is not."

"Then whose?"

She took another bite, glancing at him over the apple. "Whose are you?"

His teeth flashed white in the moonlight. "I asked you first."

There seemed little harm in answering his question.

"Eduardo is the ward of the local Señor—he was fostering the child."

"The Señor was killed?"

Gazing at him thoughtfully, she didn't answer, but waited.

The smile flashed again, in contrast to his dark beard; she noted his brows were also dark, and rather heavy. "I am Raike, from England."

"Ah," she exclaimed, as though this explained everything.

Amused, he tilted his head and regarded her, a small smile playing around his lips. "It would be best if you told the truth, you know."

"I see. Best for whom?"

The humor faded. "Everyone," he said with quiet emphasis. "Believe me."

Another man materialized behind him, although Elena had heard no sound. *Santos*, she thought, hiding her alarm—*I cannot like the odds*.

"Excellency." The newcomer sketched a respectful bow toward her. "I am Cordez. It is my great pleasure to meet you." He was perhaps forty, a stocky man whose hair was shot with grey. A shadow moved behind him, and she was aware there were other men, hanging back out of sight. *Guerrillas*, she realized with some surprise; these men must be some of the *guerrilla* fighters who'd fought the French during the Peninsular War.

"You mistake the matter." She tossed the apple core aside, and wiped her hands on her apron—much good that it did. "Who is it that you think I am?"

The *Ingles* named Raike answered. "A royal Grandee—and a refugee from the court of Charles the Fourth."

Elena stared at him in blank astonishment. "You are very much mistaken, Señor."

"A royal great-niece," added the older man, watching her closely. "Perhaps the daughter of Ana Teresa Maria de Leon, although it remains unclear."

Bemused, she reviewed the serious faces before her, and shook her head. "I am sorry, but you make a grave mistake; I am merely Señorita Elena Muta, and my family is from Castile. We are not royalty."

The two men regarded her thoughtfully as the scent of pine hung in the air, and a night bird could be heard calling in the distance. She added, "I am grateful that you warned me of the French ambush, but I am afraid your information is not correct."

After a moment, Raike continued, "When Charles the Fourth was deposed—seven years ago—he fled to exile in Rome. Many of the royals were blocked from joining him, and were forced to scatter. I am informed that you are one of these."

"I am not royal," she repeated in exasperation. "And you make no sense, *Ingles*; if I were a member of the royal court, I would not be living here, amongst the *Afrancesados.*"

The word referred to those members of the Spanish nobility who had turned coat—hoping to curry favor with Napoleon by betraying their King. Indeed, King Charles had been deposed at the connivance of his own son, Ferdinand, so that Ferdinand could ascend the throne and do Napoleon's bidding. The fact that Napoleon had promptly replaced the despicable Ferdinand with Napoleon's own brother seemed a fitting turnabout for such treachery.

Raike bowed his head in acknowledgment. "No, I don't think you are an *Afrancesado*—far from it. But I do think you are the missing Grandee, and I think Napoleon's people think so, too." He paused, studying her. "The French are searching for you because they think you know where the Spanish royal treasure is hidden."

"It is not me they seek," she insisted. "And I know of no treasure—Spanish or otherwise." After debating for a moment, she decided it would be politic to mention, "I switched my assignment today with another Postulant— Maria Lucia—but I cannot believe that she is royalty, either."

She crossed her arms before her—it was becoming a bit cool, and she was not used to being outdoors after dark.

The man called Cordez exchanged a glance with Raike, and then said in a respectful tone, "Your pardon, Excellency, but we are certain our information is correct. You are the missing Grandee, and it is rumored you know where a valuable treasure lies hidden—along with The Spanish Mask."

"What is this 'Spanish Mask'?" Elena raised her brows in confusion. "I do not understand."

Both men stayed silent, and rather than answer her question, Cordez asked, "Where is this other Postulant—Maria Lucia?"

"I do not know," Elena answered honestly. "She was supposed to work in the orchards today, and I imagine the Holy Sisters fled at the first alarm. I hope they have come to no harm."

As she watched, the older man leaned back to issue rapid instructions to one of the men who stood along the trees behind him. With a nod, the other man melted into the shadows.

Raike rose to walk over to the boy, crouching down to shake his shoulder gently. "Eduardo?"

Sleepy, the boy propped himself on his elbow and rubbed his eyes. "Is it time for dinner?"

"Have an apple." Raike produced one out of his shirtfront, and settled down next to the boy. "We will have dinner soon, but first I must hear of your adventures this day."

He is comfortable around children, Elena observed. Perhaps he has some of his own—although a guerrilla would seem an unlikely candidate for marriage.

With an effort, she pulled her thoughts away from such foolish speculations, and concentrated on the conversation between the boy and the man.

"There was smoke," related Eduardo, as he bit into the fruit. "And Señorita Elena said we should hide, and so we did. I held onto her skirt, so that no one could see."

He paused, thinking. "I found a good stick, but now I've lost it."

"Is Señorita Elena your nursemaid?"

The boy found this idea amusing, as he efficiently finished off the apple. "No; my nursemaid is Señora Montoya—although some days Señorita Maria Lucia comes to teach me."

Raike produced another apple. "What does Maria Lucia look like?"

Frowning, the boy seemed to find the question confusing as he bit into the second apple. "She looks like Señorita Elena—they are both Holy Sisters." He then added ingenuously, "Señorita Maria Lucia has a man she meets with, sometimes."

Raike raised his brows. "Is that so? And what does this man look like?"

The boy shrugged his thin shoulders. "I don't know—she says he is handsome." He then added, with all the embarrassment of a seven-year-old boy, "She kisses him, sometimes."

Listening to this, the older man named Cordez chuckled, and even Elena was hard-pressed not to smile when Raike glanced at her in amusement. "Ah—I see. Is this handsome man Spanish or French?"

The boy regarded him with a knit brow, puzzling over the strange question. "He is Spanish, of course." Scratching his knee, he added, "He is apprenticed to the vintner."

Apparently, the boy was tired of this deviation from his own adventures, and so continued, "We had to hide on the hill behind the Castillo, Señorita Elena and me. We dug beneath a log. If I had a pistol, I would have shot them, but I had only a stick."

"That's a shame," Raike agreed.

Reminded, Eduardo turned to Elena. "Should I tell him about the rabbit?"

"I would not," she cautioned. "It is far too gruesome a tale."

With his flashing smile, Raike insisted, "Come; you must tell me, now."

With great relish, Eduardo gestured with his hands. "There was a dead rabbit in our hiding place—its eyes had been *eaten out*."

The Englishman grimaced. "I shouldn't have asked."

"You were warned, *Ingles*," Elena observed.

"Are you *Ingles*?" The boy paused in confusion. "I thought perhaps you were *El Halcon*."

"No—I am much handsomer than *El Halcon*." Teasing, his eyes slid to Elena, who pressed her lips together so as to give him no reaction.

"Oh. Well, when is dinner?"

Raike placed his hands on his knees as a preliminary to standing again. "We will take you to a safer place before we feed you—perhaps I can catch you a better rabbit."

"They come with us?" The older man, Cordez, sounded a bit surprised, as he rose to his feet with the Englishman. "She may be the wrong girl—shouldn't we wait to find out?"

"They come with us," Raike confirmed, and made no further explanation, as he swung Eduardo up onto his back again.

As she rose stiffly to her feet, Elena noted that the older Spanish man appeared to be under the younger Englishman's command—a strange set of affairs, if they were indeed *guerrillas*.

The party began to hike single-file through the forest, and Elena hoped it wouldn't be much further, else she'd be tempted to ask to ride on the Englishman's back alongside Eduardo. After a half-hour of walking, Raike dropped back to fall into step beside her. "Isabella," he said thoughtfully, as his gaze rested on path ahead. "A very fine royal name."

"Do you speak to me, *Ingles*?" she asked in mild surprise.

"Ana Teresa—God rest her soul—had a daughter named Isabella. She would be about your age, I think." Elena shook her head, amused. "You are persistent—I will give you honors for that.

And I suppose I should be grateful that you have made this mistake, because now we have been rescued."

"I hope you were not planning to rally the loyalists into a rebellion," he said, as though she hadn't spoken. "It would be all-too-easily put down."

"I hope to be a Holy Sister," she replied in bemusement. "I will lead no rebellions, I promise you."

He continued, "Napoleon's people are apparently convinced that you know where a treasure lies, and they are in dire need of a treasure, just now. It would be far better to confess, and let me help you."

She shrugged. "You are tedious, *Ingles*." Her tone indicated that the subject was closed.

Although she did not look at him, she was aware that he'd turned his head to regard her steadily. "You give yourself away, you know—I can hear a thousand generations of Spanish arrogance when you rebuke me."

She made no response, and they walked the rest of the way in silence.

Chapter 3

Elena knelt in the straw, saying the Divine Office of Prayers. "Domine, ne in furore tro arguas me, neque in ira tua corripias me; Miserere mei Domine. . . ."

After their long walk over the hill, the group had arrived at a small homestead near the entry to the valley— a location apparently chosen for the strategic advantage it allowed in observing those who came and left the area. Once there, Elena became aware there were at least three other men who accompanied them—men who said nothing, but observed her from the corners of their eyes, their hats pulled down low over their faces. In response, she lifted her chin and ignored them.

Elena and Eduardo were taken into the barn, and told to climb up into the hay loft under strict instructions to hide in the straw if they heard a pre-arranged warning signal. Raike and Cordez had then gone outside, presumably to discuss the situation where she could not overhear them. One of the *guerrillas*—a big man with a stoic expression—had brought them a hamper of food from the farmhouse, and Elena ate cold roast chicken beside the boy and then washed herself as best she could in a proffered bucket of tepid water. *All in all,* she reflected, as the silent man handed each of them a horse blanket, *it is only slightly worse than the accommodations at the Convent.*

Eduardo had promptly fallen into an exhausted sleep, and Elena was eager to join him, but was determined to keep the routine of prayer that had marked her days—there was much comfort to be had in the rote recitals that never changed, despite war, or abduction, or a future that seemed more and more uncertain.

"*Benedicamus Domino; Deo gratias*. . . " Moving her lips, she whispered the prayers aloud so that her mind wouldn't wander. She had the strong feeling that she would need any divine help that *el Dios bueno* was willing to send her way; the *Ingles* seemed to be in control of the situation—in control, and unwilling to believe her. She'd heard that British forces had aided the Spanish *guerrillas,* here in the hills during the war, but it was unclear why this Englishman had remained behind, now that Napoleon was in exile.

The situation in war-torn Spain remained tense, even though the war was finally over. The allied countries who had defeated Napoleon were now involved in negotiations to redraw the territorial boundaries of Europe, and Spain had little voice in the proceedings due to her questionable past allegiances. The people of Spain had suffered mightily during the war, and it did not seem as though their suffering would be coming to an end anytime soon.

"*Amen,*" she concluded, turning her mind from these rather grim thoughts. She then leaned forward to place her hands on the straw so as to ease her knees. *I shouldn't think about it anymore*, she thought, hanging her head down so as to stretch her neck; *I should sleep—I have a feeling that tomorrow will be even worse than today.*

"You are finished?"

Startled, she turned to see the *Ingles*, waiting at the top rung of the loft ladder and watching her. "I didn't want to interrupt."

With as much dignity as she could muster, she seated herself in the straw and brushed off her skirts. She'd taken off her head scarf so that her long braid fell down her back, but it couldn't be helped—he hadn't knocked, after all. "Yes, I am finished."

He climbed into the loft, ducking his head beneath the low ceiling, and then settled to sit with his back against the wooden wall at a small distance from her—he didn't want to frighten her, she could see, and she appreciated the gesture.

He said nothing for a moment, but turned his head to watch Eduardo sleep. "I wanted to apologize; my remark about your arrogance—I'm afraid I have some prejudices left over from the war, but I shouldn't direct them toward you."

"*Ingles*," she said gently. "To a Spaniard, such an observation is not an insult."

His ready smile flashed. "I see. Then I have nothing to apologize for."

"*De nada*," she agreed in a grave tone. It occurred to her that she had never been alone and unchaperoned with a man before, and that she was rather enjoying the experience. In the light from the brazier below, she could see that his eyes were brown—not so dark as hers, though—and there was a network of fine wrinkles at their corners.

He has spent a great deal of time in the sun, she concluded, which made sense if he had spent the war here, as a *guerrilla*. His Spanish was good, but not perfect.

In the silence, he bent his head for a moment, gathering his thoughts, one arm resting on a bent knee. His hair was damp—he must have washed before he came for this visit. "I know you do not know who to trust."

There was a pause. "Aside from God," she pointed out.

"Aside from God," he agreed. "But even though you don't know who to trust, you are nevertheless going to need some help. I'm afraid—" here he paused, searching for the right words, "I'm afraid someone was careless with information, and as a result you are in grave danger."

This was of interest, and she prompted, "You said the French soldiers who came to the Castillo today—you said that they came for me."

He met her eyes. "I am certain of it. And I believe you knew it, also—which is why you hid."

She shook her head in denial, and made a gesture toward Eduardo's sleeping form. "No, *Ingles*—I had to hide the boy; he was under my charge."

He went on as though she hadn't given the explanation. "The French—I suppose more correctly, Napoleon's people—have been searching for an item known as The Spanish Mask, along with a rumored royal treasure. The Emperor is desperate to raise money, and his people will stop at nothing."

Napoleon, again. With a knit brow, she pointed out, "Napoleon is no longer Emperor, and is in no situation to be seizing anything, surely?"

The Englishman met her eyes, the expression in his own grave. "There are persistent rumors that he will escape, and attempt another conquest."

Utterly astonished, she stared at him in dismay. "No; no—*how* can this be?"

"It does seem incredible, does it not? But I'm afraid it is very likely."

"*Santos*," she breathed, shaken. "Not again."

"This is why this treasure is so important to them—the—" he rubbed his fingers together, trying to think of the word. "—the paper money—"

"The currency?" she offered.

"Yes—the currency. There is none left; not after the last seven years. Therefore, he is trying to seize upon any treasure he can—gold, silver, jewels—anything that can fund his next war."

"I see," she said, still trying to come to grips with this alarming news.

Watching her closely, he continued, "He particularly wishes to lay hands on the mythical Spanish Mask. It is supposed to be over a thousand years old, and priceless, both in value and in symbolism—apparently, it was originally worn by Alexander the Great.

Napoleon is a master of propaganda, and he would like very much to have Alexander's Mask when he attempts to raise an army again."

"He is a madman." She shook her head in disbelief; to think that the utter misery of the past seven years would be visited upon them all over again—it didn't bear thinking about.

"I wish he were merely mad. Unfortunately, he is still able to raise an army, and his people—well, I imagine you already know how ruthless they are. Again, you are in grave danger; they seem to think you know where this so-called treasure is hidden, and they will not be kind, if they want to extract this information from you."

A nuance in his tone prompted her to frown at him. "But you do not believe this tale about the treasure?"

He let out a breath, and ran a hand over his face. "No—my people have good information that no such treasure was left behind; that when the King fled there was no time.

The palace was overrun, and—if there was anything of value there in the first place—it was looted by the French soldiers, seven years ago."

Bemused, she shook her head slightly. "Then—then I do not understand; why do you take me away?"

He watched her for a few moments, and she returned his steady regard in the flickering brazier light, unwilling to look away although she knew she should. Weighing his words, he added, "Unfortunately, Napoleon is not your only problem; there is an additional danger—from King Ferdinand."

"The true King of Spain is Charles the Fourth, by the most holy grace of God," she retorted. "Not his son, Ferdinand the traitor."

He tilted his head in acknowledgement, but continued, "Be that as it may, the Congress of Vienna will almost certainly restore Ferdinand to the throne."

"*What*?" She stared at him in disbelief once again. "*Santos, Ingles*—you bring many tidings of bad news."

"And I am sorry for it," he agreed. "But there are many Spaniards who think Ferdinand is a traitor, as you do, and who will not be willing to acknowledge his claim to the throne. Ferdinand will not like the fact that you are still here in Spain; he has no heirs of his own yet, and he has already shown he will do anything to gain power."

Exasperated, she gave this theory the derision it deserved. "Even if I were who you think I am, you must know that a Grandee has no claim to the throne."

"No—but you would serve as a figurehead, which is all that would be needed. Because most of the royal family has been killed or exiled, your very presence would be a threat to him. Therefore, I have been tasked to extract you, and smuggle you to England—at least until the new allegiances are settled, and Napoleon is beaten back again.

You will be much safer in England, believe me."

But Elena only shook her head slightly. "You are mistaken—and the girl who you believe me to be must be found, if she is in such danger. You must waste no more time."

He watched her for a moment, his expression unreadable, and then sighed. "Very well, *España*—if you won't confess, I have no choice but to take you to Aranjuez."

Once again, Elena found herself staring at him in astonishment. "Aranjuez?" It was the site of the summer royal residence—a pretty little town, just south of Madrid, and the very place where the French had forced King Charles to flee. "*Ingles,* it is you who are the madman."

But he shrugged. "I think you are the girl, but on the chance you are not, I need to find a witness who would recognize you. There must be someone left in Aranjuez who can lay this mystery to rest. And I can't leave you here, certainly—Napoleon's people will not be as patient as I have been."

Struggling with her dismay at this proposed plan, she was unable to summon a response for a few moments. "And the boy?" her gaze rested for a moment on Eduardo. "What of him? I cannot abandon him."

Raike frowned. "There is no one else who can take him in?"

Elena shook her head slowly. "No—the Señor is away, and it would be too dangerous to leave him here on his own."

Thoughtfully, Raike watched Eduardo sleep, the boy's arm flung out to the side. "If the Señor was fostering him, does that mean the boy is noble? Do you know anything about his family—where they are?"

"No—I know of no other relatives." Her gaze rested on the sleeping boy for a moment, and all the revelations she'd learned this night suddenly seemed overwhelming.

It was all so unfair—*unbelievable* to think the war would resume, and that the despicable Ferdinand would once again rule the wreckage that was left of Spain; not to mention that she was to be dragged across the country through no fault of her own.

Suddenly, she turned to the Englishman. "You have a kind heart, I think. I would ask a promise of you—although I can make no promise in return. I would ask that if I am indeed captured or—or killed, you will—" her voice broke, and she ducked her chin, struggling to regain control, "—you will see to it that Eduardo is kept safe." Unable to help it, her voice choked with tears, and she raised the back of her hand to her trembling mouth for a moment.

"I promise," he said quietly and she looked up to see that he was watching her intently, a hint of surprise in his eyes.

"I lost my family in the war," she offered by way of explanation, wiping her tears with the heel of her hand. "And I feel an obligation to him—he is alone, and helpless."

Her companion leaned forward, and gently enclosed her wrist with his hand for a moment, the contact warm and reassuring. "I will see to it."

"*Gracias.*" Unaccountably shy, she was unable to meet his eyes—*santos*, suddenly there seemed to be a great deal of emotion, for such a small space.

"I will let you sleep." He rose to his feet, bending low as he made his way to the ladder. "We must make plans for the journey tomorrow."

"As you wish." Her tone was stiff and subdued, because she was a bit embarrassed by her emotional outburst.

He began to descend the ladder. "Do not rescue any more stray children, *por favor*."

"I can make no promises," she countered, and glimpsed his amused gaze before it sank out of sight.

Chapter 4

Elena was already accustomed to rising at dawn, but she could see that Eduardo was still sleepy as they stood to one side, watching the band of *guerrillas* prepare for the journey to Aranjuez. With quiet, efficient movements, the men saddled five horses in the now-crowded barn, the air suddenly moist with the heat from the stamping beasts.

"There are not enough horses," the boy whispered to her.

"I imagine we will each ride with one of the men." She was trying not to reveal her own misgivings—she was not accustomed to riding horseback. They were standing nearest to the big *guerrilla*, who was securing a sword sheath onto his saddlebow. With a practiced movement, he tugged on the hilt to ensure that the sword slid out easily, and as the blade was revealed, Eduardo made the universal sound of admiration that little boys make when confronted with such a sight.

His expression impassive, the man pulled the sword from its sheath, and then walked over to hand it to Eduardo. "If you would hold this for me, *por favor*."

Wide-eyed, Eduardo held the hilt with both hands, afraid to move whilst the man went over to retrieve his saddle bags.

"A fearsome sword, *caballero*," Elena commented, hiding a smile at the boy's reaction.

The boy's gaze slid over to hers. "Do you think he has killed people with it?"

"I shouldn't wonder."

The *guerrilla* returned to lift his saddlebags over the saddle, and Eduardo ventured, "Do you need me to hold your pistol, Señor?"

The big man considered Eduardo over his shoulder with a solemn expression, although Elena had the impression he was amused. "Have you ever fired a pistol?"

"No," the boy confessed.

"Not this day, then." The man secured the bags with a tug of the leather strap. "You must learn, first."

Excited, the boy's eyes slid once more to Elena to verify that she had heard this promised treat, and she widened her own eyes at him to acknowledge that she had, and was suitably impressed.

The *guerrilla* retrieved his sword from the boy with a word of thanks, then threw a stirrup over the horse's back to tighten the girth, whilst Eduardo watched his every move in abject admiration.

Raike had been standing at a distance in quiet consultation with Cordez, and now approached Elena. "You will ride with Catalo, and I will take Eduardo."

His gaze silently acknowledged the promise he'd made to her last night in the loft, and she could feel her color rise at the shared memory; she'd lain awake for a time, remembering how it felt when he'd held her wrist.

"Very well," she agreed with a small nod, as though she was completely accustomed to riding pillion with strange men. Raike had trimmed his beard and his hair sometime since last night, with the result that he appeared younger than she'd first thought—she gauged him to be no more than thirty, or so. She was also aware—as women are—that something had shifted between them, and that he now sought to please her. It was nothing obvious, but it was there, nevertheless.

Watch yourself, niña, she cautioned; he is an English heretic whose role in these events is unclear—except that he made the promise you rather foolishly sought, in a moment of weakness.

With a quick glance, Raike considered her much-creased Postulant's habit. "It would be best if you changed into boy's clothes and rode astride—we'd like to attract as little attention as possible."

"No," she replied calmly. "I will not wear boy's clothes, and ride astride."

He cocked his head and thought about it for a moment. "Then will you remove your headscarf? It gives you away."

She nodded, seeing the wisdom of this, and pulled the headscarf off her head so as to stuff it in her work-pocket.

"You must try to speak as little as possible—voices carry in the open air."

"I do talk overmuch," she agreed gravely.

His hands on his hips, he smiled down at her. "No—you are wary, and that's understandable. But you won't always be wary—and then we will have much to say to each other."

She blushed at the implication, as he stepped forward to place his hands on her waist and indicate he would set her up on the tall horse. "Ready? Here you go." Lifting her easily, he seated her behind the cantle. During the course of the movement, her eyes sought out his, so close to her own, and then she quickly looked away. *Santos*, she thought a bit breathlessly; *he does not even attempt to hide how he feels.*

As everyone mounted up, she held on to the big *guerrilla*'s coat, and asked, "You are Catalo?" It seemed appropriate that they be introduced, considering she'd never clung to anyone before.

"*Si*, Your Excellency."

"Not an 'Excellency'," she replied, a bit exasperated. "Only plain Señorita Elena, if you please."

He made no response, and she decided philosophically that it was just as well; she would rather not feel she had to make conversation—it took all her concentration to remain upright, and she was so far off the ground that she was afraid to look down.

The party filed through the barn door two by two; the men alert, and surveying the area with one hand resting on their weapons. As the mists rose, the early morning light began to shine through the trees—it looked to be another warm day—and the horses' footfalls were the only sound as they made a silent progress through the dense pine.

After the first ten minutes of shamelessly hanging onto Catalo, Elena began to anticipate the horse's rhythms and felt she could relax and look around her. They headed down the valley and toward the east—the sun was before them—and made a steady and silent progress for several hours. Andalusia was on the southern coast of Spain, whilst Aranjuez was located in the center, near Madrid. Elena had no idea how long their journey would take, nor what their route would be—she was unused to travel, and had only a hazy idea of geography. Nonetheless, she resolved to pay attention to her surroundings, in the event an escape had to be staged; despite the peaceful atmosphere, Raike's warnings of danger had given her pause, and after all, she could not be certain any of these men were who they said they were.

I must resist the temptation to trust him completely, she reminded herself; and I must not have my head turned by his flirtation—I imagine he is very practiced, with his ready smile and his handsome face, whereas I am very unpracticed and therefore—to be honest—a bit too willing to be beguiled. Her gaze was drawn to his broad shoulders for a moment before she took herself in hand, and firmly looked away.

Hard on this thought, Raike pulled his horse up so as to walk beside her, with Eduardo sitting before him on the saddle.

"Ah; she is still there," he said to Eduardo. "You were right."

"Señor Raike thought you might have fallen off, because you were so quiet," Eduardo explained with a smile.

"I was instructed not to speak, and I must follow my instruction," Elena responded, in a mock-prim tone.

"Such a biddable girl," observed Raike, to no one in particular. "You'd never guess she was blood-kin to Phillip the Second."

Laughing, Elena shook her head. "No—you would never guess."

He bent his head to say to Eduardo, "Alas, I have no kings in my family tree."

But Eduardo raised his face. "If you are a *guerrilla*, Señor Raike, does that mean you know *El Halcon?*"

Eduardo's tone was reverent, making it clear that such an acquaintance would rank higher than any paltry king. *El Halcon* was the legendary leader of the original band of Spanish *guerrillas* who had—almost single-handedly— inspired the dispirited Spanish citizenry to form a resistance against the hated French, their former ally who had betrayed them.

Indeed, the *guerrillas* had so harried the French supply trains that Napoleon was forced to devote time and troops to fighting them; troops that he desperately needed in central Europe.

In the end, it was said that Napoleon's defeat was due in no small part to the heroic Spanish *guerrillas,* who had fought on against all odds.

"I do not have that honor," Raike admitted. "But these other gentleman have worked with *El Halcon*."

Wide-eyed, Eduardo asked Catalo, "What is he like— is he very brave?"

Elena's escort thought about it for a moment—almost as though he weighed his words. "A clever man—very shrewd; yes, very brave."

His eyes alight with excitement, Eduardo turned to look at the path ahead again. "If only I could meet him—do you think he will come join us?"

Raike replied, "Well, I can't say, but I imagine he is just as eager to meet you."

Eduardo laughed with delight. "He doesn't know who I am, Señor."

"Is that so?" said the Englishman, as he guided their horse through the underbrush. "You astonish me."

The boy continued, "Señorita Maria Lucia said that *El Halcon* could fight ten Frenchmen at one time, and defeat them all."

Raike tilted his head, considering. "I'll bet Catalo could do the same."

As Eduardo's eager head turned to Catalo for confirmation, Elena could sense her escort's amusement.

"Perhaps not ten," the big man demurred.

"Let's not put it to the test anytime soon," suggested Raike.

"Is *El Halcon* as strong as you are?" Eduardo asked Catalo in wonder.

Catalo unbent enough to smile. "I cannot say."

Idly, Eduardo leaned to smooth the horse's mane "Why do we go to Aranjuez? What is there?"

"Castles, mainly," Raike replied easily. "Perhaps a dragon or two."

Eduardo laughed again, and Elena couldn't help but smile—the boy's enthusiasm for this adventure was touching; it seemed that he'd left his foster-home behind without a twinge of regret.

The boy tilted his head back, so as to look up to Raike. "Are you from Aranjuez?"

"Eduardo," Elena cautioned. "Not so many questions, *por favor*."

"No, I am from England," Raike replied. "A very beautiful place—England." He slid a teasing, sidelong glance at Elena.

Eduardo did not hide his astonishment, his mouth slightly agape. "*You* are English?"

"I am," the man admitted, then leaned forward to say in a loud whisper, "But I think Señorita Elena believes I am one of the dragons."

Giggling, Eduardo glanced again at her, and she arched an admonishing brow at their teasing.

"To the right," said Catalo quietly, as he held up a hand.

Raike whistled softly, and they all pulled up their horses, suddenly silent, and listening. Straining, Elena thought perhaps she could hear faint hoof-beats in the distance. Raike made a gesture, and they all melted into the forest, quietly climbing up the hill to its crest. Standing hidden in the trees, they watched as a group of French soldiers crossed the valley floor below them on horseback.

Chapter 5

"They must be going to Bailen," Cordez remarked, as they watched the troop of soldiers disappear into the distance. "It is a few miles over the next hill."

Raike nodded and picked up his reins. "Then some of us will go to Beilen, and do a little listening. We'll set up camp near here, and leave the girl and the boy under guard."

After glancing at Elena, he turned his horse back down the hill, and Catalo fell into line behind him, with Cordez and the others bringing up the rear. Elena found it necessary to clutch Catalo's coat again, as their horse carefully picked its way down the steep hill, its hooves making the rocks skitter away. The sight of the French troops had given her pause; after the uneventful morning spent riding through the sunlit forest, it was a shock to be reminded that it was all in deadly earnest. She wondered if they were the same soldiers who had called up to her, when she lay hidden with Eduardo on the hillside.

"Are you going to shoot them?" Eduardo asked Raike in a low tone. Judging from the suppressed excitement in his voice, it seemed evident that he was hopeful.

But Raike would not indulge him. "No—they are looking for Señorita Elena. If we shoot them, we give our location away, and more will then come to take their place."

"They believe she is a princess," said Eduardo with great scorn. "They are fools."

"It never pays to underestimate the enemy," Raike advised in a mild tone. "We'll proceed with caution."

The mild rebuke seemed to have little effect on the boy, who asked eagerly, "May I go listen with you at—where was it?"

"Bailen—and the answer is no. Your assignment is to guard the Señorita, and see that she eats something—I don't think she ever eats."

Smiling, Eduardo leaned around him, to look at Elena. "She eats—she ate some chicken last night."

"Did she? Then I stand corrected."

"At this point, I would eat whatever you put before me," Elena confessed. She would also give a great deal to get down from this horse, but would not complain—she wished to show the *Ingles* that she was no pampered aristocrat, although it could very well kill her. How anyone managed to sit on a horse for any length of time was beyond her comprehension.

"Soon," Raike soothed as they came to the base of the hill, and onto less rocky terrain. "Perhaps we can roast a rabbit; they should be plentiful around here."

"May I shoot a rabbit with your pistol?" Eduardo asked Catalo.

"No." The *guerrilla* shook his head. "Too much noise—it will echo in the hills. We will set a snare, instead."

The boy fell silent, happily contemplating this coming task as they continued their descent into the valley. They rode for another hour before they came into a clearing, sheltered by an outcropping of rock, which was deemed suitable for a camp. Before Catalo could do the honors, Raike came over to help Elena dismount, and she staggered upon meeting the ground again.

"Steady." He clasped her arms in his hands, his head bent to hers.

ANNE CLEELAND

"Gracias." She discreetly drew away from his hands without looking into the face, so close to hers. "I am unused to riding a horse."

With some regret, he advised, "Unfortunately, you have several more days of riding to look forward to—I will try to find a sheepskin in town."

At her look of inquiry, explained with a gleam, "To sit upon."

Blushing, she did not respond, but allowed him to steer her away from the others, who'd begun unsaddling the horses. "They'll start a fire—and there is a river down the hill. I'm afraid the accommodations will be rudimentary."

"I am a Postulant," she reminded him in a dry tone. "I am used to such."

"Ah—I keep forgetting." His amused look told her he believed no such thing. "I will leave you here with Cordez and Catalo, and ask that you do as they say—there may be more soldiers, patrolling the area, and we have to be cautious. The French may be aware that you've fled, and will be watching the roads. I'll try to find out what they know, and that will dictate what we do next."

"Very well." She would do as he asked, as it did not seem an escape was necessary—not yet, anyway—and besides, she was too stiff to contemplate hobbling anywhere.

He continued, "With any luck, the men can trap a rabbit, and you'll have roast meat—otherwise you'll have to make do with the dried provisions we carry. Tomorrow we'll do better by you. "

"I will see if there is any fruit to be had in the trees, here." She glanced overhead with a practiced eye as she pressed her hands to the small of her back. "There may be some crabapples, even at this altitude."

Amused, he observed, "I forgot; you are the royal Grandee who tends the orchards."

"You are tedious, *Ingles*," she chided him with a small smile. "I am no Grandee."

He tilted his head, as though listening. "That was better—only a hundred generations of arrogance, that time."

I should not engage with him, she reminded herself as she broke her gaze away—although it is so tempting; he is very amusing.

She looked around for Eduardo, and saw that one of the *guerrillas* had given him a knife to hack at branches whilst the men dug a fire pit.

"Don't worry—he won't hurt himself."

"No," she agreed, watching the boy. "And it is good experience; his training has been neglected, I think."

The Englishman absently ran his hand down a tree trunk, while they watched the boy's exuberant efforts. "I wonder what happened to his family."

She shrugged her shoulders slightly, and then wished she hadn't. "His father probably fell in the war, and then his lands were handed over to the *Afrancesados*. It is a sad but familiar story." Her expression stony, she looked up to him. "It is incomprehensible—that any true Spaniard would collaborate with the enemy."

With a hand on the tree, he bent his head to contemplate the ground for a moment. "I can't make excuses for them, but many of the Spanish people were not best pleased with the power of the King—or the Roman Catholic Church, for that matter. They saw the French conquerors as a means to an end."

Stubbornly, she retorted, "The *Afrancesados* are traitors—nothing more, and nothing less."

Meeting her gaze, he offered sincerely, "I am sorry for your country's troubles, *España*."

Mentally, she backed away from the ready sympathy she read in his eyes. "You are lucky that England is across the water, and remains in one piece."

He cocked his head. "Only because we had our own uprising, to remind the King that a country exists to serve its people, and not the King. Don't worry—Spain will regroup, and live to plague England once again."

She smiled. "I can only hope, *Ingles*."

He chuckled, then drew himself upright. "I must go. Remember to stay close; I will return as soon as I am able—can I bring you anything?"

"My sheepskin," she replied with a small smile.

"Don't wander off," he cautioned again. "I shouldn't be more than a couple of hours, but it all depends on what we discover."

She nodded, and after issuing orders, he mounted up and left with the other two men, leaving Cordez and Catalo behind. Elena enlisted Eduardo to gather up some wild crabapples, which were unfortunately very sour, but perhaps could be made more palatable after roasting.

They bathed as best they could in the river, and the *guerrillas* did manage to snare two rabbits—much to Eduardo's delight—so that they could anticipate a very satisfactory meal.

Elena had been remiss in keeping the Divine Office of Prayers, and since there was some time whilst they awaited their dinner, she knelt at the edge of the clearing and invited Eduardo to join her. "Do you know the prayers for vespers, *caballero*?"

"No." The boy made no attempt to conceal his extreme reluctance. "Prayers are boring."

"I am surprised to hear that you are mightier than God," she replied, and calmly folded her hands without further comment.

She was to receive support, however, from an unexpected source; Catalo approached, his black leather hat in his hand. "Excellency, may I join you?"

"I am not an 'Excellency', and of course you may."

The big man knelt down beside her in the pine needles, and Eduardo, after hesitating a moment, joined them. Elena began reciting the Office aloud, with the *guerrilla* making the responses and Eduardo joining in with what snatches he could remember.

Suddenly, Elena heard a sickening thud, and turned with a gasp to see Catalo sink forward to the ground, Cordez standing behind him and wielding the butt of his pistol.

As Eduardo cried out, Elena leapt to her feet and bolted blindly for the trees, but the older man grasped her from behind, yanking at her arm.

Twisting frantically, she struck at him with her free hand, and managed to writhe away so as to continue her mad dash into the forest—*I dare not scream*, she thought grimly; *there is no one to hear but the French*. She ran as fast as she could, clutching her skirts in her hands, but in a few strides she was tackled to the ground from behind, falling headlong onto the hard ground with a jarring crash.

"Be still," Cordez hissed from behind her head, his weight pinning her down so that she could hardly draw breath. "I would not like to cut your pretty face."

Panting, her chin pressed against the dirt, she watched as he brandished a wicked looking blade before her eyes. "Now, you will tell me where the treasure lies hidden."

Chapter 6

"I—I am not who you think I am," Elena rasped out. "I do not know, I swear it."

She could feel his breath against the side of her face, his tone menacing. "The *Ingles* is certain that you are the girl, and he would not be wrong—not about this. You will tell me, and then I will let you go, and be on my way."

"I do not know," she repeated, her eyes focused on the blade, inches away. "You must believe me."

Cursing, he yanked her arm out from beneath her, then held it pinned before her on the ground, pressing his weight against her wrist. "I will cut off your fingers, one by one. I am not a patient man." He brought the blade down, so that it was poised above her little finger. "Now, talk."

"Get away! Get off her!" It was Eduardo's voice, high-pitched and frantic, from just behind them.

Elena gasped out, "Run, Eduardo—go get help."

But her attacker had a better idea. "You won't watch the boy lose his fingers, I think." Rolling off her, he grasped her braid in his hand and yanked her to her feet. Before them stood Eduardo, standing with both hands clutching Catalo's pistol, although he propped the heavy weapon against his abdomen—it could not have been more evident that the boy had never held a pistol.

Wary, the man held out his hand. "Give me the pistol—I won't hurt you." As he slowly approached the boy, Elena gauged her moment, then twisted to grasp the arm that held her so as to sink her teeth into it. Roaring with pain, the man turned to cuff her, but she ducked, shouting to Eduardo, "Run! Now! Do as I say!"

Uncertain, the boy backed up, the pistol trained on the man. "I will shoot you," he threatened, a quaver in his voice. "I will."

Letting her go, the man instead lunged toward the boy, and Elena took the opportunity to leap upon his back, pulling her braid across his throat and yanking as hard as she was able with a hand on either side. Dropping his blade, the man staggered, clutching at her braid, then drew his own pistol, aiming wildly at Eduardo.

Elena kicked frantically at the arm that held the pistol whilst she pulled the braid tighter. "Run, Tomás!" she shouted, but then the crack of a pistol echoed, and she cried out in horror as the ground came up hard to meet her.

Slightly stunned, she raised her face to see Eduardo, still standing with the oversized pistol, his mouth agape. Beneath her, Cordez lay still; a mass of gore where the side of his head used to be. While she stared at what was left of him, other hands pulled at her, and she looked up to see Raike, his face a grim mask as he bent over her. "Are you hurt, Elena?"

"Yes—I mean, no. *Santos*, that was a good shot."

"We need to go, now," he said in a steady tone, helping her up. "The French will have heard the gunfire."

She looked behind him to see one of the other *guerrillas*—Valdez—helping Catalo as he slowly sat up, his head bent forward as he regained his senses. "Oh," she said rather stupidly. "Of course."

In a clipped tone, Raike said to the others, "Take the horses and the boy toward the south and lay a false trail— I will take the girl down the river, and we will meet up on the west end of Santa Inez."

"No." Elena drew her scattered wits together and took a breath. "The boy stays with me." Sensing his resistance to this idea, she met his gaze. "Please."

Raike considered this, glancing at Eduardo's pale face. "Can he swim?"

Reluctantly, she admitted, "I do not know about him, but I cannot swim."

"He goes with the men, then," Raike decided with a curt nod. "We will split up to confuse the enemy, and I can't handle the both of you in the water. He will be kept safe—I promise."

"You were wrong about Cordez." She brought the heels of her hands to her temples and tried to calm herself. "*Madre de Dios*."

"Excellency—I will come with you," offered Catalo, rising to his feet with an effort. "I will carry the boy."

Raike eyed him for a moment, assessing his condition. "Puente, Valdez—can you handle all the horses between the two of you?" As the two men nodded, he told them, "Go then—quickly."

With quick, efficient movements the fire was doused, and Cordez' corpse loaded onto a nervous, sidestepping horse. After reclaiming his pistol, Catalo hoisted Eduardo onto his back, and began walking toward the river through the underbrush.

"Follow them, Elena—I will be right behind you."

Elena moved forward on stiff legs, and looked over her shoulder to see Raike and the other men leading the horses over their tracks, obscuring their direction of retreat. She then hurried after the big *guerrilla* as he carried Eduardo down the ravine, the sounds of the river growing louder during their descent. As she brushed branches aside, she tried to gauge the extent of their guide's injuries. "Are you badly injured, Catalo?"

"He says his head hurts," Eduardo answered for him.

Outraged on his behalf—and on her own—she offered in a low tone, "It is despicable, to think that he would betray us in such a way."

There was a small pause. "*Si*, Excellency."

Exasperated, Elena shook her head. "Do not 'Excellency' me—it only encourages Señor Raike. I am Señorita Elena, Catalo."

As they clambered down the slope, there was another long pause before he replied, "*Si,* Señorita."

Santos; this particular man does not excel in the art of conversation, she thought, but now that she had the opportunity, she persisted, "Why are Spanish *guerrillas* being led by an *Ingles*, Catalo?"

The man responded, "I follow my orders, Señorita."

They came to the edge of the wide river, and as Catalo began wading into the current with Eduardo, Raike caught up to them, and stayed the big Spaniard with a hand. "Are you certain you can do this? If you go under, I cannot help you—not with the other two."

"*Si*, I am able."

"You have one hell of a hard head, then. Let's go."

The men slung their pistols around Eduardo's neck, and then Catalo hiked the boy up higher on his back before wading into the rushing river whilst Elena watched the procedure with some trepidation.

"Up, now." Raike led Elena into the cool water, and once they were hip deep, he indicated she was to climb upon his back, her now-heavy skirts hiked up so that her legs could wrap around his waist. "Ready?" He pushed forward, so that they half-floated whilst he maneuvered along the river bottom, making their way toward its center in the wake of Catalo and Eduardo. "I don't know how deep the river is here, but we shouldn't have much trouble.

Mainly we don't want to be tracked, so we will travel along in the water for a while."

"I see." She tried to assimilate the novel sensation of having her wet front pressed against his wet back. He was warm, and she could feel his muscles move against her; she couldn't help but remember how he'd shot Cordez with such precision, and felt a bit breathless, with her face so close beside his.

Keeping his voice low, he asked, "Do you think Cordez was acting for Napoleon, or for himself?"

With an effort, she reined in her wayward thoughts. "I don't know. I would guess he acted for himself—he wanted me to tell him where the treasure was, and he did not seek to bring me to anyone."

He was silent for a moment, then he began swimming, his arms making wide sweeping motions to each side as they floated along. Although he did not sound angry, she could feel the tension in his torso, and knew that he was. "I am sorry that I left you with that bastard, *España*."

"*De nada*. I suppose there is no honor among thieves."

"I am no thief."

Ah—this had touched a nerve, and so she tightened her arms around his neck for a moment in apology. "I know it—you are instead quite a marksman."

"That son of a bitch." He swore in a language that was unfamiliar to her—English, perhaps; she'd had never heard anyone speak English before. "Hold on with your legs, it's a little faster here." He swept his arms out before him as the water propelled them along. "All right?"

She had already come to the conclusion that it was more than all right, with his torso pressed against hers, and the water making a soft hissing sound. "*Si*. This is rather nice, isn't it? Perhaps I should learn how to swim."

"I don't think nuns need to know how to swim."

"Obviously, they do."

He chuckled, which caused a very pleasant sensation along her breast, as the river swirled around them. *I am enjoying this altogether too much*, she admitted. The moonlight glimmered off the surface of the churning river, and she appreciated the fact that she still had her fingers, since they were currently spread across the muscles of his upper chest. He was indeed very strong—she could feel it in his movements—and she remembered how he had easily lifted her when he'd found her in the orchard. *Think about something else*, she sternly directed herself, and did. "Where are we, exactly?"

"We should cross into New Castile within a few miles. I am hoping the French will assume we are headed toward the southern ports—the other men will work to help them form such an assumption."

"We did not get our roast rabbit," she sighed with regret. "I should have strangled Cordez for that fact alone."

He pretended surprise as his arms propelled them along. "You admit to being hungry? You are so slim."

"I am never fed enough—that is why I am so slim."

He chuckled again, next to her cheek, and she felt a rush of satisfaction that he thought her so amusing. *You should not seek to please him*, she cautioned herself, but then said, "Perhaps you would be good enough to catch me a fish, as you swim along."

"Don't worry; I will see you fed."

She subsided, hearing the hint of possessiveness in his tone. Watch yourself, niña, she thought yet again. You must not allow this man to think you belong to him; such a thing is impossible, no matter that he looks upon you in such a way—

"Stay quiet," he cautioned, and suddenly slowed.

Straining into the darkness ahead, she saw what he had seen; a bridge spanned the river—perhaps a hundred yards ahead—and two figures could be discerned standing guard upon it, the muskets on their backs silhouetted against the moonlit sky.

Chapter 7

Silently, with Elena on his back, Raike moved toward the steep bank that lined the river, staying low in the water until they joined Catalo and Eduardo. Raike made a hand signal to Catalo, then turned his head to whisper to Elena, his mouth against her ear, "Do you think you can hold your breath under water?"

"I think so," she whispered, and hoped this was true.

"We will practice—all right? We will duck under, and you hold your breath as long as you are able, then tap me when you must breathe again."

"*Si*," she replied, and could hear the nervousness in her own voice.

He lifted a hand and gently squeezed her wrist, his words soft and reassuring. "If you can't, you can't, and we'll turn back. But let's make the attempt—I would like to get past them unawares."

She could see the merit to this—if the French did not know they had slipped through this checkpoint, then they could travel more openly on the other side.

"I'll count to three." He tapped her arm to demonstrate. At the count, she closed her eyes and held her breath—fighting panic as the water closed over her head and she could suddenly hear the amplified roaring of the river. Focusing on keeping count, she managed twenty-five before she tapped on his arm, and they surfaced again, careful to be quiet, as she gulped for air.

"Good," he whispered. "We will do this twice, to get to the other side. We will come up under the bridge to take a breath, and then go again.

You must hang on to me tightly—don't let go, no matter what—and if you need air, tap me, and we'll come up; just stay as quiet as you can, and keep your face down and out of the moonlight."

They then sidled along the bank as close to the bridge as they dared, until he did his tapping signal and they submerged again, only this time he swam vigorously, using his arms and legs whilst she clung to his shoulders with a death grip, fighting panic. Just when she thought she couldn't bear it another instant and would have to let him know, he rose to the surface and she gasped for breath under the bridge itself, the sounds of the river echoing loudly off the stone arch.

He waited until she'd caught her breath, then repeated his tapping signal, and she steeled herself for one more session, making their silent underwater progress down the river. When they surfaced, they were near to the bank again, and he grasped a rocky outcrop with one hand, staying low in the water. He then turned her in his arms so as to whisper in her ear, "Hold, now—we wait for the others. Keep your face away from the bridge."

She nodded, and waited with her head bent, the whiskers from his beard wet against her face as he held her in his arms. Almost casually, he moved his mouth to find hers, and kissed her gently.

He then withdrew, and she could feel his gaze upon her. She did not lift her eyes, and after a long moment he turned his head to watch for the others. *It could not be helped*, she assured herself—*I cannot very well fight him off just now, which is why he took advantage. He is devious, this heretic*.

Once the others joined them, they all crept, hand over hand, along the rocky river bank for a distance, and then—as the bridge faded from sight—the men ventured out into the river again to swim.

The water was calmer, and the river became broader as they made their silent progress; the occasional distant lantern marking a homestead on the shore.

"It was only a kiss, *España*—I think I've shocked you to the core." Raike's voice was amused as he swam, his arms moving easily as she hung on to his shoulders.

"*De nada*," she replied, very much on her dignity. "I do not regard such behavior as surprising, *Ingles*."

"Don't blame my heritage—if you weren't locked away in a Convent there would be men trying to kiss you every day. Thank God I managed to get to you first."

"I will not discuss this subject," she declared. In truth, she had wildly conflicting emotions roiling within her breast, and was very much inclined to listen to his pretty compliments. She shivered—the water was cool, and although he was warm against her, she was not moving, and so was gradually growing colder and stiffer.

"Only a little bit longer," he assured her. "I have used you ill, this day."

The possessiveness in his voice had returned, but she was past caring about it, and indeed, was compelled to cling to him a bit tighter for warmth. "You could not know about Cordez," she acknowledged fairly.   "And I am glad you found me before the French did; although everyone—*everyone*—is mistaken. It makes me wonder how it all came about, to begin with."

He swam for a few moments. "It's complicated."

Yes, she thought soberly; *I imagine it is*. That he was some sort of spy for the British seemed evident; she could think of no other explanation.

He said he'd been "tasked" with finding her before the French did, and the fact that the *guerillas* seemed to answer to him only verified her suspicions—he was no ordinary soldier, to have the mighty weight of the British Command at his back.

Another reason to allow no more kisses, she thought—not that any more reasons were needed, of course.

After perhaps another hour, the men made their way to the river bank—sandier in this area, and not as steep. The lights from a village shone through the trees along the shoreline, and a dog barked in the distance. With a gesture, the two men indicated Elena and Eduardo were to stay crouched in the shallow water and wait, whilst they took a cautious survey of the immediate area.

Raike then whispered to Catalo, "It looks clear—let's get them into the barn first, and then make contact with the owners."

The *guerrilla* nodded and beckoned to Eduardo, who clambered up the bank as best he could, one hand steadying the pistols that were strung around his neck. Catalo swung Eduardo up once again and began walking swiftly across the fallow field in the direction of a large barn, silhouetted against the night sky.

After watching their progress for a moment, Raike indicated they were to follow, and supported Elena with an arm across her back. "Don't speak—we don't want the dogs to start barking." He then almost immediately broke his own admonition. "You look like a wet cat."

"I must not speak," she responded primly, her half-boots squelching as she walked.

He leaned his head next to hers. "You must get out of these wet clothes—I would be happy to assist."

Pressing her lips together, she refused to be teased, and he chuckled. Walking as quickly as she could in her sodden skirts, they traversed the stubbled field until they arrived at the barn, where Catalo held the door open only enough to allow them to slip through. They discovered, however, that their attempt at a stealthy entry was no match for the dogs in the yard, who began barking furiously.

A light suddenly shone in the homestead's window, and Raike said to Catalo, "Go." The big *guerrilla* then strode toward the house as Rake ushered Elena and Eduardo into the dark barn.

"Will he shoot them?" asked Eduardo in a small voice.

"No—the farmer who lives here often allows the *guerrillas* to use his barn. We will be well taken care of."

"We can trust him—you are certain?" Elena didn't want to sound as nervous as Eduardo, but in truth, she had already learned a hard lesson.

Raike squeezed her arm, gently. "Yes—the peasants will keep all secrets."

Elena nodded, shivering in her wet habit with her arms crossed for warmth. It was true; the *guerrillas* who had battled the French troops so ferociously—and had helped to derail Napoleon's plans for world conquest—were considered national heroes.

Catalo returned, carrying an armload of blankets, and in short order the four of them were gathered to eat a shoulder of cold ham around a blissfully warm brazier, the blankets wrapped around them as their clothes were laid out to dry.

"How will the other men find us?" Elena asked.

"They will find us." With his knife, Raike sliced off a sliver of ham and offered it to her. "They know where to look."

"Will they bring the—the dead man?" asked Eduardo, a pale crease between his brows.

"No," said Catalo stolidly as he chewed the meat. "They will bury him."

The whites of his eyes showing, Eduardo glanced up at the big *guerrilla* sitting next to him. "He—he was going to hurt Señorita Elena—I should have shot him—"

"You were very brave, *caballero*, and I thank you," Elena said softly, seeing his distress.

His face crumbling, the boy ducked his head to his chest and began to cry, his small fists rubbing his eyes. "He was going to cut off her fingers," he sobbed, his voice rising with a thread of hysteria.

Her heart wrung, Elena moved to take the boy in her arms, but was stayed by Catalo, who shook his head at her slightly and said, "Such a thing could not be allowed—you did well."

"I—I thought he killed you." The boy lowered his hands and took several gasping, shuddering breaths to calm himself.

"No—I have a hard head. And now an evil man is dead." Catalo regarded the boy steadily.

Recovering, Eduardo met the man's gaze, and made a tentative gesture toward his own head. "The side of his head was gone—it was all—all—"

"Fine shooting," said Catalo, with a nod toward Raike.

"Fine shooting," repeated Eduardo, after a moment.

"*Gracias*," replied Raike. "No one deserved it more."

Catalo brushed himself off, and made a gesture toward Eduardo. "Come, we must clean the pistols before they are needed again. I will show you how this is done."

"Can I shoot yours?" Eduardo had forgotten his upset, in the face of such a prospect.

His gaze shifting to Elena, the big man replied, "We must protect the Señorita. If we fire, it will attract attention, and bring danger to her."

Eduardo followed his gaze toward Elena. "Oh—I see. Can I pretend?"

"*Sí.*" Catalo rose and hiked his blanket around his shoulders. "You can pretend."

Eduardo leapt up, and followed Catalo without looking back.

Chapter 8

Bemused, Elena observed the boy's reaction to this dose of masculine treatment, as Eduardo and Catalo retreated to an empty stall to sit cross-legged and clean the pistols. She said to Raike, "That was indeed fine shooting, and I thank you."

In response, he picked up her hand, and held one of her slender fingers between his thumb and forefinger. "That son of a *bitch*."

"I do not know any English," she confessed.

"Don't repeat that particular phrase." He pulled her blanket tighter around her shoulders, the movement bringing his head close to hers. "Are you warm enough?"

"*Si—gracias.*" *I should move away—just a bit*, she thought; *he is a little too close.* This resolution was complicated by the fact he still held her finger.

"How can so much hair be caught up in one little braid?"

Ducking her head, she smiled; as it dried, her unbound hair cascaded around her face and down her back in long, luxurious waves. "You must make up your mind—I was a wet cat, a moment ago."

"You like to swim about as much as a cat does."

"That is unfair," she protested. "It was not a good introduction."

"I will agree. But we've covered our tracks pretty thoroughly, so that we can travel more openly, now."

"No swimming tomorrow?" In truth, she'd mixed emotions; the swimming had not been completely unenjoyable.

"No—tomorrow we will ride to the north, although riding is not your strong suit, either."

She made a wry mouth in acknowledgement. "I do not make a very good *guerrilla*—perhaps I should have been left where I belonged."

Looking at her hand, he gently played with the finger he held. "I have no regrets."

Thinking to take advantage of his soft mood—and not because she was reluctant to disengage her finger, certainly—she took the opportunity to ask a question that had plagued her from the start of this mad adventure. "What was it that made everyone descend upon my peaceful life? Some mistake has been made, and I would very much like to correct it."

He did not lift his gaze to hers, and she could see that he weighed whether or not to tell her. "A witness came forward. After Ferdinand was deposed and Napoleon was captured, this person apparently believed it was safe to reveal your identity."

"What witness?" she asked in bewilderment, her brow knit. "And it makes no sense—King Charles is exiled in Rome, Ferdinand is plotting in Vienna, and the other royal family members are at each others' throats over his betrayal—why would it be safe now?"

"I don't know who came forward," he admitted, raising his face to hers. "But my people are certain that the source's information is accurate."

She thought about it for a moment, her brow still furrowed. "But then, how did the French discover this tale?"

His expression—always slightly amused, it seemed—tightened into grimmer lines. "I'm afraid there must have been a lapse somewhere along the line.

We had a similar problem during Napoleon's retreat from Moscow—there was a leak of confidential information, and many lives were put at risk. Unfortunately, such a thing is difficult to prevent—there are always those who are willing to change their allegiances in exchange for money, or other favors."

"I see." She noted that he referred to his mysterious "people" again, and hovered on the verge of asking him outright about the conclusions she had drawn—she was convinced that he would not dissemble to her; indeed, she sensed that he had already told her more than he should. No chance was presented, however, as Eduardo approached them, carefully holding Raike's pistol.

"I have cleaned your weapon," the boy announced with a full measure of self-importance.

"Excellent," said Raike as he cocked the hammer, then peered down the barrel with a practiced eye. "Many thanks."

"I will sleep near the door with Catalo tonight," the boy explained to Elena, in the manner of a man speaking to a fragile woman. "We must keep watch."

"I understand," she agreed gravely, hiding a smile. "I will miss you."

Raike tugged playfully on Eduardo's blanket. "I will give you a commission; since you will be guarding the door, you must fetch me some coffee in the morning, from the homestead."

"Coffee," the boy affirmed, nodding as he made the mental note.

"And black powder, if the man has any to spare. Ours is now ruined, thanks to our little swim."

"Black powder," the boy nodded again. "*Si*."

Raike cocked his head. "Try not to mix the coffee with the black powder, *por favor*."

The boy laughed. "No—I will be careful."

"Very well—you are dismissed."

Whirling, Eduardo trotted off toward the door, and Elena watched him go, amused. "You are comfortable with children."

"I should be. I am the eldest of eight." He leaned forward to stir up the brazier, and the flames flickered brightly for a moment.

She found this to be of extreme interest, having no brothers and sisters of her own. "Eight? What is it like, with so many sitting at table?"

"Noisy."

Laughing, she observed, "There would be a great many rabbits to trap, with such a crowd."

He smiled down at her, his teeth flashing white in his dark beard. "It was every man for himself, I assure you."

To avoid the intimate tenderness that she read in his eyes, she looked at the fire again, and asked lightly, "What trade does your father practice, so as to feed them all?

"He was a Baron—a Señor. He is dead, now."

"I am sorry for it," she said softly, glancing up in sympathy. She could tell from the timbre of his voice that he missed his dead father.

"So now, I am the Baron."

She met his gaze, which was serious upon hers in the flickering firelight, and thought, niña, you are reckless beyond measure and this man is not—definitely not—a suitor or even a potential suitor.

Hard on this thought, she stole a glance at his bare chest, a portion of which was visible if one looked from the side, where the blanket gaped.

"You are careless with your father's honors. I think." With an effort, she turned from the covert contemplation of his chest, and brought her gaze once again to the fire. "Did he know you were a spy?"

Taken by surprise by the bald question, he ducked his chin for a moment, but then answered, "I think he guessed."

She glanced at him with interest. "Can you speak of it—of your work?"

Raising his head again, he met her eyes. "I'm afraid not."

She nodded philosophically, and faced the fire again. At least she had verified her suspicions and it was just as well—*completely ineligible*, she reminded herself.   A shame, but there it was—not to mention it was entirely possible that his task was to sweeten her into thinking she was dear to him so as to beguile her secrets. If this was in fact his assignment, he was very skilled and should be promoted immediately.

He touched her knee where it rested beneath the blanket—which was not objectionable in any way, as the blanket was quite thick. "I believe you said your family name was 'Muta'."

"*Si,*" she nodded. "From Castile."

"I suppose you will tell me it is only a coincidence that 'Muta' is the goddess of silence."

"You are tedious, *Ingles*," she responded absently, watching the fire. How annoying that they were back to this exasperating subject again, and that he had left off any further attempts to hold her finger.

He chuckled, and said nothing for a few moments, content to sit with her in silence, rather than press her on the topic. *He is probably afraid I will stand up and leave*, she thought, *which I should—I should not allow this intimate conversation with this heretic spy.* She was unable, for some reason, to put this thought into action.

"You are old for a Postulant, I think—shouldn't you be a Nun, by now?"

She flicked her gaze toward him in mock-contrition. "My Abbess is concerned that I have no true vocation; it is very distressing."

"It would be a ridiculous waste; you are a beautiful girl."

The intensity behind the words made her lift her face to his in surprise. He leaned in toward her, lifting his hand to gently caress her cheek. Breathlessly, she waited, immobile—he was going to kiss her again, and she was powerless to resist.

His mouth touched hers as his fingers traced the contours of her face, and then he lifted away for a moment, as though gauging her reaction. For good or for ill, she could muster no reaction, but only sat completely still, her eyelids lowered because she didn't know where to look—certainly, she could not look at him.

He bent to meet her lips with his own again, this time with more urgency, as his hand moved to the side of her throat. She lifted her lashes to see that his eyes were closed, and in turn closed her own eyes, so as to sink into the sensation of it all—this indescribable feeling of longing, mixed with exhilaration. His hand trailed down within the blanket, and the touch of his fingers on her collarbone woke her from her haze. "You mustn't," she whispered as she pulled away. "Please."

He withdrew his hand, and made no response for a moment. "Your pardon," he finally said.

Oddly, she felt it was she who had transgressed, and she met his gaze. "I am sorry."

"Don't be," he replied. "I am a stubborn man."

Chapter 9

As Raike had predicted, early the next morning the other *guerrillas* appeared with the horses and two additional *guerrillas,* which left Elena—who was unused to the company of men—the sole female amongst six of them. *If nothing else*, she assured herself, *the Ingles will have no further opportunity to take the gross liberties he attempted last night*. She then urged herself to remember that this was something to be desired, as she sat with Eduardo to eat their breakfast whilst the men stood by the door and conversed in low tones, the newcomers occasionally glancing her way with barely-concealed curiosity.

Shafts of intense sunlight filtered through the cracks between the wooden boards that made up the walls of the barn, making visible the motes of dust which floated in the air. The horses' heads were lowered as they crunched on their oats; an occasional hoof stamping on the wooden floor.

"Are we going to Aranjuez, still?" asked Eduardo, who seemed concerned that this plan might have been changed due to the betrayal they'd experienced, and the perilous escape by river.

"I think so." Elena tentatively tasted the coffee, and decided that the flavor was not at all to be desired.

"They are anxious to find a witness to identify me, so that they will understand they have made a mistake."

The boy watched the men discuss their plans, even though their voices could not be heard. "It might take a long time."

She sipped at the coffee again—as there was nothing else—and marveled that Raike had managed to consume two cups without a pause. "Perhaps." She did not want to think about why she was as reluctant as the boy to have their adventure come to an end, and so she firmly did not do so.

"Do you think Señor Raike will let me ride my own horse?"

"I don't know," she responded diplomatically. "We will have to wait and see."

His eyes agleam, the boy glanced up at her sidelong. "He likes you. He told me he thinks you are pretty."

"You mustn't tease me, Eduardo."

"Are you going to marry him?"

"I am going to be a Holy Sister," she reminded him. "We do not marry." She set the cup down, unable to drink any more, and decided it was an opportune moment to broach the subject. "He is a good man, Eduardo—even though he is *Ingles.* If I am called back to the Convent, or—or if anything should happen to me, you must not be afraid to go with him."

Pressing the remaining bread crumbs between his fingers, the boy thought this over. "Would Catalo come with us?"

"I shouldn't be surprised." She hid a smile that he made his preferences clear; she had become extraneous, which was as it should be—it was time for the boy to join the world of men.

After sucking the last crumbs off his finger, Eduardo lowered his voice. "I asked Catalo if he thought you were pretty, but he said I mustn't say it—he said that you must be respected."

"He thinks I am a princess, too." Her tone invited the boy to share in the foolishness of such an idea.

"Like the French soldiers," he laughed. "But they didn't find us, because they were fools."

Fondly, she hugged him to her. "We were good little rabbits, you and I—deep in our burrow."

"We were good rabbits," he agreed with a smile, discreetly freeing himself from her embrace.

"You are cheerful this morning." Raike approached to crouch down beside them, cradling his tin cup between his hands. "And I hardly recognize Señorita Elena—this is the first time I have seen her looking so clean."

Lifting a hand to his mouth, the boy stifled his amusement as Elena primly crossed her hands in her lap. "There was little help for it; between the dirt, the blood, and the betrayals, I have been ill-used."

But Raike only shook his head with regret, and ran a casual hand over Eduardo's head.

"More ill-usage to come, I'm afraid—I think it best to avoid the main roads for the time being; with any luck the French have lost our trail, but I would like to be certain."

Eduardo asked, "Were you a soldier in the war?"

"In a manner of speaking," Raike replied easily, as he took the last piece of cornbread from Elena's plate. "The English make excellent soldiers, you know—none better." This, with a teasing glance at her.

"Did you kill many people?"

Raike leaned toward the boy, and lowered his voice. "We should discuss this later, and not in front of the lady."

But Eduardo found this warning amusing, and scoffed, "Señorita Elena is not afraid—she tried to kill Cordez with her hair."

At this, Raike laughed aloud, the movement causing some of his coffee to spill. "I agree—she is not like any nun I have ever known."

"And you have known so many," she observed.

Still smiling, he cocked his head, as though trying to remember. "Now that I think about it, perhaps the girls I'm thinking of were not, in fact, nuns. But they were all very pretty, and lived together in a fine house in Barcelona."

Struggling to control her laughter, Elena gave him an admonishing look over Eduardo's head.

"I would not want to be a nun, and have to say prayers all day," opined Eduardo, oblivious to any byplay.

Raike contemplated the dregs of his coffee cup. "No—we must convince the pretty Postulant that there are better options available."

"Such as?" She arched a brow, wondering what he would say in front of the boy.

But he was equal to the challenge, and met her eyes in amusement. "Speaking for myself, I have need of an orchard-keeper."

She shook her head. "I am not surprised; you are rarely at home, it seems."

"Ah—but had I an orchard-keeper, I would be at home more often."

She ducked her head to hide a smile as Eduardo protested, "I would not want to work in an orchard all day, either."

Thinking it past time to change the tenor of the conversation, Elena asked, "What would you like to do, Eduardo?"

"I want to be a *guerrilla*," the boy announced, with supreme conviction.

Raike nodded his approval. "I am glad to hear it—you will make an excellent *guerrilla.*"

Slyly, Eduardo glanced up at him. "Then, can I ride my own horse, today?"

"Not a chance." The man gave him an affectionate cuff. "Now, go ask Catalo if he needs any help."

They watched him run toward the others, who were loading-up the saddlebags with new provisions. "Who are the new men?" asked Elena. "Can we trust them?"

He followed her gaze. "They are all *El Halcon*'s men, and we can only hope not to repeat our experience with Cordez. I suppose there's always the chance someone gets greedy, and wants to seize this so-called treasure for himself."

"This treasure that does not exist," she observed with some irony.

He idly fingered his cup. "Oh—there's no question that Napoleon's people seem to think it exists, which is why you are in immediate danger. It is a bit surprising— the tale is a little too fantastic, for my taste."

With a quick gesture, he tossed the remaining contents of his cup onto the ground. "It may well be that there is something else at work here, and if that's the case, I'd like to find out what it is." He rose to his feet and held out a hand to help her up. "Come, it's time to be on our way."

She rose and brushed off her much-abused skirt, stoically preparing for another rugged day.

"Don't repeat anything I've told you to the other men," Raike cautioned, as he steered her toward the horses.

"I will not—my promise," she assured him, lifting her gaze to his—*santos*, but the man was honest to a fault with her; she couldn't help but be pleased that he felt he could trust her.

He slid his fingers under Catalo's saddle girth to check its tightness. "The longer we remain here—in Spain—the more dangerous it is for you. If you could see your way to telling me the truth, then we needn't look for a witness.

Instead, I can quietly bundle you off to England, and all problems will be promptly resolved."

In exasperation, she shook her head. "I am sorry, *Ingles*—"

"Don't answer yet," he interrupted, moving to allow Catalo to gather up the horse's reins. "I know you want to trust me. Follow your instinct."

If I followed my instinct, she thought honestly, *I'd be trying to catch a glimpse of his bare chest again*. Further thoughts along these lines were curtailed as they mounted up, the horses moving restlessly in anticipation. Elena was grateful to see a sheepskin secured behind the saddle, and as Raike hoisted her aboard, he advised, "Tell me if you need to rest, or if you are hungry, all right?"

"*Si*," she replied, a bit embarrassed that he was so protective of her in front of the silent Catalo—although Catalo seemed very protective of her also, the only difference being Catalo was not making romantic overtures.

However, she was soon to discover the reason for the big *guerrilla*'s attitude, after they'd quietly melted into the cottonwood trees. "Señorita," he said, as she held on to him and resigned herself to another difficult day. "I must tell you something about myself—I did not know whether to say, but I think it is important that you know."

"I listen," she replied, surprised that he would broach a conversation.

"Years ago—before the King was forced to leave—I served as a household guard at the Palacio Monteleon."

There was a small silence, as the horse walked a few steps. "I am not who you think I am, Catalo. Do you understand this?"

"*Si*, Señorita." He said nothing further, and neither did she.

Chapter 10

The day was spent riding toward the north and slightly west—as far as Elena was able to determine—and it seemed to her they were in no particular hurry; instead riding along the crest lines of the rolling hills or crossing the occasional river—some so deep that she had to draw up her legs to avoid a wetting—with little sense of urgency. She saw no signs of pursuit, but then again, she was not certain what to look for. The men rarely spoke among themselves, and when a light rain began to fall, Raike pulled alongside Catalo's horse without comment, and handed over his black leather hat, which she accepted with a small nod.

The landscape flattened as they entered the New Castile region; the vast plain of farmland was interrupted only by scattered vineyards, and the occasional windmill provided the only break in the monotonous horizon. To the west, the flatland was bordered by low hills, and it was along these foothills they began to travel, the men keeping a sharp watch as there was little cover.

They stopped for a midday meal, and Elena carefully lowered herself to sit on a sandy patch of ground, stretching her legs out before her, and flexing her feet in her half-boots. She was not surprised when Raike settled in to sit beside her, and—as the rain had ceased—she returned his hat with an expression of thanks.

He smiled as he adjusted his hat on his head. "I can't seem to keep you dry."

"*De nada*; I am becoming accustomed." In truth, she longed for a bath and a warm fire, but for reasons which did not bear scrutiny, she did not wish to complain to him.

"At least it not too hot, this time of year."

"Spain is always too hot." He leaned back on his hands, and squinted up at the sky. "England is much more pleasant—you will see."

But she had done some thinking—as they rode hour after tedious hour this morning— and had come to the regretful conclusion that matters could not continue as they had. "You must not tease me," she said gently. "Especially before the others—they may reach a conclusion that is not true."

He met her gaze for a long moment, the expression in his eyes suddenly serious. "It could become true—you must try to keep an open mind."

"I do not wish to cause you pain," she told him with all sincerity. "Please."

But with an impatient shake of his head, he persisted—the man had warned her that he was stubborn, after all. "It is not so very impossible; either you are a Postulant without a vocation—in which case everyone will be relieved that I take you off their hands—or you are who I think you are." He paused for a moment.

"Yes?" she prompted softly.

"A royal Grandee," he continued evenly. "But it is not as though you are in the line of succession, and it is not as though the royal house is not in a shambles, anyway."

"My poor country," she agreed sadly.

He added with quiet intensity, "The enemy knows you are alive, that you are somewhere in Spain, and sooner or later they will find you. Even if they gave up on finding the mythical treasure, they would no doubt arrange for your marriage to an *Afrancesado*—someone who will serve Napoleon in the next war. You can't wish for such a fate."

Without flinching, she responded with dignity, "I do not contemplate marriage to anyone. I hope to become a Bride of Christ."

After watching her for a moment, he broke the tension with his ready smile. "Then good luck to Him."

Struggling not to laugh, she said severely, "You mustn't blaspheme."

The smile lingered, and he ducked his head for a moment, willing to change the subject to something less controversial. "How did you come to be the orchard-keeper at the Convent?"

She demurred, "I am only an apprentice; Sister Margarita is the orchard-keeper—she is very knowledgeable."

"I see. And I suppose if you are out in the orchards all day, there's little chance that a visitor would accidently see you." His glance was keen.

But she refused to be discomfited. "You have a very strange idea of Convents, *Ingles*, if you think we have visitors coming at all hours."

His gaze moved up to check the sun's location. "Did you have orchards, where you grew up in Castile?"

"Yes." She looked over the flatlands, barren and unappealing. "When I was a girl, I used to climb the trees, and wait for the birds to come eat the fruit so that I could watch them. I had to sit very still, amongst the branches."

He smiled at her, well-pleased with this small insight. "Did you? More a bird-watcher than an orchard-keeper, then."

With a reminiscent smile, she gazed into the distance, remembering the almost overpowering scent of apple blossoms—or ripened apricots, or oranges—and the sun, making her hair warm on her back as she rested a cheek against the roughened bark.

"There were few other children my age, and I was very shy. I suppose it was a retreat, of sorts."

She glanced at him, only to quickly look away at the depth of feeling in his eyes as he watched her—*santos*, she was not following up on her resolution very well. "I should check on Eduardo," she announced. This was an excuse, of course; Eduardo was sitting with Catalo, and from all appearances hadn't spared her a stray thought.

As she stood a bit stiffly, he offered, "You should consider Eduardo's future, too. A boy with no family will have a rough time of it, when the next war breaks out. He'd be safer in England, too."

"I will not go to England, because I am not the Grandee," she replied steadily, aware that he was shrewdly using the boy as an incentive. "Although I am certain it is a beautiful place." This last was added to spare his feelings.

He shifted his hat further back on his head so that he could look up and meet her eyes. "If I find a witness who positively identifies you as the missing Grandee, will you agree to take Eduardo to England?"

"You will find no such a witness." And then—because his words had indeed shaken her a little—she added, "I must remind you of your promise—your promise about Eduardo."

"I haven't forgotten. I do not break my promises."

His eyes was grave upon hers, and she dropped her own gaze to examine her hands. "I meant no insult; it is only—I suppose this talk of danger alarms me. It seems so peaceful here, that I forget what is at stake. I would not like for him to be caught up in it."

He rose to stand beside her. "We are dealing with dangerous people, Elena; make no mistake. Will you at least think about what I have asked?"

"I will. But you must also remember what I have said—how we—how you and I cannot—"

She struggled to couch the rebuff as gently as she could, but he spared her, and interjected, "I know. Believe me, I know."

As she walked away, she was left with the very strong feeling that nothing had, in fact, changed. She couldn't decide if she was chagrined or relieved by his stubbornness—if all the *Ingles* were like him, it was a small wonder they had won so many wars. And she was not helping matters by speaking with him alone and at length, but she seemed to have no will to stay away from him; to refuse to listen to his plans for a mutual future, although it was what she must—*must* do. How alarming it was, to discover that temptation was so very tempting; it was of all things unfair, and the Convent truly did not prepare you for it. Despite her best efforts, she had replayed in her mind again and again those two occasions when he'd kissed her. With steely resolve, she turned her mind to other matters.

They rode almost due north for the rest of the day, and when evening began to fall, the group stopped to make camp on a hillside overlooking a town, the sparkling lights visible in the near distance.

"Where are we?" Elena asked Catalo, as they dismounted.

"Cuidad Real, Señorita." He did not expand on the subject, and she did not expect him to; he kept his thoughts to himself, did Señor Catalo.

Stretching out her back, she cursed all horses, and then began to follow Eduardo as he happily gathered wood, using Catalo's knife to hack with abandon. Grateful for the mindless task, Elena helped him—no easy thing, with so much of the brush wet from the rain.

His wet curls plastered against his head, Eduard seemed none the worse for their long ride, as he wielded the too-large knife against hapless branches.

"We will have a good fire," she remarked, collecting what he harvested in her apron as she followed along behind him.

"Catalo said we'll have fresh meat—chicken. He said he is hungry."

Such a meal seemed unlikely, and Elena smiled as she glanced around them. "I see no chickens, Eduardo."

"It is what Catalo said," the boy insisted stubbornly. "He said he is going to teach me to set a snare for a rabbit, but it will not be needed tonight."

"He is a good friend."

Eduardo paused in his endeavors to meet her eyes with a beguiling smile. "May I trade with you, and ride with him tomorrow?" It was clear he'd been awaiting the right opportunity to broach this plan.

Elena firmly quashed the jolt of anticipation she felt at the thought of riding with Raike—*Madre de Dios*, he would probably consider them betrothed, after she'd spent a day clinging to his waist. "We must do as we are told, Eduardo—and it is apparent that Catalo's horse is the stronger." The boy turned away, hiding his disappointment with only moderate success.

Elena reminded him, "At least Raike will talk to you; Catalo says very little to me."

The boy nodded vigorously, finding another branch to hack. "He says he doesn't say much, because he must listen, instead."

"I wonder what he listens for," Elena asked idly, then stood up in alarm as she saw they were being observed by a man who stood among the undergrowth, watching them at his ease, his hands on his hips.

Grasping Eduardo's hand, she backed away, thinking to call for the others, but the man held up a reassuring hand.

"Do not be alarmed, Your Excellency."

This was more easily said than done; the man was middle-aged, with a dark beard shot with gray, and a grizzled head of hair pulled back into a queue. An angry looking scar ran across his face, and he regarded them with piercing, hawk-like eyes. All in all, he was a most fearsome sight.

"*El Halcon*," breathed Eduardo in awe.

Chapter 11

As Elena stared in astonishment, the visitor bowed his head in amused acknowledgment. "And who are you, *niño*?"

"I am Eduardo." The boy's words tumbled over each other. "I—I am going to be a *guerrilla,* too." His eyes wide, he brandished the knife for emphasis.

"Pray God that by the time you are grown, we won't need you." The man's gaze moved to Elena. "I am sorry if I startled you, Excellency—my men were expecting me, but it seems that you were not informed."

Elena found her voice. "No; I was not, Señor."

"Are you hungry, Eduardo?" The *guerrilla* indicated several dead chickens, tied together and lying on the ground at his feet. "Help me with these."

But Elena stayed the boy with a hand. "Señor Raike," she called out, without taking her eyes from the newcomer.

The man spread his hands in a disarming manner. "I will wait—you do well to be cautious, Excellency."

"I am no 'Excellency'," Elena responded, almost absently. "Instead, a terrible mistake has been made."

Raike strode over, and spoke in a reassuring manner. "It is all right—he is an ally. Allow me to introduce—"

"*El Halcon*," she finished. "Yes; I am aware."

Raike greeted their visitor in the manner of men, cuffing and cursing each other affectionately, whilst Elena watched, holding Eduardo's hand and thinking over this rather alarming turn of events.

Raike must have forgotten that he'd once told her he'd never met *El Halcon,* since it seemed clear that the two men were well-acquainted. That, and the legendary *guerrilla*'s support must have been enlisted to bring pressure to bear on her because she was not revealing her supposed secrets, and who could be more trustworthy, then such a hero of Spain?

After the chickens were dressed and roasted, the men withdrew to eat and have a low-voiced conversation around the fire, punctuated by snatches of laughter or dramatic gestures as they exchanged the tales of their trade. Eduardo chafed, clearly wanting to join them, but Raike had indicated he was to remain with Elena—which was probably wise, considering the subject matter and Eduardo's tender years. On occasion she could feel Raike's gaze upon her, but Elena did not meet his eyes. Instead, she awaited the interview which surely was coming, and wished she were anywhere else.

"Do you think he has killed a lot of people?" Eduardo's gaze rested on the famous *guerrilla*.

Elena had to smile. "You are a bloodthirsty *caballero,* I think."

But the boy's hesitant answer surprised her. "I think about Cordez, and how the side of his head was gone—and I wonder how anyone can do it; can kill someone."

Meeting his eyes, she carefully picked her way through this thorny issue. "I suppose—well, I suppose it depends on why you must. If you are a soldier, and you must kill the enemy, for example. Or when Cordez was going to shoot you—I would have gladly killed him three times over." Inspired, she suggested, "Perhaps you should ask Catalo." The big *guerrilla* had handled Eduardo very adroitly the other night—she had little doubt he would say whatever was appropriate.

Ducking his head, Eduardo confessed, "I don't want him to think I am afraid."

Elena touched the small boy on the shoulder. "He would not think the less of you—I am certain of it."

Eduardo's gaze rested on Catalo, who could be seen in the light of the fire, sitting with the other men and saying little. "Catalo says I should not be here—that it is dangerous, and I must stay close to him. He wanted me to ask if I could switch horses."

"He did?" This gave her pause; Catalo did not strike her as an alarmist. But before she could mull over this unexpected revelation, she saw Raike and *El Halcon* rise to approach her, and so straightened her back and folded her hands in her lap. Raike indicated that Eduardo should go join the men, and then he crouched before her, the worried brown eyes searching her face—he knew she was not happy about this development. "He wants to speak with you—just for a few minutes."

"Of course." She lifted her eyes to his with barely concealed annoyance. "How can I possibly refuse?"

He didn't respond, but watched her for a moment. "Elena—don't be angry; I must do what I think is best."

"Best for whom?" she asked in a neutral tone. "England?"

He covered her hand with his. "Best for everyone."

She nodded, her gaze on the hand on hers. It was impossible to be angry with him; in her heart of hearts, she knew he would never act to her disadvantage. He wanted her to be safe—or at least safer than she was now, when through no fault of her own she was suddenly a prize for evil men.

"I'll stay with you; all right?"

She nodded again, and then looked up to the *guerrilla*, who had been watching them without comment. "Señor; I am pleased to make your acquaintance—I have heard much about you."

As Raike stepped back, the other man bowed his head. "And I have heard rumors of you, also—rumors that I am grateful to behold are true."

"They are not," she replied steadily. "I am not who everyone seems to think I am."

The *guerrilla* hoisted a foot on the log she sat upon, and leaned on his leg to contemplate her thoughtfully, his expression unreadable in the dim, flickering light.

Elena sat quietly with her own unreadable expression; there was an advantage to having been trained as a postulant.

"Your Excellency—"

"Please, Señor," she interrupted. "I hold no title; I am not who they believe me to be."

With an ironic smile, the man contemplated her silently for a moment. "I must disagree. I am certain you are. You are Isabella, daughter of Ana Teresa—may *el Dios bueno* rest her soul, and the souls of all the others, too. You disappeared the night of the escape to Brazil, and you are the missing Grandee."

"No, Señor." She shook her head. "You are mistaken."

He looked into the distance for a moment, then continued as though she hadn't spoken. "The French—they seized the saint's medals off the bodies of our dead soldiers, and then tied them to their horse's tails in mockery. You cannot allow such as they to seize The Spanish Mask."

"God forfend, Señor."

There was a small silence, whilst she had the feeling that he awaited her confession, but she had learned stoicism at the feet of her Abbess, and did not seek to fill the silence.

With a nod of his head, the *guerrilla* continued, "Your devotion is commendable—but the *Afrancesados* are now aware of your role in all this. They will not rest until they find you, and extract your secrets. They will not be kind; allow us to secure the treasure before they do."

At this, she deigned to raise her eyes to him. "How did the *Afrancesados* come to believe that I know such a thing, Señor? What happened to set this—this rumor in motion?"

The *guerrilla* rested his chin on his chest for a moment, weighing what he would say. "I am not at liberty to reveal this, Excellency—you understand that we must protect our sources."

Elena dropped her gaze again, and nodded. No one wanted to say who the source was, or what had happened to set off this perilous course of events. On the other hand, Raike had told her that the English were skeptical that there was a treasure in the first place, and instead felt that Napoleon's people were desperately hoping the rumor was true. It was all very confusing.

"You have nothing to say to me, Excellency?"

"There is nothing I can say, Señor."

He sighed and straightened up, making a conciliatory gesture with his hands. "I ask that you think on it—much is at stake." She made no response, and so with a small bow, the man turned to return to the others, his eyes meeting Raike's for a brief moment.

Raike remained standing near to her, saying nothing, and so she rose to her feet. "I should put Eduardo to bed."

"Will you think about what he said?"

She met his eyes briefly, and then looked away, finding it too painful. "Yes, *Ingles*; I will think about what he said."

As she turned away, his hand stayed her arm. "I am sorry to put you on the spot like this—"

"*De nada;* I know you do what you must."

And so do I, she thought, as she brushed by him. It is my best chance, with the lights of Cuidad Real so close.

She could feel the interested scrutiny of the assembled men as she extracted Eduardo from their midst, and then steered him toward a likely sleeping spot. Once bundled in a blanket, she struggled to stay awake despite her weariness, whilst the men doused the fire and settled down for the night, two of them taking the first watch.

With intense concentration, she watched the guards patrol the perimeter, gauging the timing of the rounds. Next to her, the moonlight illuminated Eduardo's face as he slept peacefully, one arm out-flung, as usual. *He is safe*, she assured herself; *between Raike and Catalo, no harm will come to him.*

Choosing the moment when the closest guard was at a maximum distance, she slipped out of the blanket, and tried to arrange the folds so that it appeared she continued to lay close to Eduardo. Then—bent down almost double—she ran as light-footed as she was able, down the hillside and toward the lights, expecting at any moment to hear a shout of discovery.

Chapter 12

There was enough moonlight illuminating her descent that Elena could avoid stumbling, but it was nerve-wracking; there was little cover to hide her progress, and so she breathed a bit easier when she finally made it to the edge of the vineyard that was spread out over the foothills—the plants were only waist-high, but at least she was no longer so exposed, against the barren hillside.

Because there would undoubtedly be a pursuit, her best chance lay in speed—once she came to the town it would—hopefully—be a simple matter to find the church. She had stayed there before, when she was traveling to the Convent.

Her foot caught on a root, and she stumbled but didn't go down, using her hands on the ground to steady herself. Straightening up, she brushed the dirt from her hands and listened, but could hear only the night insects and her own breathing, the scent of the vines woody and pungent.

Gathering up her skirts in her hands, she began to run again, but was suddenly seized from behind and lifted from her feet, a hand over her mouth. "It's me, Elena," Raike's voice said beside her ear.

She didn't struggle—in an odd way, it was similar to the first time he'd seized her in the Convent orchard—she had trusted him even then, when she knew nothing of him. Tentatively, she tugged at his arm because she needed air; he was in his shirtsleeves, and she could feel the muscles of his forearm beneath her fingers.

"Will you stay quiet?"

She nodded, and he lifted his hand about an inch from her mouth to test her. Gasping, she caught her breath; no easy task, with his arm tight around her.

He said nothing, and into the silence she pled, "Please, *Ingles*—"

"William," he interrupted, an edge of anger in the voice next to her ear. "My name is William—not that you've shown the slightest interest."

He was very unhappy with her, and she found—despite everything—that she wished to placate him. "Please—Wiyam—"

"William," he corrected her.

"Will-i-am." She repeated the unfamiliar pronunciation, then said impatiently in Spanish, "What is the Spanish—"

"No—not in Spanish," he said grimly. "As hard as that may be to accept."

"I am sorry to be so unkind," she said softly. "After you have been so kind to me."

But he was not to be cajoled. "Where do you go?" he asked from behind her head, and shook her gently by her waist. "Who do you go to?"

Hesitating, she wondered how to respond, and he said against her head, "You will tell me, Elena—do not think I will spare your fingers."

He then belied this alarming threat by turning her in his arms so as to kiss her, rather roughly. Surprised, she allowed this gross impertinence, mainly because she seemed to have no control over her response. His mouth probed hers, his beard prickly against the delicate skin of her chin as he set her on her feet, his arms pulling her hard against him. *It is safer if I do not resist*, she decided—*he is in an uncertain mood, this Ingles.*

He broke away, his breath coming hard. As though there had not been a passionate kiss in the interim, he repeated, "Where do you go?"

"I cannot tell you." She drew an uneven breath. "I shouldn't trust you."

With a sound of exasperated frustration, he lowered his head and kissed her again, his mouth open upon hers, his hands moving from her waist up her ribcage, to her breasts.

"Oh.'" She broke away in confusion. "You mustn't."

"Your pardon," he murmured, and then bent to kiss her neck, his right hand moving to completely cover her left breast.

This is a very strange sort of conversation, she thought, and lifted her chin so as to aid him in his endeavors—if she did not have a rash after such treatment, she would be very much surprised.

"Please; let me go into the town—it is important."

"Tell me why," he murmured into her throat, "and perhaps I will."

"I am afraid to tell you."

His busy mouth paused and he pulled away to face her, which caused her to stagger a bit, as she'd been leaning into him. After steadying her by the elbows, he met her eyes. "Why? Why are you afraid?"

"I know you have not been honest—I know you are trying to trick me." She was going to use his name for effect, but she was not certain she remembered how to pronounce it.

He shook her gently. "What the hell are you talking about?"

Unable to hold back the words, she burst out, "I have met the true *El Halcon*."

Thunderstruck, he stared at her.

"It was not well done of you." *Santos*, it was a shame the kissing was finished, and they were on to serious matters again.

Taking a long breath, he ducked his head, and ran his hands through his hair. "Look, if we continue on to Aranjuez, you remain in danger. I want nothing more than to send you to England, and let my mother feed you for a few months—"

"You like your women lush, then; I am sorry to disappoint." Crossing her arms under her undeniably small breasts, she refused to look at him.

"I thought to protect you, Elena—"

"You thought to trick me, and yet you tell me I should trust you—Wiyam," she added tentatively.

"William." He lifted a hand to run his knuckles down her cheek. "William."

"Will-i-am," she repeated. "Your pardon." Naturally, he would have a name that was almost impossible to pronounce.

"You'll get it." They stood together in silence for a few moments, and she wondered hopefully if perhaps the kissing was to recommence. "You were going to leave Eduardo without a word?"

She could tell that it was not necessarily Eduardo that he thought of, and she hastened to assure him, "I was going to write to you—to explain. I was not going to leave without a word."

"What is the explanation, then?"

Carefully feeling her way, she ventured, "It is as you said earlier—I do what is best for everyone. If I continue to travel with you, I bring danger; to me, to you, to Eduardo, to the men. I need to hide away until this—this foolishness about the hidden treasure passes."

He lifted a hand to hold the side of her face against his palm. "I would have torn the country apart to find you."

"You would be too busy fighting Napoleon," she corrected, rather pleased by this show of devotion.

"I can do two things at once." He drew her into his arms, and rested his chin on her head. "I know you are in a damnable situation—I do understand, and I cannot be angry, Elena. But I wish you would allow me to help you."

"You are a heretic spy," she reminded herself as much as him, leaning so as to breathe in his scent.

"I love you."

His arms tightened around her, and she found she could make no response, emotion closing her throat. How very difficult everything was—how unfair.

"We will come about," he whispered into her hair. "My promise on it." He bent to kiss her again—gently, this time; although she rather enjoyed the rough ones, too. "How did you meet *El Halcon*?"

"I do not think I should say," she admitted.

He searched her eyes for a moment, and then remarked, "I believe the religious houses were instrumental in supporting the *guerrillas* during the war—there was a silent network of aid."

"I should not say," she repeated.

He drew away from her, and said very seriously, "Promise me you will attempt no more escapes. In return I will promise you—on my sacred honor—you are much safer with me than without me. The British hold the whip hand now; no one dares antagonize us."

"I promise. But no more deceptions, Will-i-am."

"No more deceptions." He lifted her hand in his to kiss it, and then held it as she followed him back up the hill.

They returned to the camp, Elena keeping her gaze downcast so as to avoid the curious scrutiny her brief escape evoked from the guards. Eduardo slept on, undisturbed, and she lay beside him for a time, unable to sleep, and thinking about Raike, and how his warm hands had felt on her body.

There was really no question of leaving Spain—despite his intent to carry her off to his home in England. It was a ridiculous notion; her place was here. Although she would like to see what England looked like—brimming with heretic churches, and with no decent wine, from what she'd heard. But he would be there—which made all other drawbacks completely irrelevant. *Except,* she reminded herself ruthlessly—*except when he wasn't there, because he was be pursuing his spying business, somewhere dangerous. You are foolish, nina—he speaks of love with soft words and you believe him, even though he lies for a living.*

With a sigh, she pulled the blanket closer around her and faced the sad fact that she *did* believe him, which made it all a thousand times more difficult. He was frustrated, and exasperated, and she could well understand it—she felt the same; something was at work here that neither one of them understood. This—attraction—between them was not slated to end well, but she refused to dwell on this unfortunate fact; not now, when she needed to keep her wits about her. She had been swept up in dangerous events that she didn't invite or comprehend, and even if he could be nothing more, at least he was an ally.

No more kisses, she promised herself, then sighed again; aware that she would break this resolution at first opportunity.

Chapter 13

"We go to Toledo." Eduardo's eyes glimmered with excitement. "Señor Puente says there is a *corrida* there— he says his uncle was a *torero*." The boy picked up a stick and made a motion as though he was stabbing at a bull, complete with a rather gruesome sound effect. "I would like to see a bull fight; I hope we can go see one."

Surprised, Elena asked, "We go to Toledo?"

"*Si*; I heard the men speak of it." He took another imaginary stab.

They were seated on a river bank, drying off from a cleansing dip into the river—although Elena was so used to being grubby that it almost didn't matter, anymore. The group had traveled rapidly across the lowlands and were now several days into the more rugged Montes de Toledo. Clothed in her wet shift, Elena sat with a blanket wrapped around her whilst her habit was spread out in the sun to dry.

A bird trilled overhead, and the boy squinted up into the tree branches. "A finch?"

"Yes; very good—you would make a fine gamekeeper, I think."

"I am going to be a *guerrilla*," he reminded her with a touch of impatience, ducking his head to watch his toes wiggle on the sand. "Will Catalo stay with me in Toledo?"

Smiling, she shook her head. "You will not stay in Toledo, Eduardo; instead you must resign yourself to staying with me and Señor Raike."

His brow knit, the boy glanced up at her. "When they thought I was asleep, I heard the men talking about what should happen to me, when they came to Toledo."

This was unexpected, but Elena did not wish to alarm him. "You must have misunderstood, Eduardo. You will stay with me—and Señor Raike. I have not heard of any plan that would leave Catalo behind in Toledo."

The boy leaned to grasp another stick from the river bank. "Señor Raike says that Catalo makes a good nursemaid. He is funny—he is always saying something to make me laugh."

"*Si.*" She felt a wrenching pang of sadness. "He is very clever, I think."

"Señor *Ingles,*" Eduardo smiled at the joke, as the second stick followed the first.

"Señor *Ingles,*" she agreed. "You must do as he says, Eduardo—he will see that you are kept safe."

"But Catalo says it is our duty to keep *you* safe."

Elena was unable to resist throwing her own stick into the river.

"Then we will all watch out for each other, like good soldiers."

Raike approached from upriver, his hair wet from bathing, and his shirt still damp and clinging to his chest. "May I approach?"

"You may." She made a show of drawing the blanket closer around her, and when his teeth flashed in appreciation, she met his gaze with her own amused one and managed—only with a mighty effort–to keep her focus on his face and not on the wet outlines of his chest.

"Can I watch a bull fight?" Eduardo rose to his feet and began wading into the water, searching for stones to throw.

Raike rested his hands on his hips. "I do have need of a *picador,* to help me catch a fish or two for dinner."

"I will help." Excited by this prospect, Eduardo dropped the stones back into the river. "Shall I fetch Catalo's sword?"

The Englishman raised his brows. "I think not; Catalo loves his sword more than man or beast, and he would faint dead away if we put it to such a use."

While Eduardo laughed, Raike directed the boy to follow him. "Instead we will build a dam with stones, and scare the unsuspecting fish downriver. Then you can stab at them with my knife, as long as you don't stab yourself in the process." He looked up to Elena. "You may join us, *España*; we need an assistant to scare the fish."

"Very well—let me dress, first."

"Not at all necessary."

Eduardo covered his mouth with both hands and giggled, as Elena fetched her damp habit and—after admonishing them to turn their backs—wriggled back into it. She then followed Raike and the boy to a likely place where the two waded into the stream, treading lightly on the slippery rocks in their bare feet.

The sunlight filtered through the trees and reflected off the gurgling water, as she watched Raike and Eduardo build a dam with stones, the two discussing placement and strategy with a great deal of seriousness.

"What am I to do?" called Elena from the shore.

Raike gestured to her. "We are almost ready—go upriver, and then splash toward us."

Elena eyed him doubtfully. "But the water is cold, and I am finally dry again."

His hands resting on his hips, the man said to the boy.

"Do you hear, Eduardo? We will not have fish for dinner, because the Señorita thinks the water is too cold."

"*De nada*," she called out, laughing, and tied her skirts up, knowing that she put an immodest amount of leg on display. "I will follow orders."

She then waded out mid-stream and splashed about as best she could, her arms spread wide to keep her balance. As she came closer to the dam, she could see the fish, flashing silver in the sunlight as they leapt about against the stones.

With a great deal of excitement, Eduardo happily began stabbing them, and in short order there were a dozen or more on the river bank.

Raike surveyed their catch, and then with a wink at Eduardo, tried to convince Elena that she should carry the fish back to the camp in her apron.

"No," she protested, laughing. "I would smell of fish for days."

Crouching, Raike produced a string, and strung the fish through the gills with quick efficiency. "Can you carry them all?" he asked Eduardo.

"Don't let them touch your clothes," Elena implored, and the boy hurried back to the camp, carefully holding the string of fish high off the ground.

As she watched the boy leave, Elena took the opportunity to ask, "Is it true that we go to Toledo?"

Glancing at her, Raike nodded. "Yes—it's a bit of luck, in fact. We've located a witness at a Monastery; a former servant at the Palacio who should be able to verify your identity. We can clear up the matter without risking a trip to Aranjuez, and the French won't guess that we'd go to such an out-of-the-way place."

Skeptical, she quirked her mouth. "A secret witness? Is this another trick, Will-i-am?"

"No—I gave you my word, no more tricks. Hopefully, the witness will tell me what I need to know, and then we will plan from there."

Hesitating slightly, she asked, "Is your plan to take me to England, and leave Eduardo in Toledo?"

Raike looked at her in surprise. "No—of course not. When we go to England, Eduardo comes with us." His tone told her he was a bit exasperated that she still didn't trust him to keep his promise.

Hastily, she explained, "I only ask because he thought he overheard something to that effect."

Surprised, he shook his head. "No—he must have misunderstood. I promised you that I would take care of him, and I will."

They began to walk slowly back to the camp, and she knew they were both reluctant to end this interlude—this chance to be alone together, even if only for a short while.

Squinting against the sun, she asked, "I wish you would tell me what prompted this mad race to find me, that day at the Castillo. Can't you say?"

Willingly, he tilted his head toward her. "Mainly, our people were reacting to the enemy. We intercepted communications about this mythical treasure—Napoleon has an urgent need to lay hands on any fortune he can find—and so they thought to send a unit to check it out. That's why the enemy came calling, that day."

Elena glanced up at him. "And Napoleon seeks The Spanish Mask."

Raike made a derisive sound. "A fantastical tale—the people at the British Museum know their antiquities, and they've never heard of such an artifact. No one has located Alexander the Great's tomb—and it's not for lack of trying, believe me.

If such a Mask actually existed, it would be beyond priceless."

With a knit brow, she remarked, "How strange; the French think there is a treasure—and are much determined to find it–but the British think it is all nonsense."

"It *is* nonsense. Charles' overthrow happened too suddenly—it was too unexpected. We have excellent sources, and no one has heard a whisper about anyone who managed to get into the strong room and hide the royal treasure before the French overran the place."

Puzzled, she glanced up at him. "I don't understand, Will-i-am; why do you wish to take me away from here, if you are not seeking this treasure?"

He sighed. "You won't like hearing the reason, Elena."

"I would like to hear it, nevertheless."

Carefully choosing his words, he explained, "The fact that you have surfaced at all is a concern for my superiors. The British delegation at the Congress of Vienna wants Ferdinand back on the Spanish throne, and wants the Roman Catholic Church's power cut back. But there will be a deep resistance to Ferdinand's restoration as King—as you can well imagine–and if you are indeed the missing Grandee, you could serve as a rallying point for the opposition.

So when my people heard this tale about the missing Grandee, the Home Office decided to extract you before any harm could be done to the negotiations. Or any harm to you, too—you are in grave danger, if Ferdinand decides to eliminate the threat that you pose."

She was silent for a few steps, thinking this over. "It is a terrible thing for my people—to have no voice. To have no choices, except to suffer under the rule of one foreigner or another."

"I can't disagree," he said sympathetically. "But that very attitude is exactly why the Home Office is concerned about a popular uprising—one that could create new chaos, which would only help Napoleon in his plans to raise an army again. We can all agree that Napoleon—or someone like him—shouldn't be the one to hold power in Spain again."

"True," she agreed a bit sadly. "But that does not make it any easier—to have so few choices left."

He touched the small of her back with a reassuring hand. "Spain will endure, *España*—this situation is only a temporary setback for her. But the world is changing, and the old ways are being shaken off."

"So it would seem," she agreed, and then they were back at the camp, and there was no further opportunity for private conversation.

Chapter 14

They ate a fine dinner of roasted fish, but did not make their camp as usual; instead Raike and the men held a low-voiced discussion before he approached her.

"We will stay the night at the Monastery; it will give you a chance to sleep in a bed. The route requires that we cross some farmland, so if we come across anyone, say nothing unless you are addressed. You will ride with Catalo and pose as his wife—the rest of us will watch from the perimeter."

"*Si.*" She would gladly follow any and all instructions if it meant she could have a bath and sleep indoors—although she imagined that a Monastery's guest quarters were not much better than the Convent's. Still, it was not as though she was accustomed to luxury.

With an easy movement, Raike lifted her to her usual perch behind Catalo. "I don't anticipate any trouble, but we do not want to incite any interest—there may be patrols in the area, watching for us."

As twilight fell, they began the journey down the mountainous terrain toward a road that cut through the valley, with the distant lights of a small village beginning to twinkle up ahead—their destination, presumably.

Thinking over this mysterious visit, and what lay ahead, Elena decided she should make an attempt to ask some questions of her escort, now that there was no one to overhear. "Who is it that we seek out, Catalo?"

"I am not certain, Señorita."

With some skepticism, she eyed the back of his head. "I do not think I believe you. You know much more than you say."

There was a pause whilst he reconsidered his answer. "I would rather not say, Señorita."

She didn't press him, since it seemed fruitless, and instead offered, "You are very kind to Eduardo—he tells me he would like to be a *guerrilla,* just like you."

The man unbent enough to say in a warmer tone, "He is a good boy."

With a smile, she observed, "He is having a wonderful adventure, and will never wish to return home."

For the first time, Catalo was bold enough to broach a question. "Do you know where will he go, Señorita? He tell me his parents are dead."

"I am not certain. Perhaps—"

"Señorita," he interrupted in a low tone. "We are to be stopped. You must say nothing, *por favor.*"

Dismayed, Elena saw that there were several mounted men awaiting them on the road up ahead, their hands resting on their pistols. As they came abreast, Catalo pulled up with no show of alarm. "*Buenas noches, Senores.*"

There was a pause whilst the men looked them over. One issued a brief phrase in French to a Spanish translator, who then recited, "Please identify yourself."

A Frenchman, thought Elena in alarm—although the man did not wear a soldier's uniform. She lowered her gaze, so as not to reveal her concern at this turn of events.

"I am Mateo Cordoba. I travel with my wife to her sister's."

After this was translated, the Frenchman asked a brief question of the translator, and Elena recognized the word "*Anglais.*"

"*Non,*" said the translator immediately.

Elena glanced up to see the Frenchman's gaze upon her, so she quickly lowered her eyes again. For a tense moment, she wondered who had the faster horses, but with a word, the man pulled out of their way and his Spanish translator indicated they could continue down the road.

Catalo made no comment as they resumed their journey, and after a moment, Elena asked, "They were seeking an Englishman?"

There was a pause. "I do not know, Señorita."

Elena subsided, but remained uneasy. She was certain that the man had asked the translator whether Catalo was English. Was it a coincidence, that there happened to be an Englishman nearby? Could the French know about Raike's involvement in her disappearance? Impossible, she decided immediately; Raike was posing as a guerrilla and in any event, what he'd told her was true; no one dared to make a move against the British, now that the British held the upper hand in the negotiations.

Subdued by the encounter, she spoke no further until—with a quick glance around them—Catalo departed from the road, and began to circle around a large field; no easy task in the darkness. The horse's footfalls crunching on the dried grass, they crossed over a fallow field which had been long neglected—only a cursory attempt had been made to scythe the weeds. After a time, a high wall loomed up before them, and over its crest Elena could see the graceful arches of steeple bells, outlined against the starry sky—they had arrived at the Monastery.

Catalo walked the horse along the perimeter of the wall, until they came to a halt at what appeared to be the entry gate. He whistled softly, then waited in silence. In a moment, the glow from a lantern could be seen approaching from within, and with a grating sound that echoed in the silence, the gate swung open. Catalo prodded the horse into a graveled courtyard, where two monks came forward to help her dismount.

"Others will follow me," said Catalo to the monks, who nodded without reply. One of them bowed his head and stepped forward to address Elena. "Señora, allow me to escort you to the woman's quarters; your husband will stay in the main building."

With a nod, Elena followed her escort across the deserted stable yard. It was very quiet, and she had the general impression of disuse, as though the Order was struggling to survive. It was a good-sized property, but there were obvious signs of neglect; plaster that had gone unrepaired, and weeds that had gone unpulled. The monk led her into a small outbuilding—women were necessarily segregated from the community—and Elena wondered if she would be in the company of females, for a change. "Have you any other guests?"Without looking at her, the monk shook his head. "No, Señora. Before the war, we would house many pilgrims, traveling the Way of St. James, but there are few willing to travel openly in these times." He paused. "A woman from the village will come to assist you—she should be here shortly."

Standing in the dormitory hallway, her escort opened the door to the spartan cell that was to serve as her quarters—it appeared very similar to her old accommodations at the Convent—and as she walked within she was surprised to see that Raike stood in the shadows behind the door, smiling at her.

Struggling to keep her countenance, she turned her gaze back to the monk. "*Gracias, hermano.*" As the door closed behind him, she tried to give Raike a disapproving look, but could not suppress a smile. "*Santos*, Will-i-am— you made my heart stop; how did you manage it?"

"I had plenty of incentive." He took her into his arms to bring his mouth down to hers.

She did not resist his kiss, thinking instead that it had been far too long, and she was tired, and it was so very nice to have a few moments of privacy—but as his mouth began to move down the side of her throat, she broke away. "You should not be here. If they find you, they will assume—"

"They will admire your ingenuity—a husband in one building, and a lover in another."

She laughed softly while he continued to nuzzle her neck. "Will-i-am; be serious for a moment, *por favor*."

"Oh, I am utterly serious." His mouth met hers again.

Reluctantly, she broke away. "You must go—a woman from the village is coming soon."

"Perhaps I should stay, then; she may need help with your bath."

"You would only be disappointed, I think," she teased.

He leaned to kiss her quickly, one last time. "Impossible; every inch is perfection."

There was a perfunctory knock, and then the door opened to reveal a stout, older woman who looked from one to the other with raised brows. "Your pardon—I believed you to be alone, Señora." With a roguish smile, Raike bowed to the woman, and then exited without a word. Having no acceptable explanation, Elena did not offer one, but instead said with as much dignity as she could muster, "I would very much appreciate a bath, if it is possible."

"By all means," said the woman in a dry tone.

Chapter 15

As the other woman poured a bucket of steaming water into the hip bath, she directed a curious glance at Elena. "Where do you hail from, Señora?"

Elena decided it would be best to offer as little information as was politely possible. "I am from the Andalusian area."

"Ah." The woman nodded. "And the gentleman?"

Uncertain of how much to say, Elena replied, "The gentlemen is a *guerrilla,* who is providing us escort." To change the subject, Elena asked, "What is this place called?"

Straightening up, her companion offered, *"San Vicente de los Reyes.* I come from the village to help, whenever there are female guests—my brother is one of the monks, here."

"I appreciate your assistance, Señora. Once I bathe, may I visit the chancel?"

Her companion nodded. *"Si*—I will show you the way."

The woman offered a steadying arm to help Elena climb into the hip bath, and with a happy sigh, she consigned herself to the bliss of the bath—in the Convent, bathing was a cursory process, and it was heavenly to immerse herself in the warm water.

Later, as she combed out her hair beside the hearth, she wondered where Raike and Eduardo were, and hoped the boy would behave himself, since the monks were no doubt unused to the company of an energetic little boy.

Despite this latest alarming turn of events, she felt confident that Raike would keep them safe, and so was not overly-concerned one way or another about the supposed witness who could identify her.

I am a walking contradiction, she admitted to herself; *I am steadfast in saying that I am not his to direct, and yet I willingly place myself in his hands.* That the future was fast approaching—and that it would almost certainly include a very painful parting—she refused to think about.

Dressed once again in her Postulant's habit—brushed as clean as it could be, after so much misuse—she braided her hair and then followed the Señora across the garden path toward the cloisters. It seemed abnormally hushed, to Elena; at the Convent this time in the evening, one would hear the sounds of the kitchen work, and the other Sisters going about their final evening chores.

"It is very quiet," she remarked as they entered the cloisters.

"The war took its toll," her companion replied, an edge of bitterness to her tone. "The Brothers aided in the resistance, and many paid for it with their lives."

"I am sorry for it," Elena offered with sympathy. "We must hope they wear a martyr's crown."

But the woman only continued with low heat, "The war was not the end of it. The new authorities seized half the lands, here—even taking over the mill, because it was the most profitable. There was little left as it is, but the vultures in Vienna will jump at any chance to weaken the Church."

Sadly, Elena could offer no comfort. "Yes; I have heard that the British do not want the Church to hold as much power as it had."

"The British are the strong horse, now, but they are heretics." The woman pressed her lips together, as though she regretted saying too much.

Being as she was very fond of a certain heretic, Elena offered, "I suppose we must be grateful they helped us defeat Napoleon, regardless of their religious beliefs."

Immediately, the woman smiled in contrition. "Forgive me; there are many here who resent the British, and I listen to gossip overmuch—it is my besetting sin."

They paused at the arched stone entrance to the chancel, and after nodding her thanks, Elena pulled open the ancient wooden door to enter the Monastery's chapel area. It was nearly deserted—she could see only one monk, kneeling near the front—and so she slid into a pew and knelt to pray, covertly assessing her surroundings with some dismay—clearly this sacred place had been looted, and probably more than once. The altarpiece had been removed, only empty niches remained where the statues of saints had once stood, and Elena noted with alarm that there were what appeared to be musket ball holes scattered across the walls.

Lowering her head, she breathed in the scent of old wood faintly mixed with incense, and felt as though she was in a familiar and safe place. *Miserere mei, Deus*, she began. *Help me to know what is best to do.* She did not mention Will-i-am by name, because there was no need—surely almighty God was aware of her conflicted feelings on that subject. And there was no doubt that He had set something in motion—it seemed unlikely she would ever return to her old life at the Convent, and could only trust that this was for the greater good.

After a few minutes of profound prayer, she rose to genuflect, and then turned to see that Raike sat with Eduardo, a few rows behind her. Smiling, she slid in to sit beside the boy, and resisted the urge to hug him. "Are you behaving, *caballero*?"

The boy kicked his legs, impatient with the inactivity. "*Si*—I ate a flan in the refectory. The cook said he will make me *palmeras,* in the morning."

Keeping her voice low, Elena laughed, "Make certain you save one for me—I love *palmeras*." She raised her eyes to Raike, who was watching them without comment. "You are strangely silent, Señor."

"Have you seen the walls in here? I am waiting for gunfire to break out at any moment."

She quirked her mouth. "In truth, I am surprised you suffer to stay in a Monastery, Señor Heretic."

"Not struck by lightning, as yet."

She bent her head to stifle her smile, as Eduardo asked, "What does that mean, 'heretic'?"

Elena chose her words carefully. "It means that Señor Raike does not belong to our Church, he belongs to a different Church."

Eduardo found this of mild interest, and looked up to Raike. "How is it different?"

The man answered readily, "The Postulants are not as pretty."

The boy laughed aloud, and Elena had to admonish him to be quiet, even though she was inclined to laugh herself. "Señor—you must not jest about such serious matters."

He met her gaze and shrugged. "Some matters are more serious than others."

Shaking her head, she chided softly, "You are rarely serious about anything, I think."

"Now, there you are wrong." The hand that rested on the back of the pew stole up to tug on her braid.

Rhythmically kicking the back of the pew before them, Eduardo announced, "Catalo says we leave tomorrow morning."

Surprised, Elena looked to Raike for confirmation, and he nodded. "I think it best if we keep moving."

"But, what has happened to your mysterious witness? Was there a change of plans?"

His gaze was steady upon hers. "No. In fact, the witness awaits at the Chapter House. Shall we go?"

Suddenly wary, she took Eduardo's hand and followed Raike out the chancel doors into the cloisters that surrounded the central courtyard—the place was silent, and there was no one else in sight. It occurred to Elena that she had seen only the two monks who'd met them at the gate, and a third–the one who'd knelt in prayer in the chancel. Truly, the placed seemed deserted.

"Catalo gave me a coin, and I threw it in the fountain," Eduardo announced, as he leapt from square to square on the paving stones.

"Did you? Did you make a wish?"

"Yes. But I can't tell you what it was, or it won't come true."

If only all problems were so easily resolved, she thought. "Very well—you must not say, then." She could take a good guess what his wish involved; the boy was inseparable from his taciturn hero, and it appeared he had left behind his old life without a shred of regret. "I hope your wish comes true, Eduardo."

"What would you wish for, Señorita Elena?" Curious, his little face turned up to hers.

Unsure as to whether Raike could overhear, she replied, "I suppose we all wish for happiness."

With a small hop, the boy added, "I will be happy if there are *palmeras* in the morning."

Laughing, she agreed. "*Si*—that would make me happy, too."

As they reached the end of the courtyard, Eduardo spotted Catalo, waiting outside the Chapter House door. The boy released her hand to run toward him, and the big man hoisted Eduardo over his shoulder and then carried him off to bed, the boy pounding the man's back in delighted outrage.

Elena watched them leave for a moment whilst Raike stood silently beside her, and she could sense the sudden tension between them. He said in a quiet tone, "You are my priority, Elena. But I must discover what is afoot here, because I confess it makes little sense to me."

She nodded, having a perverse desire to help him, even though it might not be to her own advantage. He opened the door, and they entered the Chapter House to see that a young woman sat at the far end of the long oaken table. The Señora from the dormitory sat beside the young woman, and the kneeling monk from the Chancel was seated across the table from both of them.

Ah, Elena thought, carefully schooling her features. *It all begins to fall into place.*

The monk stood to bow his head to her in greeting, but Elena's attention was drawn to the young woman, who rose and held out her hands in greeting. Nothing loath, Elena enfolded the girl in a warm embrace. "Maria Lucia—*santos*, but I am glad to see you."

The other Postulant held Elena tightly for a moment, and murmured the Latin word from the daily prayers, "*Cave*." Beware.

No need for the warning, thought Elena, who continued to smile as she faced the other girl and clasped her hands between her own. "Are you well? Where did the sisters go—is everyone unharmed?"

"Yes; when the soldiers came, everyone fled to Murrilla and remained for a week, until it was safe to return. What of you?"

With a small smile, Elena confessed, "A group of *guerrillas* took me across Spain on a wild goose chase."

"*Guerrillas*? This is so? It does not look to have been such a terrible hardship." Maria Lucia slid Raike a flirtatious glance, and Elena had to quash a jolt of annoyance.

Elena continued, "It is all a misunderstanding; this gentleman is under the impression that I am the missing royal Grandee."

Maria Lucia laughed and turned to Raike, her dimples on full display. "You are regrettably mistaken, Señor; Señorita Muta is not the missing Grandee—I am."

Chapter 16

"I tried to tell him this," Elena noted into the silence.

"*You* are the daughter of Ana Teresa?" Raike raised his dark brows in surprise.

The girl regarded him with gentle amusement. "I am. You will understand that my identity has necessarily been kept secret—a Grandee of the ancient bloodline can only be a threat to Ferdinand, and to the *Afrancesados*."

Raike indicated they should all be seated, and as he held Maria Lucia's chair he observed, "Yet, all this time you've made no attempt to join King Charles's court in exile?"

"Impossible," the girl pronounced, as she settled into the chair. "There are spies everywhere—it was far safer to stay hidden, and await events rather than attempt the journey to Rome. How could we know the war would last for so long?"

Raike cocked his head. "But now—unfortunately– your secret is out, Excellency, and Napoleon's people are searching for you. How did this happen; were you betrayed?"

Maria Lucia shook her head with an irritated gesture. "I do not know. One day all was quiet, and the next the soldiers were at the Convent, stomping about."

"How fortunate that you managed to escape—and find your way here." His tone was mild, but Elena gave him a sharp glance.

The other girl explained, "The religious houses have their own secret network, Señor–thanks be to God."

Raike bowed his head, studying the table as he considered this turn of events. "You may not be aware—Excellency—that the French soldiers who descended on the Convent are attempting to seize the Spanish royal treasure. There is a persistent rumor that you know where it is hidden."

Maria Lucia stared at him in genuine surprise. "Why, that is ridiculous—I know no such thing."

Raike raised his eyes to meet hers. "Do you know how such a rumor got started, then?"

Composed, the girl meet his gaze with her own steadfast one. "I know not—perhaps there was an error in translation."

Watching her, the Englishman explained almost apologetically, "Yet—they believe you have this information, and they are scouring the area for you, hoping to seize the treasure. It seems they are very determined."

She lifted a hand in a dismissive gesture. "I cannot control what the French may or may not believe, Señor."

Raike leaned forward, and said with quiet emphasis, "You cannot wish that Napoleon hold The Spanish Mask in his hands."

"Napoleon seeks The Spanish Mask?" The girl stared at him. "You speak nonsense, Señor. Napoleon is in exile—he is a prisoner."

Holding her gaze, Raike shook his head. "Not for long, I'm afraid—he is planning an escape, and will soon attempt another conquest."

The monk sat, unmoving, but the Señora gave a gasp of alarm, and Maria Lucia objected with an incredulous shake of her head, "No—no; I will not believe it."

"I'm afraid it is not an error in translation." Watching the other girl, he waited a few moments for this alarming information to be assimilated. "And whether you know the treasure's location or not, you are in danger–the men who seek you out are ruthless, and will stop at nothing to discover what you know."

It was clear that the news of Napoleon had shaken Maria Lucia, and she considered Raike with a hint of incredulity. "Surely, the Congress in Vienna would not allow Napoleon to march through Europe again."

"I believe the former Emperor does not much care what the Congress will or will not allow. But in any event, I stand ready to offer my assistance, on behalf of the British Crown. I will guarantee your safety to the coast, where a ship will take you to England until it is safe to return to Spain again." Almost as an afterthought, he nodded toward Elena. "Señorita Muta would accompany you."

Ah, thought Elena with grudging respect; this wily heretic, he seeks to deliver me to his mother, one way or another.

Her brow knit, Maria Lucia regarded him for a long moment. "I must think on this."

But Raike persisted, "It would be best if we left quietly, after breakfast—perhaps with you disguised as a boy."

Maria Lucia blinked in surprise. "A boy?"

Raike flashed his charming smile. "An impossible task, I agree. We can only hope that no one comes too close."

"You are impertinent," Maria Lucia rebuked him, but the appreciative gleam in her eyes seemed to belie the words.

"I hope you will trust me, Your Excellency; I would very much like to act as your escort." This, said with an underlying nuance.

"I would very much appreciate your assistance, Señor." Maria Lucia gave him a glance from beneath her lashes that made Elena long to shake her.

Into the ensuing silence, the monk spoke for the first time. "Although I am sorry to make mention of it, your news is most alarming, Señor, and our Abbot wishes that no more trouble be brought down upon our heads." He shook his head ruefully. "Our Order cannot withstand any more ill treatment."

Raike nodded in understanding. "Of course—your hospitality tonight is much appreciated. You have my promise that we will clear out after breakfast tomorrow; the enemy will never be aware we were here."

"*Deo Gratias,*" observed the monk with good humor, and then he leaned back to clasp his hands over his abdomen. "I will see to it that sufficient provisions are made ready for your journey. What route will you take? I can send word to other Orders along the way—they can offer shelter."

"We haven't the Grandee's consent as yet," Raike reminded him, and then brought his attention back to Maria Lucia, a smile playing around his lips, and the full force of his charm brought to bear.

The girl lowered her gaze to the table. "I shall have to think upon it overnight, Señor." Her eyes then flicked up briefly to meet his.

"Very well, Your Excellency. I promise you will not regret it."

Outraged, Elena inwardly fumed at the unspoken agreement to rendezvous later. *Brazen heretic*, she thought with barely-controlled fury; *and not surprising, considering he has always been so brazen with me.*

As this thought created a feeling of acute unhappiness within her breast, she refused to dwell on it.

Rising to his feet, Raike formally bowed to Maria Lucia. "I will see you tomorrow, Excellency."

"Yes—tomorrow." This with another glance at him from under her lashes.

Almost before the door closed behind Raike, Maria Lucia grasped Elena's hand. "Walk with me; I have missed you, and I will hear of your adventures with this Englishman."

The two girls headed out together into the cloisters, and Elena wasted no time before demanding in a tart tone, "*Madre de Dios*, but *Tio* has much to answer for. What on earth is he about?"

But Maria Lucia pleaded, "First, tell me of Eduardo, is he well?"

At the other girl's obvious concern, Elena softened her tone. "He is enjoying himself hugely, and now he wishes to be a *guerrilla*."

Maria laughed, but Elena was still unhappy about the flirtation she'd witnessed, and asked in a constrained voice, "Tell me, what has happened to *bello* Roberto? He would not be pleased to see you beguile this *Ingles*."

"Bah—Roberto is a boy; the *Ingles* is a man." The girl lifted her face to the stars with an anticipatory smile.

Stifling a sharp retort, Elena attempted to assure herself that Raike—surely—would not take liberties with Maria Lucia in a Monastery, no matter how high the stakes. Surely not.

But it was evident that Maria Lucia harbored a different opinion, as she announced, "We should return to the women's quarters, I think—I am very tired."

ANNE CLEELAND

Out of the corner of her eye, Elena noted that the monk who'd attended their meeting drifted on quiet feet back into the chancel. "I think I will go say the Divine Office—it will be a relief to say it in a proper chapel, for a change."

Clearly torn between duty and pleasure, Maria Lucia asked with no real enthusiasm, "Shall I join you?"

"No—go and rest. I will pray for both of us." This last said in a grim tone, as it seemed that the other girl was a little too inclined to sin. That Elena suffered from the same inclination, of course, was neither here nor there.

Chapter 17

Once again, Elena entered the battered chancel and knelt to pray, this time directly behind the monk, who was bent devoutly over his hands with his cowl hiding his face. With a glance around to be certain no one could overhear, she chided, "I have never seen you so quiet, *Tio*—you must be ill."

Even from the back of his head, she could sense his smile. "You must hush, *Pajarocita*—I am a holy man, and cannot be distracted."

"You are a fraud," she pronounced. "And you have shaved your beard—I nearly did not recognize you."

In truth, she'd recognized him the moment she saw him, seated at the table in the Chapter House, and could not say she was surprised. There were only two people in the world who knew where the Spanish royal treasure lay hidden, and the other one now knelt before her. Since she'd told no one, that left only the one possibility; but why *Tio*—now known as the famous *El Halcon*— would allow Napoleon to learn their secret was a question to which she had no answer.

The man before lifted his head slightly. "How was your apple crop? I hear that Andalusia had a terrible problem with rust, this season."

"The apples trees thrive, and I will not be diverted from this topic," she replied ominously. "What is at play here, *Tio*? I have been much abused, and I would have some answers from you."

"The *Ingles* is a shrewd man," the other observed thoughtfully. "I am fortunate Maria Lucia has no information to give him."

"Is the *Ingles* right about what will happen? Napoleon looks to escape?"

Her companion leaned to spit on the stone floor, which did not seem appropriate behavior for a holy place, but Elena let it pass. "Bah; that miserable creature is like my falcons—there can be no taming him. The British were fools not to hang him the moment he surrendered."

Her gaze fixed on the altar before them, Elena could only shake her head in dismay. "Who would believe it? That he'd be allowed to escape, and bring down another round of misery upon us?"

"It is unbelievable." He sighed heavily. "And this time we stand helpless against him—no thanks to the *Afrancesados*, who infect our country like a plague."

"You are many things, *Tio*," she replied with a small smile. "But there is not a soul alive who would call you 'helpless'. Instead, you will be busy, yet again."

He bowed his head, and did not refute this.

Tio had been the Royal Gamekeeper at the Palacio during Elena's childhood, and he'd patiently allowed the inquisitive little girl to follow him around as he performed his duties, which included training the falcons for the royal family. It was he who had anticipated the betrayal by Ferdinand, the King's son, and who had raced to hide the royal treasure on that disastrous night at Aranjuez, when everyone else had fled in disarray.

Almost single-handedly, *Tio* had then inspired a *guerrilla* war among the peasants, a movement that had spread throughout their dispirited country, making warriors of ordinary citizens and causing such havoc to the French forces that much of Napoleon's *Grand Armée* was forced to stay in the hills and fight when they were much needed elsewhere.

El Halcon became a legendary patriot, shrewd and fearless; and for reasons she did not understand, he had divulged the one secret he'd made her promise never to tell another living soul.

"I know you serve Spain," she continued. "No one can doubt that. But I do not understand—*surely* I am not to tell this *Ingles* of the treasure."

"No." He lifted his head to gaze at the crucifix. "Instead, you will be returned to the Convent tomorrow, and continue on as you were before."

Frowning, she stared at the back of his head in abject surprise. "But—but you heard what he said; the *Ingles* thinks to send me to England, to go with Maria Lucia. He is a very determined man, *Tio;* even you cannot defy the British."

"We shall see." With a sigh, her companion contemplated his hands, resting on the pew. "I am sorry for your troubles, *Pajarocita,* but there is much at stake. Our country is weak, the jackals at the Congress are circling, and Napoleon—cursed be his name—will exploit the situation to the hilt. Desperate measures are sometimes necessary, for the greater good."

She considered this in bewilderment. "What measures? I do not understand; how did they find out about the treasure?"

But he didn't answer her directly, and instead replied, "I will resolve this problem—my promise on it. Along with my apologies for the many indignities you have suffered."

So; he was not going to tell her what was afoot, and why he'd broken his silence about the treasure. That the jackals were circling was inarguable, but it was unclear why he had encouraged them to circle around *her.* Very well, then; she was used to keeping her own counsel, and trusting him. She rose to genuflect. "*Buenas noches, Tio.*"

"Buenas noches, Pajarocita."

Once back at the women's quarters, Elena donned the cotton nightdress laid out for her, and— after scrambling into bed—was not at all surprised to hear a familiar low whistle, sounding from just outside the door.

Quickly, she drew the blanket around her and watched as the door opened just enough to allow Raike to slip through before it was carefully closed again. In truth, Elena was rather relieved to behold him here–instead of other places he could be–and so made no protest.

Arms crossed, he propped his shoulders against the door and did not approach—which was just as well, since she was in her nightdress. A shame, that she hadn't thought to brush her hair out of its braid.

"What is it you wish?" she asked formally. She wanted to make it clear that she was annoyed with him, over his flirtation with Maria Lucia.

"Tell me of the Señora."

This was unexpected, and Elena blinked. "She isn't fond of the English, and she very much resents the situation in Vienna, but I know little else."

"Would she betray you?"

Staring at him, she knit her brow in puzzlement over the strange question. "How—how do you mean?"

"Would she betray you to Napoleon's men?"

Taken aback, she stammered, "I—I don't think so."

He persisted, "For a great deal of money?"

Slowly, Elena shook her head. "I honestly don't know. It seems unthinkable—they have suffered much, here."

He looked aside, and thought about it for a moment, and she waited in respectful silence, wondering what had inspired this line of questioning.

"Something isn't right," he finally said. "But damned if I know what it is."

"I tried to tell you I was not the Grandee," she ventured.

He shot her a look from beneath his brows that clearly conveyed his opinion on the subject. "Can I believe anything that girl will tell me?"

This question raised some alarm within Elena's breast, and she could not suppress a tart response. "I do not know what she will say, but you are *not* to seek her out."

His smile flashed white in the darkness. "If only you were half so avid."

"You won't seek her out—will you?" She could not be easy; he was avoiding any assurances.

With a wry mouth, he shook his head. "You are the dog in the manger, *España*."

Considering this for a moment, she confessed, "I do not know what this means."

"It means you can't have something, and so you won't let anyone else have it, either."

She felt her color rise, but insisted, "I just don't want *you* to have it—and I will have your promise."

He heaved a sigh, and contemplated his hands. "I may have to kiss her, *España,* but I promise I won't enjoy it— although she does resemble you, which is probably why she was chosen to be your mask. She also copies your mannerisms very well; is she a less-royal cousin?"

There was a small, silent pause. "Will-i-am," she whispered, her voice breaking. "I am so unhappy."

Responding to her tone, he moved over to the cot, and crouched down beside it, taking her hands in his, and looking up into her face. "We are going to be married," he said softly. "And everything else will have to fall into place."

She trembled on the precipice of throwing herself on his capable shoulders, and refrained only with a mighty effort. Unable to speak, she did not disclaim, and wondered if she was making a monumental mistake, to even allow him to think such a thing.

"What should I call you?" he whispered, his dark eyes intent upon hers.

"Isabella," she replied, all resistance gone without a shred of regret. "Elena was my nurse's name, and when I hear it, it only reminds me how much I miss her."

He kissed her hands, one after the other. "Go to sleep, Isabella. We are going to steal away before the sun rises, without telling the monks or the Señora. Don't be alarmed when I wake you, and be ready to leave immediately."

"Yes, Will-i-am." She watched as he rose and slipped out the door, on his way to his rendezvous with Maria Lucia.

Chapter 18

As Raike had forewarned, their party crept quietly away before dawn the next morning, the guerrillas keeping the horses quiet until they were well beyond the gates. To Isabella, it then appeared that they traveled north and rather quickly, keeping away from the main road. And instead of her usual place behind Catalo, she'd been hoisted up behind Raike; apparently, he wished to have private conversation with her.

"I will put you and Eduardo on board the next ship to England, because it would be best if you were away from Spain for the time being."

Torn between relief and exasperation at his high-handedness, she explained, "It is not such a simple thing, Will-i-am." She clung to his waist and relished the sensation of being so close to him—it rather reminded her of their swim in the river. For a moment, she was tempted to rest her cheek on his back, and firmly had to take herself in hand.

"Not so complicated that it won't be done."

It was a novel experience to be ordered about, but she allow him this moment of mastery and decided to change the subject. "How went your assignation?"

He chuckled, unrepentant. "That girl will never be a nun—I feared for my virtue."

"There will be no more of this type of behavior," Isabella declared. She could be masterful, herself.

"Pray that there is no need; I must ply my trade as best I can."

Reluctantly she acknowledged that this was only fair—she should not seek to constrain him, since he was evidentially very good at whatever it was that he did. "Can you tell me any tales of this trade?" She was hungry to hear more about him, and how he had come to be in the orchard behind the convent on that oh-so-memorable occasion.

"One fine day, you and I will share a bottle of Madeira and I will tell you the tale."

"*Bueno*." He probably could not tell her much of importance, which she took in good part; after all, she was in the same position as he was, with some secrets more important than others.

He added, "In any event, all my hard work was in vain. Maria Lucia doesn't know much, does she?"

Watching over his shoulder as the sky began to lighten, Isabella admitted, "No, but she is loyal, which is at a premium, these days."

They rode for a few minutes in silence while she contemplated the fact that—strange as it seemed—she was more loyal to Raike than she was to *Tio*, or at least she trusted him more.

After all, she'd allowed Raike to steal her away in the pre-dawn—which must have come as a surprise to the *guerrilla*—and wondered if she would indeed step onto a ship bound for England, despite the fact that such an idea was incomprehensible, a few short days ago.

Raike interrupted her thoughts to ask, "How did you come to be tucked away in the Sierra Moreno? You must have been young—who brought you there?"

After considering, she decided there was no harm in telling him as much as she was able. "That day at the *Palacio*—when the King was forced to step down—no one had anticipated that Ferdinand and his *Alfrancesados* would betray us all.

We all feared for our lives, and many of the royals fled to the coast, planning to sail to Brazil to join the Portuguese court—they were already in exile, there."

She could sense his surprise. "Wasn't that the ship that sank?"

"Yes," she replied in a quiet voice. "I survived only because I'd been sent on a last-minute errand at the Palacio, and they didn't realize I wasn't with them when they left. It was deemed too dangerous to attempt to catch up with them, and so instead I was taken into hiding."

She could hear the surprise and disapproval in his voice. "They left you *behind*? How old were you? Your mother set sail without knowing you were aboard?" She could see that he found this incredible, and felt a pang of sadness that it was not so very incredible, after all.

"I was twelve, but my mother was not in Aranjuez at the time—she was visiting in Asturias, with her retinue." She paused, then explained, "We were not the same as an ordinary family, Will-i-am. My parents traveled a great deal, and often I did not see them for months at a time."

"My family will love you."

He made the pronouncement as though such a course was inevitable, and for a moment, Isabella tried to picture it—living amongst so many others who would no doubt find her strange, and who would speak a language she did not understand. "You must make no assumptions, Will-i-am."

He did not press her, but instead said with sympathy, "I am sorry you lost your parents in such a way."

"Yes—it was very hard."

She was silent for a few moments; she hated to be reminded of those days, and so didn't think of them very often.

After the *Alfransecaros* had overrun the Palacio, *Tio* had smuggled her to the nearby convent in Aranjuez— where the Holy Sisters had nervously hoped her presence would not be discovered so as to invite the attention of the invading French army. And then—whilst hurried plans were being made to transfer her to a remote corner of the kingdom— word came that the royal refugee ship had sunk in a storm, losing all souls aboard. Isabella could still remember numbly listening to the sound of quiet sobbing at the Memorial Mass, as the Holy Sisters wept for yet another calamity that had been bestowed upon their ravaged country by a God who must be trusted, even though He did not seem to be paying much attention.

After a moment, he asked, "Who else knows who you are?"

"Maria Lucia. My Abbess at the Convent." She paused. "Catalo."

Slowly, he raised his head and she could feel the sudden tension in his back. "*Catalo*? How is that?"

"He said he was a member of the household guard at the Palacio Monteleon; he recognized me." Gauging her companion's reaction with some uneasiness, she explained, "I suppose he thought to respect my wishes, and that is why he did not betray me to you."

He was silent, and she'd the sense he was gravely uneasy; that this news was not welcome to him seemed evident.

He began to pull his horse up. "I think it best that you switch, and ride with Catalo—we'll move Eduardo over to Valdez."

In some alarm, she asked, "What is it? Should I be wary of Catalo?"

Glancing at her over his shoulder, he smiled reassuringly, even though the expression in his eyes did not match his smile. "No—it's just a precaution."

They halted, and he explained to the others that they would need to switch, as he was concerned that his horse was coming up lame. He helped Isabella dismount, then lifted her behind Catalo whilst Eduardo was moved behind Valdez. This development seemed ominous to Elena; if he was worried about Catalo for some reason, it seemed strange he'd surrender her over to him.

She tried to catch his eye, but he only announced in a casual tone, "We'll have to divert to Reyna, and I may have to find another horse, depending on how this one does."

The others nodded their understanding, and then Raike wheeled his mount to head toward the west, instead of the northern route they had been taking. It seemed to Isabella that their pace was considerably faster as she shamelessly clung to Catalo, and wished she could have a few moments alone with Raike to ask the questions that were tumbling about in her mind.

They plunged ahead for at least an hour—the land in this region was flat farmland–and in the future, Isabella would never again catch the scent of ripe wheat without experiencing a grim sense of foreboding.

On occasion, Raike would look back at her over his shoulder, and then scan the horizon behind them as the horses thundered toward the hills that rose in the distance.

Suddenly, Isabella heard one of the *guerrillas* behind them whistle sharply, and then the horses came to such an abrupt halt that she was thrown against Catalo's back. Alarmed, she followed the gazes of the men as the horses sidled nervously; a company of mounted men could be seen in the distance, heading toward them from the left at a fast pace.

"Split up," Raike commanded. "Two groups; two directions." He indicated who was to go where with a curt gesture, and immediately they took off at a dead run, Raike's group headed toward the distant village nestled in the hills, and Catalo's group wheeling away at a right angle from their pursuers.

Frantically looking for Eduardo, Isabella saw with relief that Valdez followed Catalo, and then was surprised to realize that no one had followed Raike—they must have misunderstood his command.

Holding tight so as not to lose her balance, Isabella turned her head to watch Raike recede into the distance. Despite the double load, Catalo's horse surged away, opening up a distance between them and the pursuers until she realized there was, in fact, no pursuit; all of the enemy were following Raike, even though it must have been evident she was the only female amongst the group.

"Catalo," she shouted frantically, tugging at his coat. "Raike—they are after Raike. We must help him."

The big man took a look over his shoulder, but did not slow down. "No—he knows what he does."

They continued at a hard pace, whilst Isabella silently gripped Catalo, trying to convince herself that she was mistaken; that something nefarious was not unfolding, as all the other guerrillas raced away from Raike and the pursuing horsemen. Then, when she could not be comforted, she tried to assure herself that Raike was very skilled at his trade, and that he would elude his pursuers. She'd heard no gunfire, so this was to the good—they must never have come within range. He was a warrior, and shrewd for all his light words—surely they would meet up again this evening, and laugh about his narrow escape. *Por favor Dios*.

Chapter 19

Isabella sat unmoving in the pew, her eyes fixed on the crucifix and her mind completely empty. She could not think of the words to the Office—could not think at all--but could only sit, imploring God on a fundamental, unspoken level. Although her gaze did not waver, she was straining to listen; waiting for a familiar footfall, *willing* for it to be heard.

She didn't know how much time had passed when she heard other footsteps behind her, and Catalo's voice, subdued. "Señorita; I am sorry to disturb you, but we must leave."

Without looking at him, she replied, "And where do we go, Catalo?"

"I am to return you to your convent."

She took a long breath, and remarked bitterly, "Now that my usefulness is at an end."

The *guerrilla* stood silently by, and made no reply—but then again, what reply could he make? When they had returned to this cursed place, dusty and disheveled, she had immediately looked for *Tio,* but he was not in evidence.

Instead, the Señora had indicated that she would take Isabella and Eduardo to be washed and fed, but Isabella had angrily jerked her elbow from the woman's hand, and had come directly here to the chancel, to begin a desperate vigil.

She pressed her lips together for a moment, and then said, "He is not coming back, is he?"

"Señorita—"

"You will answer me. Catalo."

She turned to fix her gaze upon him, a white-hot rage suddenly stirring within her breast. The time for cowed acceptance was over, and an unfamiliar fury rose up within her, powerful and fearless. "Speak," she commanded.

After hesitating a moment, the big man admitted, "I cannot say."

"You mean that you will not say." Coldly furious, she rose on stiff legs to face him. "You will tell me what has happened to him—why this trap was set."

With an unreadable expression, the big man replied stoically, "I cannot."

Implacably, she held his gaze with her own. "I command you, Catalo."

There was a small silence, and then the words were quietly spoken. "It is war, Excellency."

She flashed at him, "I am well-aware it is war—better than most, I think. Who has bribed you?"

Almost imperceptibly, he flinched. "No—no." He ducked his chin for a moment. "It was important— something was needed to offer the *Afrancesados*."

Staring at him in horror, she bit out, "You—and *El Halcon*—are aiding the *Afrancesados? Madre de Dios*, I will not believe this."

The door to the chancel opened, and the two monks entered, only to pause in surprise as they witnessed the confrontation.

"*Leave* us," Isabella commanded with an angry slash of her hand, and the monks retreated in confusion.

The *guerrilla* continued as though there had been no interruption. "The French Emperor will try to rise again— and so it is necessary to make sacrifices. More, I cannot tell you."

She struggled to maintain her poise in the face of this horrifying disclosure. "*How* can this *be*? Raike is an English lord; the *Afrancesados*—or even Napoleon himself—do not dare hold him prisoner."

"No one is to know of it, Excellency."

This seemed ominous, and she stared at him. Such a seizure was extraordinarily reckless, even if they hoped to keep it secret—why, such a hostile action could conceivably derail the delicate negotiations in Vienna. "I don't understand—why would they dare to do this?"

Choosing his words carefully, the man explained in a constrained voice, "The *Ingles* knows valuable information." Catalo hesitated for a moment, then added, "Those who serve Napoleon seek to learn what he knows."

Grasping the back of the pew, Isabella steadied herself as a blackness descended, and she breathed in air, fighting faintness. *Madre de Dios.* The monsters would extract the information—and not kindly—and then kill him; they dared not allow him to live so as to tell this tale.

Her head snapped up. "*You*—" she breathed, incredulous. "*How* could you allow this? What kind of—of *Judas* are you—he fought for our country, at your side."

Without flinching, Catalo withstood her scorn, but she could see from the expression in his eyes that he was stricken. "It is war, Excellency, and I must follow my orders. Sacrifices must be made; it is unfortunate, but it is the way of it."

Staring at him in utter incomprehension, she pulled herself together. "Where do they hold him?" Seeing his hesitation, she furiously insisted, "You will tell me, and tell me *now*."

"I believe they took him to the Alcazar—it is perhaps ten miles from here, near Santa Luisa."

This, of course, meant nothing to her, but she commanded, "Then you will take me there, and immediately."

He ducked his head for a moment, then admitted, "It will be too late, Excellency."

In a cold fury, Elena bit out, "Then I will return his body to his mother, along with my abject apologies for the shame of my countrymen."

Struggling, Catalo met her gaze, and did not respond. Sensing her advantage, she continued, "You will find the men in your group who are still loyal to Spain—if any exist—and bring them with us when you take me to where they hold the *Ingles*. You will obey me in this Catalo—we must hurry."

"Yes, Excellency." His resigned tone was that of a man who has agreed to a hopeless cause. "I will do it."

She started to pace, to relieve her tumultuous emotions. "Tell no one. Fetch Eduardo; let these fools think you are returning me to the convent."

But Catalo could not find this plan sensible, and stared at her in dismay. "You cannot mean to take the boy to the Alcazar, Excellency?"

Although she had turned to leave, she whirled to face him once again, her face aflame, and her eyes narrowed in scorn. "Do you suggest I leave him *here*, in the company of dishonorable men?"

He bowed his head. "No, Your Excellency."

"Go, then, and fetch him."

After flinging open the chancel doors, she then slowed her stride, walking through the cloisters with a bowed head and chafing at her impotence, knowing only that she must go to Raike.

He'd once said he would tear the country apart to find her, and she found that she could do no less–how foolish she'd been, not to have poured out her heart. And now— now it was too late—

No, she scolded herself. Enough of such thinking; I will find him if I have to tear down this Alcazar, stone by stone.

She was vaguely aware there were British military garrisons in Spain, but any attempt to find the nearest one and ask for help would take too much time—and it was unlikely anyone would admit to the abduction, anyway— too much was at stake.

Picking up her pace, she turned a corner and came face-to-face with the Señora, who halted in surprise. Isabella remembered Raike's suspicions that the woman was complicit in the plot, and had to restrain herself from shoving her to the ground.

"Señorita." The woman greeted Isabella with a respectful nod.

"No; not 'Señorita'," Isabella corrected her in an ominous tone. "Isabella Maria Teresa Eugenia de Léon; royal Grandee of Spain and great-niece to his majesty, the rightful King of Spain."

Agape, the woman stared at her in confusion, then curtseyed low. "Oh—oh–"

Her cheeks aflame, Isabella towered over the cringing woman, tempted to strike another person for the first time in her life. "And if I am *ever* returned to power, I swear upon my mother's soul that you will feel its sting."

Brushing by the woman, she strode out through the garden gates and proceeded directly to the stable yard. Catalo was there before her, ordering that their horses be brought out, with Eduardo standing beside him. On sighting her, the boy ran over, a worried expression on his face.

"Catalo says we must ride out again—where is Señor Raike? Did the bad men take him? Catalo won't say."

Reining in her fury, Isabella crouched down before the boy and looked into his eyes very seriously. "Señor Raike is in trouble, *caballero*, and we must ride very quickly to rescue him. But you must tell no one of this, on the honor of Spain."

"*Si*, Señorita," he agreed, his little face solemn. "I probably should have my own pistol."

"We will ask Catalo," she equivocated, and stood to see that two of the other *guerrillas* had arrived, strapping on their weapons and striding forward—Valdez and Puente. There was no point in worrying whether they were loyal; she had no options left. After deciding that she couldn't trust herself not to strangle Catalo with her bare hands, she strode over to Valdez, and was mounted up behind him as Eduardo took his place behind Catalo.

"Do you know our errand?" she asked her escort, as they clattered out of the courtyard in the bright sunlight.

"*Si*, Excellency," Valdez answered in an even tone, as though neither her newly-acknowledged status nor the prospect of three men making an attempt to storm the Alcazar inspired the slightest concern. "Hold tight, if you would; we will go quickly."

The horses sped away, but necessarily slowed once they came to the foothills, which had to be crossed to make the most direct route to Santa Luisa. Isabella tried not to chafe at their progress as the sweating horses were urged up the hill, or think about how every passing minute may have been Raike's last on earth. *It is a sin to despair*, she reminded herself; *and I must not start to weep, or I will not stop, and then I will lose all authority over these men.*

It is time to take my fate into my own hands; the old ways will never come back. All these years I have been silent and obedient–waiting for the world to right itself– without ever considering the possibility that it might never do so. And then—and then this laughing man came, and— by the grace of God—loved me; and I never told him—I never told him. But he knew—he knew without my saying; he was so patient with my foolishness. It is a sin to despair—he is yet alive; I know it. I will not believe otherwise.

Chapter 20

Isabella and the *guerrillas* carefully led the horses to the edge of a copse of trees, where they could stay concealed as they observed the Alcazar, which was situated in the middle of a broad meadow. It was an old military installation, the white-washed walls gleaming in the fading afternoon light as their party assessed the wooden entry gate with its two posted guards.

"I need a knife that I can conceal in my sleeve," Isabella said quietly. "I am going inside."

"Excellency—" Catalo could not conceal his alarm at this proposal.

But she would not be moved, as she smoothed out her headdress, and tied it under her chin. "We cannot fight them, and there is little time. If I pose as a holy sister, I can walk about unnoticed, and at least I can discover where they hold him. Watch for me to return to this gate—I don't know how to whistle, so you will have to watch."

"Excellency, it is not safe; if the *Alfrancesados* discover your identity—"

She turned on him, and said coldly, "You have no right to tell me what to do, Catalo. It is by your doing that we are here, and if I do not survive, then the fault is wholly yours. That is the terrible price of treachery."

He bowed his head, unable to meet her eyes, as Eduardo watched this exchange with a worried crease between his brows. "Treachery?"

Hard on this remark, she was compelled to say to Catalo, "If I am—if I do not return, you must deliver Eduardo to *El Halcon.* I will have your promise, upon your soul, Catalo." That neither *El Halcon* nor Catalo could be trusted was unfortunately beside the point; she was running out of options, but she did know, as a certainty, that Catalo would never put the boy in jeopardy.

"Si."

"And you will give him his own pistol," she added. This, to brighten the boy's stricken expression, as he watched them. "Now, give me a knife," she repeated. "Quickly."

A few minutes later, her hands folded into her sleeves so that the knife was concealed, she smiled a serene smile at one of the guards at the gate. "I am sent from my Prioress to arrange for food baskets." She did not specify for whom these mythical baskets were intended, although she imagined she could make a vague reference to orphans if the need arose—there were plenty of war-orphans nowadays; indeed, she was one, herself.

With an indulgent nod, the guard allowed her to enter, and she glided through the assembly yard toward the east wing, as though she knew where she went. From long experience with various palaces, she looked to find the kitchens, where the servants would have a keen interest in anything that was happening on the premises. With any luck, someone would know of a new prisoner who had not been processed through normal channels.

"*Hermana,*" a soldier greeted her respectfully as he passed her by, and she nodded, as she had seen her Abbess do on countless occasions.

The man's greeting heartened her in an odd way—it was unlikely, after all, that the common soldiers were sympathetic to the *Afrancesados;* more likely they were loyal Spanish men, who would be very unhappy to hear about the Napoleonic plot that was going forward. As a last resort, she could always attempt to rally them to help her, and hope there were enough of them who still loved their country.

As she arrived at the servant's entrance near the back of the main building, Isabella stopped a pretty maidservant to ask for directions to the kitchens. With a friendly smile, the girl offered to escort her there. "Who do you seek, *Hermana*?" she asked over her shoulder, as they passed through the door.

"I am to fetch a jug of water," Isabella replied vaguely. Then, aware that it was unlikely a nun would be sent on such an errand, she added, "To assist a priest; I am not certain why it is needed."

Her eyes wide, the girl asked in alarm, "Has someone died?"

"Perhaps," Isabella equivocated, and fervently hoped it was not so. Thinking she may as well confess her ultimate aim, she explained, "I believe he visits the prisoners, and so perhaps holy water is needed."

"I will accompany you, then." The girl's sudden spark of interest led Isabella to understand she had her own reasons for volunteering.

This was to the good; if Isabella was accompanied by a servant, her story would be more plausible—whatever her story was going to be.

Imitating a nun's demeanor, Isabella nodded. "*Gracias.* What is your name?"

"Ines, *Hermana*."

"*Gracias*, Ines; I appreciate your help; I am not sure where they house the prisoners."

They came to the kitchen, busy at this time with the preparation of the evening meal, so that no one had time to show much of an interest in them, except for a young man who laughingly teased Ines as she fetched the stone jug. The girl smiled at him and seemed inclined to tarry, until Isabella reminded her they were needed, and sooner rather than later.

The flirtation was broken off with good grace, and Ines led Isabella toward the back of the enclave; past the curing room, down a set of stone steps, and then through a narrow, windowless hallway that smelt of unwashed bodies. It was evident from the grim atmosphere that they were approaching the prisoners' cells, and Isabella soon beheld a guard who was stationed beside a heavy oaken door, his expression brightening upon catching sight of Ines.

"Juan," the girl greeted him with an arch smile. "What have you done, to have drawn such an assignment? You are in trouble, I think."

The man shrugged in a philosophical manner. "They needed someone to substitute for the guard—only for a little while. I am awaiting a Frenchman, and then I can go."

So—matters were pressing. Isabella broke into their conversation, trying to contain her impatience. "I have been sent to pray for the prisoner."

"There is a priest here, somewhere," Ines explained to him. "The *Hermana* was asked to bring water to him."

His brows raised, the young man reviewed both of them with open skepticism. "There is? He must have come in before I came. Which prisoner?"

"All of them," Isabella answered promptly. "It is the feast of San Pedro, after all." He did not appear to be of a religious bent, and so hopefully he would be unaware that this was not, in fact, the feast day for the patron saint of prisoners. Inspired, she turned to Ines, and took the jug of water from her. "You should stay here with Juan, while I am within; there may be sights which are inappropriate for a young girl."

With this added incentive, the man readily stood to unlock the door so as to allow Isabella entry, and she turned to confront the narrow, damp passageway flanked by cell doors, four on each side. As she breathed in the scent of mold and stale urine, she thought, *courage; he is within, and you are nearly there.*

Juan called out helpfully, "There is no priest visiting in the last cell on the right. That one has his own guard, and I was told not to enter."

She nodded, and then as soon as he shut the heavy entry door, she ran light-footed down the dim hallway to the cell on the end. After straightening her headdress and composing her features, she knocked firmly on the thick wooden door.

After a moment, the face-plate slid back to reveal a rough-looking soldier, who stared at her in surprised silence—she was clearly not who he was expecting.

"I am here to pray for the prisoner," Isabella announced.

Astonished, the man stared at her for a moment. "Who allowed this?"

Improvising, Isabella explained, "It is on the orders of the Frenchman."

"*Bueno*," the man conceded immediately, and opened the door.

137|P a g e

Isabella slipped inside, and suppressed a gasp as she reviewed the scene before her. Raike was suspended in the center of the room, his wrists manacled by chains that were affixed to the ceiling. He had been beaten, and his face was bloody and bruised, one eye swollen shut. The other eye, however, met hers. He was shirtless, his chest covered in blood and several long, ugly red welts. The horrible scent of burnt flesh lingered in the air, and a hot brazier with several pokers stood at the ready. Isabella dragged her gaze back to the guard, fighting a feeling of light-headedness.

He peered behind her, out the door. "Where is the Frenchman?"

"He is coming," Isabella assured him. "He is a religious man, and has asked me to pray for the soul of this heretic."

Openly incredulous, the man stared at her. "*Rochon* is a religious man?"

"Everyone must answer to God," she reminded him severely. "Even you—please kneel for a moment, and join me, *por favor*." She made a gesture, inviting him to kneel on the bloodstained stone floor.

With extreme reluctance, the man shifted his bulk to kneel down, whilst Isabella hesitated; on coming up with this plan, she had entertained a vague idea of stabbing the guard with the knife, but now found she did not have the wherewithal to take such an action. Fortunately, there were other means at hand, and so with all her strength, she brought the stone water jug down on the back of the man's head.

Chapter 21

The guard slumped to the floor, and Isabella dropped the jug and looked up to Raike. "Key," he croaked through swollen lips. "On the wall."

Quickly, she leapt to snatch the key, hanging on a hook by the door, and dragged the guard's stool over to stand upon it so as to unlock the manacles around his wrists.

"I love you." She paused to look into his good eye, and repeated sincerely, "I love you."

She then struggled to twist the key in the rusted iron lock—no easy task for her slim fingers—and heard a low, rasping sound emanating from him. He was chuckling, she realized, and had to smile herself, despite the harrowing situation. *He must think me crazed, and in truth, I think I am.*

 The first manacle released and his arm fell, then the second followed suit and he collapsed to his hands and knees onto the stone floor.

"Stay awake," she implored, scrambling down from the stool, and trying not to think of the disaster that would ensue if he lost consciousness—there was no chance she could support his weight.

"Water," he rasped, and she lifted the jug and released the stopper, tilting it to his mouth as he drank greedily. "Hurry," she urged. "Someone named Rochon is expected, and he does not sound like a kind man."

He grasped the bucket used for cooling the pokers, and with an effort, poured the water over his head. She watched him nervously, and explained. "I have a knife—I thought you could hold it to my throat, and pretend that you have taken me hostage."

"It is a good plan." He rested for a moment on his hands and knees, his tone almost kindly as he carefully took several short breaths. "But you would have a dozen musket balls in your breast before we went five paces."

"Oh." She was a bit shocked by this revelation. "I thought they would respect my vocation."

"I am certain they would be sorry for it, but you would be dead, nonetheless." Suppressing a groan, he began to rise to his feet and she rushed to steady him. He gestured toward the fallen guard. "Help me put his uniform on."

Her nimble fingers flying, she unbuttoned the unconscious man's coat and yanked it off his arms, then carefully slid it on Raike, who grunted with pain as he helped him with the sleeves. "Give me the knife—I am going to take a great deal of joy in killing this bastard."

She found she was unable to stifle a protest. "Is it necessary? Perhaps if you just hit him again—"

"He knows you are complicit." He gestured to her. "Best turn aside—if you faint, I can't carry you."

Stung, she retorted, "I'll not faint—I am worried it is you who will faint." Nonetheless, she averted her eyes as he crouched, and winced as she heard the sound of the blade slicing through the man's throat.

"How many guards outside?"

"There is one, at the entrance to the hall—but he is young, and not the usual one." She thought of Ines and the guard, and tried not to dwell on the widening pool of blood that was suddenly spreading on the floor. "Can you spare him? He has been helpful."

Rising to his feet, Raike leaned an arm against the wall for a moment, gathering his strength. "You must distract him—keep his back to me—understood?"

"*Si.*" Straightening her skirts, she opened the cell door to walk down the passageway and knock on the heavy entry door. Juan opened it, and Isabella noted that Ines was no longer in evidence; he must have been worried how it would look when the important visitor arrived.

Passing through the door, she left it ajar, and circled to stand before the guard. "I am finished with my prayers." Hoping to spare him the same fate as Raike's guard, she smiled in a friendly manner. "Perhaps you will escort me back to the kitchens, Juan—I forget how to go."

"I cannot leave my post, *Hermana,*" he replied in apology. "Where is the priest—is he not with you?"

"Here he is." Raike's arm snaked around the man's neck as he pressed the blade against his throat. With a swift movement, he pulled the man's pistol from its holster. "Don't move."

Watching the terror in his eyes—he was not much older than she was—Isabella was moved to assure him, "Be easy; he will not kill you."

His voice low, Raike said near the man's ear, "No, but the Frenchman will. They can have no witnesses—that is why you were brought in, instead of the regular man. I suggest you say nothing, leave this place, and do not come back." He pressed the blade against his throat. "Do you understand?"

Isabella added with all the sincerity she could muster, "It is because of *El Halcon* that I am here—I swear it by all the saints and holy angels. You need only leave, and say nothing." She nodded toward Raike. "You can see that he is *Ingles*—he should not be a prisoner here."

Juan swallowed, and nodded. "What of the other guard?"

"He is dead," said Raike. "Do you join him, or do you leave?"

"I leave." Juan turned to walk quickly down the hall, and did not look back.

Raike then paused to draw a careful breath, bending over with his hands resting on his knees. He looked up at her sidelong, and she could see that his hair was matted with blood. "Quickly, now—take the habit off; you're too noticeable. You'll be a prostitute, and I'll be a soldier." He straightened up, and sighted down the barrel of Juan's pistol.

She wasn't certain this was a good idea even as she obeyed, quickly pulling the habit up over her head so that she stood in her linen sheath. While it was true that a nun would draw attention, so would a prostitute, surely. "I don't think I have the bosom for it," she confessed.

"Shake your hair down, and no one will care," was his labored reply. "What's at the top of stairs?"

"Nothing—a hallway. It leads to the kitchens."

"Who do we have within the walls?"

"No one," she replied steadily. "Only me."

His eyes met hers for a quick moment, calculating. "Is it light out, or dark?"

"Getting dark."

"Good." Gingerly, he straightened up, and tucked her under his arm. "We're drunk—if we are stopped, you must do all the talking."

"*Bueno.*" Isabella had never been drunk, but she knew what it looked like, thanks to the convent's woodcutter, who was forced to retire when he unfortunately chopped his foot.

They began to navigate up the narrow stairs, Raike leaning heavily upon her. "If I go down—" he paused to take several short, cautious breaths. "You get out."

"No," she replied stubbornly. "I stay with you."

He said nothing further, and they emerged into the back hallway, the clanging from the kitchens echoing in the low-ceilinged area. Supporting Raike, Isabella moved toward the back door, nervously expecting to be found out at any moment.

Apparently unconcerned, Raike lowered his face to hers so that no one would see his injuries, and Isabella smiled and laughed as though he was speaking to her as she steered him toward the exit. Just when she thought they would make it outside with no one the wiser, she heard an incredulous voice ask, "*Hermana?*"

It was Ines. Isabella tried to ignore her, but the girl followed them out the door. "What has happened? Who is he?"

Raike paused to lean against the wall, and Isabella saw his hand move to the knife at his waist. Seeing this, she turned to face the girl. "You must stay quiet," she whispered in an urgent tone. "I rescue this prisoner from the French."

The girl's dark eyes looked from Isabella to Raike. "*Si.* If you wait a few minutes, the guards will change out for the evening meal. I will fetch Juan, to help." She then turned and slipped back into the kitchen.

"Keep moving," Raike rasped. "We can't trust either of them."

Her arm supporting him once again, Isabella began to move along the shadows next to the building, heading toward the same gate through which she had entered.

Two soldiers approached, and Raike swung her against the wall and lowered his head to kiss her, his hands roaming over her breasts. Isabella stood completely still, trying not to be shocked, and could hear one of the soldiers chuckle as they passed by.

Raike lifted his head, and then rested his forehead against hers. "Next time, try to be more convincing."

"I'm sorry—I am afraid I will hurt you." Diplomatically, she did not mention that he tasted of blood.

"I'll survive—just don't squeeze too hard."

"I love you," she repeated sincerely. She could not tell him enough.

He lifted his head, and took a quick survey of the area. "Don't worry—I am completely convinced."

They kept moving until they stood directly across from the gate, Isabella a bit daunted by the sight of the two guards who manned the post, their muskets slung across their backs.

"We will wait to see if what the girl said was true— that they are going to change out," Raike whispered. "If there is only one guard, it will alter our strategy."

Sure enough, a minute later a bell was heard from the kitchen, and with a cheerful comment, one of the guards walked off in that direction.

Lowering his head, Raike indicated the remaining guard at the post. "You must distract him—remember that you are a prostitute. Try to lure him into the shadow along the wall, so that when I take him out, it will not be as obvious."

Nervously, she pulled her shift lower at the bosom. "What if he will not dally with me?"

Taking her hand, he brought it to his groin. "Touch him here."

144 | P a g e

She blinked. "Oh—won't he think it strange?"

"No—believe me."

"You mustn't kill him," she said in a rush. "He is just a soldier."

"Agreed." He paused to lean his head back so that it rested against the wall—she could see that he was gathering his strength. "Now, go."

Casually, Isabella approached the soldier, and—remembering what Raike had said about her hair—she ran her fingers through it, walking toward him with a slow smile. Meeting his bemused gaze, she halted. "What has happened to the other man? I was to meet with him."

The guard offered an appreciative grin. "He has gone to eat, *nena*."

Imitating Ines's manner with Juan, she tilted her head to one side and eyed him. "Ah—that is a shame.

He was going to walk with me." She fingered a curl that rested on her bosom and then walked past him, into the shadows by the wall.

Without hesitation, the guard followed her. "Will I do, instead?"

Apparently she needn't have worried about any reluctance on his part, and Raike's suggestion wouldn't be necessary—which was just as well, as she wasn't certain she could bring herself to do it. Instead, she leaned her back against the wall and smiled. "I will see how you kiss me, first."

With a quick glance around, the man stepped into the shadows and lowered his head to kiss her. He was the second man to have done so, and it was quite a bit different from Raike's kiss, because he seemed intent on forcing his tongue in her mouth, and she wasn't certain that she should allow such a liberty, no matter how noble the cause.

Fortunately, she didn't have to worry about this for very long, because Raike cracked the back of the man's head with the butt of his pistol and with a grunt, the guard slumped down to the ground.

"Let's go," Raike gasped. "Quickly."

Isabella struggled to slide the wooden gate-bar just enough to allow them to slip through, and then propped-up Raike as she urged him out into the darkness, listening to his labored breathing and hoping for a miracle.

Chapter 22

As the darkness closed around them, Isabella was conscious of a feeling of euphoria, despite the fact that Raike was leaning more and more heavily against her. She'd managed to get him out of the Alcazar, but her slender frame would not be able to support her companion much longer and so, when she gauged they were far enough away from the walls, she called out softly, "Catalo."

Raike came to an immediate halt, swaying on his feet. "No," he muttered. "Not Catalo."

Urging him onward, she soothed, "It is all right—he will not betray you again." She hoped that this was true, but there was little choice, in any event. "He brought me here—it is all right, Will-i-am."

But instead of replying, her companion staggered, then slowly dropped to his hands and knees. Alarmed, she knelt beside him, listening to his rasping breaths. "Oh—oh please; only a bit further, Will-i-am—"

Suddenly she felt the movement of men all around her, silently converging on Raike, and carrying him away into the darkness. She followed as best she could, stumbling over the uneven terrain until they were within the cover of the trees.

Her own breast heaving with exertion, she strained in the darkness to make out the huddled figures, crouched around the fallen Englishman.

"Señorita?" Eduardo said, as he stepped toward her. "What has happened to your dress?"

Reminded, Isabella pulled the bodice of the linen sheath a bit higher. *Santos*, she must look a sight—she'd forgotten, in the press of events. "I had to pretend to be someone else, *caballero*."

The boy turned to watch the others, his voice anxious. "Señor Raike is hurt?"

"*Si,* Señor Raike is hurt."

The men worked in silence, not even speaking to each other, whilst she waited for some sign that it wasn't all in vain—it would be ridiculously unfair if the wretched *Ingles* died after all this effort—*por favor, por favor Dios*.

Catalo turned his head to address her. "Did you see his injuries?"

With an effort, Isabella pulled herself together. "He has burns on his chest, but I think his legs and arms are not injured. He has been beaten, and he has trouble breathing."

Valdez was probing, which elicited a groan from the unconscious man. "Ribs, I think. He should not ride until we have a doctor see to him—otherwise it may do serious damage."

Catalo nodded. "We cannot stay here. To the village, then; we will find a stable to hide in."

"They were waiting for a Frenchman named Rochon." Isabella had the impression this was important, for some reason.

There was a small silence, and she was given to understand that this was an ominous sign. "They will look for him, then," Valdez said in a flat tone. "They cannot allow any to know that he was captured by them."

"They will not find him," said Isabella firmly. "Come—where do we go?"

"*Hermana?*" It was Ines, softly calling from the meadow, and instantly, the sound of many pistols being cocked could be heard as the men crouched to aim.

"Come out, *Hermana*; I am here with Juan. We will take you to a safe hiding place."

Isabella put a hand on Catalo's shoulder, and whispered, "One of the kitchen maids—and a guard. They helped me take the *Ingles* out, and so I think we can trust them."

"Raise your hands," Catalo directed, and the two servants obeyed, moving cautiously toward the wary *guerrillas*.

While the young man looked nervously from Catalo to the other men, the girl said in a low voice, "Juan will take you to his uncle's house; he was a Grenadier, and they do not dare to search there."

Faintly, they could hear raised, excited voices drifting up to them from the Alcazar. "They know he has escaped," breathed Isabella in dismay. "Hurry."

Catalo said to Ines, "Go back and listen; come later to report what you have learned." To Juan, he said, "Show us the way."

For Isabella, the half hour that followed was in some ways worse than the past one—up to this point, her only concern was to get to Raike and hope that he was still alive; now she had to worry that it was all for naught. With silent speed, the unconscious man was carefully hoisted upright behind Catalo—they dare not lay him down on the horse— and with one hand, the big *guerrilla* grasped Raike's wrists around his waist, to keep him secure. The rest of them mounted up, and followed Juan toward the lights of the village, their eyes straining in the darkness, and no one speaking as they listened for sounds of pursuit.

The boy directed them to a comfortable house, situated at the head of the main street, and they circled around to the back where the dark shape of a stable loomed up before them.

A man stood watching for them, and silently signaled that they were to move inside the structure. Catalo turned to address the other *guerrillas* in a low voice. "Go—lay a false trail. I will leave a mark on this tree when it is safe to return."

The two men lowered Isabella and Eduardo onto the ground, and then quietly melted away into the darkness.

Isabella turned to face their guide, and saw that he was surveying her appearance in the lantern-light and trying to hide his astonishment with only moderate success. "*Hermana?* Please come with me."

"No; I stay with the *Ingles.*" She was not going to leave Raike again, having learned a very hard lesson about who could be trusted. "He has need of a doctor."

The other's manner became more conciliatory. "Your pardon, I should have explained; I am Señor Tello, and I was a surgeon during the war. I will see to him, but first he must be hidden. Come—I will show you."

Carefully, the two men slid Raike down from the horse and onto Catalo's shoulder, the movement eliciting a groan from the unconscious man. "Tie my horse somewhere else—hidden in the trees," the big man instructed Juan. "Quickly." He then looked around him. "Eduardo?"

"Here," the boy said.

"Stay close."

"I will see to him." Isabella could not be easy with Catalo's management of the situation–although it did appear as though he'd repented of his treachery, since he hadn't taken the opportunity to deliver Raike to the *Afrancesados* in the meadow.

And in any event, she had little choice but to enter into an uneasy truce; if they survived this night, there would be time enough to refuse to speak to him ever again.

"Whose is the boy?" asked Tello, a bit taken aback.

"I am protecting the Señorita," Eduardo explained importantly. "I had a stick, and soon I will have my own pistol."

"I see," said the doctor, who clearly did not. "Come, now."

They followed him into the house, Catalo carefully carrying Raike, and Isabella following with Eduardo. An older woman in a plain, high-necked black gown held a candle at the foot of the stairs, watching their entry with an impassive expression. She made no comment, but turned to follow them up the stairs.

"There is a hiding place—behind the wall on the landing," Tello explained, as he stopped to press on a wooden panel. The outline of a narrow door was revealed, and the surgeon pushed it open to reveal a small room within; Isabella could see that a pallet had already been set up on the floor.

As he ducked through the door with Raike balanced on his shoulder, Catalo said to Isabella, "I will stay with him."

"No, you will not; I will stay with him."

"Excellency—"

Isabella's voice was icy. "I would not be so foolish as to leave him alone with you."

Before the argument could escalate, Tello intervened. "Allow me to stay with him, *Hermana*—I must examine him, anyway." He turned to the older woman. "If you would have a basin of water fetched, and my kit."

The older woman's gaze rested on Isabella's face, and then she said in a low, dry voice, "If you would not mind—" she hesitated for a moment, "Señorita, it would be best to change your dress. It is possible the house will be searched, and you would invite unwanted interest."

Isabella lifted her chin, noting that the woman had concluded that she was not, in fact, a nun. "Yes. I'm afraid there is every likelihood there will be a search; the injured man is *Ingles*, and a valuable prisoner. And Juan must hide, also—the *Ingles* said the French will want to kill him, because he is a witness."

With some alarm, Tello told the woman, "Send Juan in, then, as soon as he returns." With a decisive click, he pulled the panel door closed.

"I will go outside to fetch him." Catalo offered, and his boot steps echoed as he hurried downstairs.

The woman lifted her candle, and turned to ascend the stairs to the second floor without comment, leaving Isabella and Eduardo to follow in her wake. Wary, and wishing she knew more about their rescuers, Isabella asked, "Who is the master of this house?"

"He fell, during the war." The woman made no further remark, as she continued her silent progress.

"I am sorry to hear it. Who holds the house now?"

"I do."

Startled, Isabella said, "Your pardon; I believed you were a servant, Señora."

"*De nada;* I dismissed the servants, when I heard you were coming. I am Doña Francesca." She led Isabella into a small bedroom. "You may wash, although the water may no longer be warm. I will bring a dress and a comb for your hair in a moment, but first I must fetch Señor Tello's kit to him."

"Eduardo—" Isabella took the boy's hand in her own. "Could you help Doña Francesca while I change out of my clothes, *por favor*."

The boy left with the woman, and Isabella quickly bathed her face and wriggled out of her sheath. As the garment was now streaked with Raike's blood, she bundled it up and shoved it beneath the straw mattress.

After a perfunctory knock, Doña Francisca re-entered, carrying a dress over her arm. "It is outdated, but anything else I have would hang on you. Quickly—your escort says there are soldiers in the street, coming door to door."

"Shouldn't I pose as a servant?" Isabella noted the dress was a fine one, as she stepped into it and turned around to be buttoned up.

"No one would mistake you for a servant," the woman explained in her dry voice, as her stiff fingers struggled to close the buttons. "We will say the man is my nephew, and you are his wife and son. Downstairs, quickly."

The woman produced a tortoiseshell comb, and Isabella used it to secure her braid on the top of her head as she hurried down to the dining room, where Catalo and Eduardo were already seated.

As Isabella and Doña Francesca quickly took their places, Ines began to serve up a stew.

Into the silence, a sudden knock could be heard at the front door. As Ines went to answer, the Doña turned to Isabella to suggest in her dry voice, "If you would, Señorita, you must make an attempt to appear frightened."

Chapter 23

"Say nothing, Eduardo," Isabella warned.

"*Si.*" The boy spoke through a mouthful of stew, which wasn't a surprise, since he was hungry, and being pursued by marauding soldiers was not at all unusual.

They all looked up when they heard voices approaching, and Catalo rose to his feet, as though concerned.

A soldier appeared at the doorway, his cap in his hand. "I am sorry to disturb you, Doña Francesca; a prisoner has escaped from the Alcazar, and we believe he is dangerous."

The woman turned to Catalo in alarm. "*Dios Bueno*—are the doors locked?"

"*Si, Tia,*" Catalo replied, "And I have my pistol."

The soldier's gaze was drawn to Isabella, still seated at the table. Remembering the woman's advice, she kept her eyes averted, and turned to pull Eduardo onto her lap.

"We must make a quick search—only to ensure the prisoner is not hiding in the house, without your knowledge." The man's tone was deferential and apologetic; it was apparent he was sorry for the intrusion, and greatly respected their hostess.

"By all means," agreed the older woman, and made an elegant gesture with her hand. "I thank you for your concern." She then remained calmly seated beside Isabella, whilst Catalo moved to the foot of the stairs, a hand on his pistol as he watched the soldiers begin their search.

Again, Isabella had to hope that Catalo would not betray them, and also hope that Raike would not groan again—although the panel door seemed very stout. *If worst comes to worst,* she thought a bit grimly, *I will tell them who I am, and I will tell them they will have to shoot me before they take the prisoner back—they are Spanish soldiers, after all, and so they may be willing to listen.*

"May I have more stew?" asked Eduardo into the tense silence.

Doña Francisca looked down her narrow nose at the boy, and Isabella had the impression she was greatly amused, despite the tromping footsteps overhead. "Of course." She indicated that Ines should ladle more stew into his bowl.

"*Gracias,*" Isabella prompted.

"*Gracias,*" repeated the boy dutifully. "Do you have any *palmeras*?"

"*Madre de Dios.*" The woman shook her head. "You have cool nerves, just like your sister."

Eduardo corrected, "The Señorita is not my sister, Doña."

"No, of course; she is too young." The shrewd old eyes rested thoughtfully on Isabella, but Isabella was looking to the stairs, where Catalo kept a silent vigil, one boot on the lowest step as he listened carefully.

Fortunately, the search was a perfunctory one and the soldiers clambered down the staircase, apologizing for the inconvenience as Catalo bowed his head, assuring them that he completely understood, and that he would remain on guard.

As the door closed behind them, Isabella released the breath she did not realize she'd been holding. "I must go to see how the *Ingles* does."

She stood, and said with all sincerity to Doña Francisca and Ines, "*Milles de gracias*—I owe you all a debt I can never repay. How did you know to be ready for us?" She had puzzled over this, ever since Tello had been watching for them at the stable—somehow, word had been sent.

"I sent the spit-maid ahead," Ines replied as she cleared away the dishes. "I told her we were needed to help *El Halcon* make a rescue."

Isabella nodded, grateful, but uneasy with the idea that so many already knew of their presence here; all it would take was one traitor to seek favor with the *Afrancesados* and they would be lost.

"Is it true, that *El Halcon* is involved?" The older woman inquired.

"Assuredly," lied Isabella in a grave tone. "But the stakes are very high, and I can say no more."

Catalo had been standing to the side of the front window, lifting the lace curtain with a finger to covertly watch the soldiers, but now he walked over to join them, and asked Ines, "What did you hear at the Alcazar?"

The maidservant turned to him, eager to share what she knew. "There is much confusion—it was not clear which prisoner had escaped, and I don't believe anyone knew that he was *Ingles*."

"Is there a Frenchman—newly arrived?"

The girl looked at him in puzzlement, her pretty brow knit. "A Frenchman? I do not believe so. There was a visitor who had urgent business with the Commander, but he had to wait while the grounds were searched."

"What did this visitor look like?" asked Catalo.

The girl shook her head. "I only caught a glimpse—an ordinary man; I do not think he was a soldier."

They were interrupted by Tello, speaking out from the landing. "*Hermana*—I would like to give this man some laudanum, but he insists he speak to you, first."

Needing no further urging, Isabella lifted her skirts and hurried up to the hidden room. "His injuries—how does he?"

The doctor smiled his reassurance. "Not too bad—cracked ribs and burns, but nothing that will not heal; merely a few more scars, to add to his collection."

Closing her eyes for a brief moment, Isabella silently breathed her devout thanks. The sullen guard at the Alcazar must have been waiting for the Frenchman before beginning his terrible work in earnest; thank *el Dios Bueno* that the man had been delayed.

"Do not stay too long—he has lost blood, and needs to rest," cautioned the doctor as he stepped aside.

Isabella slipped through the door, her anxious gaze drawn to the figure on the pallet. Raike had been bathed, and his bare chest was bound tightly with linen strips. His face looked much better—it was still swollen and bruised, but the blood had been wiped away, and the gash near his eye had been stitched. One eye was still swollen shut, and the good eye that met hers held a full measure of concern, so she carefully schooled her expression to be reassuring. "All is well; we are in a safe place."

"Who are these people?" His voice came out in a hoarse whisper as she knelt beside him.

I have no idea, she thought, but said with confidence, "They are friends, Will-i-am. The soldiers from the Alcazar have already searched, and have left. You are safe."

He nodded, a small crease appearing between his brows. "Catalo—"

"I would not like to trust Catalo an inch; but at present I am forced to." She gently took his hand. "I have little choice, Will-i-am, but I am being very careful."

"Don't go anywhere with him."

"I go nowhere without you, my friend. I love you." She lifted his hand to plant a soft kiss on a knuckle.

Carefully, he took a shallow breath. "If you love me, Isabella, I will have your promise—"

"No," she interrupted. "Don't even bother."

He closed his eyes and she could see that a smile quirked at his mouth, despite everything. "Eduardo?"

"He is here—he is safe. Valdez and Puente are laying a false trail." She was well-pleased to think she sounded like a veteran *guerrilla*.

He nodded, then opened his good eye to whisper, "There is a Frenchman—"

"Rochon," she interrupted. "I know—you must not worry; he will not find you. You must rest, now; the doctor will give you laudanum."

He closed his eye for a long moment, then opened it again, meeting her gaze. "*Gracias*," he whispered. Thinking to make a light comment, instead her face crumbled and she began to cry, leaning forward to sob, her forehead resting on his bandaged chest while his hands gently stroked her head. After the storm had passed, she sat up, wiping her cheeks with her palms and ashamed of herself for worrying him. "Forgive me—I am overwrought."

"You are tedious, *España*," he whispered, a soft gleam in his eye. "It is you who are tedious, *Ingles*," she retorted. "Now, go to sleep."

Chapter 24

Isabella left Señor Tello with Raike, and returned to the table to find Doña Francesca sitting with her hands folded on her lap. "I put the boy to bed—he was asleep on his feet."

Isabella took a wary glance around. "Where is Señor Catalo?"

In her dry voice, the older woman replied, "He went outside, and Ines could not resist the challenge and so she followed him. Should I warn her to be wary?" The woman's sharp gaze met Isabella's.

Frowning, Isabella thought it over, appreciating the Doña's forthrightness. "I believe that you—and your family—have nothing to fear from Señor Catalo." When the woman lifted a brow at this lukewarm assurance, Isabella added, "I'm afraid I am reluctant to explain exactly what has happened to bring us here."

The woman offered her thin smile. "Pray do not concern yourself, Señorita—I have not had such an adventure in an age. Tell me, how does the *Ingles*?"

"He—he has broken ribs, and some wounds, but he should recover." Thinking of how Raike had looked, she could feel her mouth began to tremble, and firmly closed her lips, refusing to start weeping again. "It is difficult to see him so."

"I do not doubt it. You have known him long?" The woman's thoughtful gaze rested on her face.

Be wary, Isabella reminded herself. "I am afraid I am not at liberty to say." She tried to convey the unspoken impression that *El Halcon*'s secrets must be protected.

"*Si*," the woman agreed without surprise. "It makes no sense that the Alcazar would treat an *Ingles* in such a way—there must be evil forces at work."

"Indeed, there are." Isabella agreed. "And thank you again, for taking us in. What purpose does the hidden room serve?"

Lifting her gaze to the stairway, Doña Francisca explained, "It was originally a lock-room to store valuables, but during the war my husband became involved in the resistance to the French, who'd commandeered the Alcazar." After a moment, she added, "The *Ingles* is not the first escaped prisoner who has been hidden within—nor is he the first *guerrilla*."

Isabella had already surmised as much; when the hated French betrayed Spain, the furious populace had taken matters into their own hands—no doubt there were many such hidden rooms in many a home. "I understand your late husband was a Grenadier."

"Indeed, he was. After the French betrayed us, he worked to disrupt the supply trains, when they came in from the coast. He fell at Cadiz."

Isabella nodded, having heard many tales of the bravery of the citizens who rose up to fight their former ally—even taking to the streets, to battle hand-to-hand. She thought of the ominous news of Napoleon's next war, and could not bear to think that it may all have been for naught.

As if reading her thoughts, her companion's mouth tightened. "And now everything is so uncertain; our King is a fool—"

"The true King is in Rome," Isabella interrupted firmly. "Ferdinand is nothing but a despicable puppet."

At this pronouncement, the older woman spread her hands in reluctant acknowledgment. "Indeed—but King Charles is unlikely to return, and we've no choice in what is to happen to us."

Stubbornly, Isabella shook her head. "It matters not what they do. We did not fight off one oppressor to accept another; we are Spaniards—it is not in our nature."

Lifting her brows, Doña Francesca regarded her thoughtfully. "You are right, of course. I hadn't looked at it in quite that way."

Footsteps could be heard descending the stairs, and Tello joined them, nodding at Isabella, and helping himself to coffee. "He is asleep, but we should watch him this first night; Juan will sit with him for a time, and then I will take a turn."

"I will also take a turn," Isabella said.

The surgeon gently shook his head. "You will need your rest, *Hermana*—and you must not be closeted with him alone."

Isabella regarded him as though he had said something completely nonsensical. "I will take a turn," she repeated. "Only tell me what I must do to care for him."

After intercepting a glance from the older woman, the man capitulated. "*Si, Hermana.*"

They sat in silence for a moment or two, and then Tello glanced at Isabella, fiddling with his coffee cup. "I am given to understand—that is, Juan mentioned that *El Halcon* was involved in these matters."

"Indeed, he is," Isabella agreed. Involved up to his eyeballs, the black-hearted scoundrel.

"Will he come here?" The man could not quite conceal this fervent hope.

"I do not know, Señor," Isabella equivocated. "Much must necessarily be left unplanned." Which reminded her that she should best make an exit, before the aforementioned scoundrel could make an unwanted appearance and seize hold of Raike again. "How soon can the *Ingles* travel?"

The surgeon shrugged. "A few days—with ribs, there is little to be done, except to try to keep him quiet. He's a strong man, we will see how he does." He looked up to Doña Francisca. "I will take Juan a bowl of stew—he has not yet eaten."

"Allow me to relieve him," Isabella offered, as she rose. "What should I watch for?"

"Fever," the surgeon responded. "Or if he seems overly restless—come fetch me."

As she crossed the floor toward the stairs, Catalo returned through the front door with Ines by his side, the girl's pretty mouth sulking. *I could have warned her*, thought Isabella dryly as she mounted the steps. *Catalo is not one to dally—he follows orders, and does not indulge himself.*

After sending Juan downstairs, Isabella closed the door to the hidden room and then knelt on the floor next to Raike, who was sleeping soundly. His forehead was cool to the touch, and so she settled in next to him, leaning against the wall, and shifting to try and find a comfortable position—she would have liked some laudanum herself; it had been a long and thoroughly miserable day.

She watched Raike breathe for a few moments, and then gently placed her hand atop his arm—he who was so capable, so confident; now helpless and surrounded by those who had betrayed him.

Indeed, she would not be over-surprised if Catalo and the other *guerrillas* were trying to contact *El Halcon* this very night—they would certainly obey him before they would obey her, no matter their regret in the matter.

She pressed her lips together, thinking that it all made little sense; if she had not seen *Tio*'s duplicity with her own eyes, she would never—never in a *thousand* years—have believed it of him, that he would conspire with the *Afrancesados* so as to allow Napoleon to access Raike's secrets.

Tio must have a reason, she decided; but whatever it is, it is no excuse. No matter the stakes, one does not sacrifice an innocent ally to such a fate.

Meanwhile, she had a helpless man and a little boy to protect while *El Halcon* and the *Afrancesados* were determinedly searching for them; and as the *guerrillas* were expert at such things, she imagined they would be indeed be discovered, and sooner rather than later.

I need leverage, she decided, watching Raike's chest rise and fall, and then toyed with the idea of heading to the nearest British garrison—surely even *El Halcon* would not dare flout the mighty British. The problem, of course, was logistical—she could not make the attempt alone, because she could not leave Raike with Catalo, and she could not transport Raike and Eduardo without Catalo, either. *I am helpless*, she thought in acute frustration. *It is beyond vexing, that there is nothing I can do to put a stop to Tio's treachery.*

Frowning, she gently stroked Raike's arm, watching the dark hair spring up after her fingers had passed over it, and then her hand suddenly stilled, as she lifted her gaze to watch the shadows dancing on the wall. *That is not true—I am not so very helpless,* she realized.

I have been so distracted that I've forgotten I have the best leverage of all; the British aren't the only ones who hold the whip hand.

Leaning forward on her hands and knees, she carefully kissed Raike's forehead. "I will be back," she whispered, then exited the room to stand on the landing and address the others, seated at the table below. "Doña, is there a priest nearby who can be trusted?"

Aghast, they turned to her with one accord, and she quickly reassured them, "No, no—the *Ingles* is well. It is just that I have a mind to be married, this night."

Chapter 25

As could be expected, this announcement was met with a stunned silence. Isabella repeated, "I must marry the *Ingles,* and immediately. Is there a priest who will be discreet?"

Doña Francesca considered the request, but shook her head with regret. "The local *Padre* drinks to excess—he would not be discreet, and at this time of night he may not even be coherent."

"*Hermana,*" interrupted Tello in astonishment. "Your holy vows—"

"I am merely a postulant, I have taken no holy vows." She thought it over for a moment. "Is there a civil servant who could marry us?"

"You cannot be married outside of the church," protested Tello in undisguised horror. "Please—it is unthinkable."

"I can be married in the church at a later time," Isabella pointed out. "But it is important that I be married to the *Ingles* as soon as possible." Better not mention that the bridegroom was a heretic; one shock at a time.

"Is such haste necessary?" asked the older woman, as though she was merely curious. "Perhaps he should recover a bit."

"Tonight," said Isabella bluntly, and allowed her gaze to rest for an accusatory moment on Catalo. "He must be made my husband this night."

"I am a priest," said Catalo.

Staring at him in astonishment, Isabella could not find her tongue for a moment. "This is true?"

He met her gaze, his own unreadable. *"Si.* I can perform the marriage."

"I thought you said you were a palace guard," she accused him with some suspicion.

He bowed his head in acknowledgement. "And a priest."

"You are a very strange sort of priest," she bit out, conflicting emotions roiling within her breast. If he was indeed a priest, she must respect his vocation and—regrettably—no longer harbor fantasies of murdering him. "If this is some sort of trick—" she began in an ominous tone.

"It is not."

"Hermana—er, Señorita," Tello ventured, obviously distressed by these developments. "The *Ingles* has been drugged—he will sleep for hours."

"We will wake him up for this," Isabella replied firmly. "He need only agree to it. Come, Catalo."

Catalo nodded, and rose to his feet. "A witness will be necessary."

"I will witness," said Doña Francesca, who rose to follow Catalo. "Señor Tello, if you would keep a vigil outside the door, please." As she followed Isabella, the woman murmured in an undertone, "Tello would be a too-exacting witness, I think."

They crowded into the narrow room where Raike slept, his head turned to one side on the pallet. Isabella knelt beside him, and said softly, "Will-i-am; can you wake up for a moment?" She tentatively patted his bearded cheek, and he turned his head toward her, murmuring something in English.

Isabella looked up to the others. "Does anyone speak English?"

"Some," said Catalo. "But I do not know what it is he said."

"Perhaps we should proceed," suggested the Doña, gracefully settling in to sit on the stool, "and we shall see how he does."

Thinking this good advice, Isabella sat back on her legs and cradled Raike's hand in both of hers, looking up to Catalo expectedly and trying not to think of how she would have to explain to Raike that the traitorous *guerrilla* presided at their wedding.

Catalo hesitated, then asked, "Are you certain—that is, can we be certain this man is not already married?"

"*Si,*" Isabella said calmly, and hoped it was true. "Indeed, he offered marriage to me as recently as yesterday." How strange, that yesterday seemed like it was two lifetimes ago.

"And his Christian name is—?"

"Will-i-am."

"Ah—*Guillermo,*" remarked Doña Francesca.

Intrigued, Isabella turned to her. "Is it so? He did not wish me to say it in Spanish."

"I suppose you must learn English, then," the older woman replied.

"He will be my husband; of course I will learn his language." Glancing down at him, Isabella's gaze lingered on the planes of Raike's cheekbones, on the eyelashes fanned out against his skin, so much paler than usual. Without conscious thought, she gently smoothed a lock of hair back from his bruised forehead. "Of course," she repeated.

"Let us proceed, then," said the Doña in a satisfied tone.

Catalo made the Sign of the Cross, with the women following suit, and then he began the abbreviated ritual. They came to the portion that required vows to be spoken, and—as Raike had not yet moved—Isabella began to experience some doubts that she would be able to elicit a response from him—or at least enough of a response to pass muster, no matter how compliant the witness. With some urgency, she repeated Catalo's promptings, bending her head to her bridegroom so that she spoke very close to his ear. "I, Isabella, take you, Will-i-am—"

Raike moved suddenly, shifting his face on the pallet toward her voice, and his good eye flickered open for a moment as he tried to focus on her.

Delighted, she smiled at him. "*Querido,*" she said softly. "You will marry me, *si*?"

"*Si,*" he whispered, the syllable barely audible as he closed his eye again.

"That will do," pronounced Doña Francesca.

Catalo raised his hand, and as he gestured a blessing over the couple Isabella bent her head, trying not to think of the confrontation to come between the two men— although the confrontation would necessarily have to wait until Raike found his feet.

"Many blessings," said the older woman, as she rose to formally kiss Isabella's cheeks.

"Thank you, Doña. We will leave for Aranjuez tomorrow—as quietly as possible." Isabella turned to Catalo. "You will take us, and if you dare—if you *dare* to speak of this to anyone—"

"I will not," Catalo replied, stone-faced, and aware that she referred to *El Halcon*.

Hopefully, she'd secured his cooperation, although it was a gamble; with any luck, the same bone-deep loyalty that compelled him to obey her would now compel him to protect her husband, but in the end, she couldn't be certain–his loyalty to *El Halcon* may trump all other considerations.

The tense confrontation was interrupted by Doña Francesca, who thoughtfully tapped a finger against her cheek.

"A carriage would be best, perhaps; otherwise, the injured man will draw attention. He could lie down on the floor, out of sight."

"I'm afraid we have no carriage," Isabella pointed out.

The woman met her eyes. "You will; have no fears about being given whatever is needed." Frowning, Isabella considered the merits of this plan. "We could pose as a family, as we did when the soldiers came—it would serve us well; no one would be searching for a family, and no one would mistake Catalo for Raike—they are not the same size."

"A wagon, then," suggested Catalo. "It would be best if the boy is visible."

"It shall be done," the woman assured them. "There are many who will give you aid, and never speak of it—do not fear." She then said to Catalo, "Go down—I will join you in a moment."

After the *guerrilla* stepped onto the stairway landing, the Doña leaned in to Isabella, and advised her in a low tone, "You must close the door, and remain behind for a time with your new husband. It is important that you attempt to consummate the marriage—or at least lead everyone to believe it could have been consummated. Otherwise, it could be set aside."

"Oh," said Isabella, a bit taken aback. "I did not realize—"

"And you will need a wedding ring," the other woman added, as she began to remove the wedding ring from her own finger.

Chapter 26

"Doña Francesca," Isabella protested, "I cannot take your wedding ring."

"Nonsense; what good does it do me?" With her dry smile, the woman worked the thin gold band over her knuckle, and handed it over to Isabella. "It may be too large for you, but you must have a ring, if you are to pose as a wife."

Torn, Isabella held it between her fingers. "I feel that I should not wear it—your husband—"

In response, her companion folded her hands before her, with her gaze fixed upon the thin, gold ring. "My husband was awarded a medal—the *Medalla al Valor*—in Madrid, after the Battle of Talavera. The Queen herself bestowed the honor upon him, and it was the proudest day of his life. He never tired of speaking of it—how Queen Maria Luisa had taken his hand in her own, and had spoken so kindly to him. He told me in that one moment, he could feel the presence of King Leovigild himself, along with all the ancient and mighty Kings of Spain; he was overcome with humility, to receive such an honor in their presence."

The woman paused, her low voice suddenly rich with emotion. "He wore that medal every day of his life, and I am certain he was wearing it when he fell at Cadiz."

Lifting her eyes, the woman concluded, "He would be honored to know that you are wearing his ring."

Bowing her head, Isabella slid the ring on her finger. "I will see that it is returned, then, and I thank you."

"*De nada.*" The woman gestured with her head toward the hidden room. "Now, go along—I will keep the others away."

Isabella carefully shut the door behind her. Raike lay as he had been during the wedding ceremony, pale and unmoving, but breathing evenly, and she knelt beside him to feel his brow, which remained thankfully cool.

She watched him for a few moments, her brow knit. "I must consummate the marriage," she whispered into the silence, and wished she knew exactly what was meant. She was aware that married people behaved in some mysterious way that involved taking off one's clothes and lying together in a bed, but she was unclear on the particulars. There had been scandal at the Convent— quickly hushed up—when one of the novices had been found in such a state with the stable hand, and while the postulants knew that a grievous sin had been committed, the whispered discussions behind the sacristy did not resolve exactly what had happened.

She gently touched Raike's cheek. It would certainly feel very strange to remove her clothes, even with Raike sleeping soundly. She watched his chest rise and fall for a moment, and then sidled closer, finding she had a vague desire to lay her head on his broad chest, but resisted this inclination because the movement might hurt his ribs.

Instead, she brushed a hand gently along the linen bandages that bound his chest, noting there was an old scar on his shoulder—the doctor had remarked that he had a collection of them. It occurred to her that she was married to someone she knew very little about, but then brushed the thought aside immediately; from the beginning, she'd known him and he'd known her on a fundamental level that defied where they had come from, and what their lives had been beforehand.

There would be plenty of time—God willing—to discover all the details.

Above the linen bandages, there was a triangle of sparse dark hair in the middle of his chest that thinned out between his collarbones, then disappeared on his throat until his beard began. Fascinated, she admired the masculine thickness of his Adam's apple, and then leaned in to tentatively press her fingertips against the hollow of his throat, feeling the warm skin. He didn't react, and emboldened, she leaned forward on her hands, and lowered her head to gently kiss his mouth. His mouth moved slightly in response, and he made a soft sound—barely audible.

Pleased to have evoked a reaction, she kissed him again, but this time he made no response, his parted lips unmoving. Watching him, she suddenly remembered how the soldier at the gate had put his tongue in her mouth—he had thought her a prostitute, and she knew that prostitutes were sinners who led married men astray; perhaps that was the consummation, then. Tentatively, she lowered her mouth to his again, and gently touched her tongue to his.

His reaction was immediate; he turned his head toward her, and murmured something in English against her mouth. Her own reaction was also immediate—she felt an urgent desire to climb aboard him, and press herself against the length of his long, masculine body. As she was unable to indulge this urge, she kissed him again, more boldly this time, and elicited a gratifying sound that emanated from deep within his throat.

This must be it, she thought, feeling a heady new excitement course through her veins. No wonder everyone seems to enjoy it so much; there is such an intimacy—such a warmth—it quite takes one's breath away.

He winced—she was putting too much weight on his chest—and so she reluctantly pulled away, trailing soft kisses down his throat and onto his chest, feeling very pleased with herself because she'd figured it out, all on her own. She smoothed his hair back over his ear and then, unable to resist, bent to kiss his earlobe.

"'sabella—" he murmured, the word a bit slurred. "Sweetheart," he added, and then his head sank to the side as he settled back into sleep.

She smiled with delight—she didn't know the word, but she definitely recognized its tenor. "Sweetheart," she repeated softly, and carefully laid her cheek against his chest.

Chapter 27

"Are you awake yet?"

Isabella opened her eyes to see Eduardo's face, inches from her own. Sleepily, she smiled at him, and pulled the quilt closer around her shoulders against the morning chill. They'd shared the narrow bed last night, both of them so tired that neither had been inconvenienced by the confined space. "I'm hungry," the boy announced. "Are you still angry with Catalo?"

Santos; she thought—here's a dilemma. It would be nice to be seven years old, and not bothered with treachery, or betrayal, or the fate of Spain. Rather than answer directly, she decided to divert the subject. "I must tell you a secret, caballero, and you must promise not to tell a living soul."

She said it with just enough solemnity to catch his full attention, and he stared at her, wide-eyed. "What is it?"

"We must do some playacting, you and I. We will leave here in a wagon with Catalo, and pretend that we are a family."

"I am going to go live with *Catalo*?" She could see that he could hardly credit this piece of good news.

Rather than disabuse him, she continued, "Remember when the soldiers came to the house last night, and we pretended at the table—pretended we were a family? We must continue to do so. If anyone speaks to us, you must say nothing, though. Do you understand?"

He nodded, and asked with excitement, "Does Catalo know of this—should I tell him?"

"Yes, you should tell him." She felt a sudden pang, thinking of how eager the boy was to share this plan with his flawed hero—this fatherless boy, who'd been fostered since he was a baby. "You must caution him to be careful not to give us away."

Eduardo scrambled out of bed, and pulled his clothes on, not bothering to button the buttons in his haste. "Don't forget to wash," Isabella reminded him, sinking back into the pillow and thinking it a hopeless cause.

"In the kitchen," the boy promised over his shoulder, and slammed the door behind him.

Isabella lay for a few more moments in the warmth of the bed, fiddling with the too-large ring on her finger, and listening to men's voices drifting up from downstairs—she'd slept longer than her usual. She would like to check on Raike, but didn't wish to interrupt if the doctor was with him, and so instead she dressed, and made her way down the stairs to hear of his status.

Tello was speaking to Catalo in the kitchen, holding several small glass vials.

"Keep him as quiet as possible; I will give you some laudanum—use it as necessary—and an infusion that will ease his aches; it should be mixed one-part-to-four with water."

"I will take these," interrupted Isabella smoothly, unwilling to trust Catalo with such a task.

As he handed her the vials, the doctor added, "We are packing provisions and clothes donated from the neighbors with their good wishes. Doña Francesca is outside with the boy, supervising, so that none will be surprised by your departure. Do you need a map of your route?"

Catalo did not respond, and Isabella glanced over at him only to see that he stood stock-still, his hands spread out to either side as the barrel of a pistol was pressed against the back of his head. With a gasp, she saw that Raike had been concealed behind the door; he was upright and—thanks be to God—seemed to be much stronger. She turned to address Tello, who was staring, speechless. "Leave us." It was probably best there be no witnesses to whatever was to come.

"*Señores*, I—I beg of you—" the man faltered.

"Out," ordered Raike in an ominous tone, and so Tello backed away, and closed the door behind him.

"Stand away, Isabella."

She obeyed, moving over toward the hearth, and then Raike addressed Catalo. "Start talking, you son of a bitch, or I will blow your head off."

Catalo had not moved. In a quiet voice, he replied, "I had my orders."

"Whose?" In the ensuing silence, the pistol was cocked with a loud click against the base of the man's skull. "Speak, unless you want the boy to have to step over what is left of your head."

"My Prior."

Raike assimilated this statement for a moment. "What the hell does that mean?"

"I am a Knight—a Hospitaler."

In some surprise, Isabella glanced at Raike, who made no response. Although she was not familiar with the particulars, she knew that the Knights of Malta had absorbed the old order of the Knights Templar after they'd been forcibly disbanded. In recent years the Knights' leader—the Grand Master—had foolishly allowed Napoleon to capture Malta, with the result that their Order was now scattered, with no home base.

Nevertheless, the Knights of Malta was still a powerful force, often working behind the scenes in support of the Roman Catholic Church, and combating the evils of slavery.

"Why would the Knights work with Rochon?"

Catalo lifted his chin slightly at this reference to the notorious Frenchman. "No—they do not." The words were said with quiet vehemence.

"Then who was behind this?"

Into the silence, Isabella ventured, "Is it *El Halcon*? You will tell me, Catalo."

Raike glanced at her in surprise, and then back at Catalo, a frown creasing his brow. "What the hell does *El Halcon* have to do with any of this?"

After a moment's hesitation, the *guerrilla* confessed, "I am under orders to monitor *El Halcon*—to watch what he does, and report back to my Order. I am sorry for what happened to you, but I could not give myself away."

Slowly, Raike lowered the pistol so that it was no longer pressed against the man's head. "Are you saying that the Knights of Malta suspect that *El Halcon* is throwing in with Napoleon? And you expect me to believe this?"

Doña Francesca carefully opened the kitchen door, and then paused upon beholding the tableau before her. Isabella held up a palm, and the woman quickly withdrew.

As if there had not been an interruption, Raike voiced his scorn. "What you are telling me is preposterous."

"I am not so certain he is wrong," Isabella offered. "*El Halcon* was at the Monastery, posing as a monk."

"*What*?" Raike stared at her in astonishment.

"And I think—I think that he was aware of the coming ambush."

There was a profound silence. Catalo began to turn around, but with a swift movement, Raike raised the pistol again. "I told you not to move."

Isabella continued, "I think he is telling the truth, Will-i-am; he is a priest."

There was another profound silence. "*You* are a priest?" Raike repeated the words in amazement. "The devil!"

"*Si,*" Catalo replied, with just a trace of irony.

"I should probably mention—" Isabella swallowed, "—I should probably mention that he married us last night."

Raike slowly lowered the pistol. "He *married* us? You and me?"

"Yes, I thought it best.   He would not kill you, if you were my husband."

For the first time, Catalo displayed some emotion, his jaw working. "I would not have killed him regardless, Excellency—"

Coldly angry, Raike raised the pistol on him again. "No—but you would step back, and allow someone else to do it."

Speaking quickly, Isabella sought to defuse his renewed anger. "Doña Francesca was a witness to the ceremony, and I have consummated the marriage, so that no one can attempt to undo it."

There was a small silence, while both men stood unmoving. Lowering the pistol, Raike turned to face her. "You consummated the marriage?"

"Yes." She felt her color rise. "The Doña told me it was important, but I didn't wish to wake you."

Raike ducked his head for a moment, and Isabella had the sudden impression that he was amused—and that Catalo was amused, also, although he did not betray it outwardly. In an odd way, it broke the tension between the two men, as Raike tucked the pistol in his waistband. "If that is the case, it appears my fate is sealed. Come, Lady Raike."

"Oh," she said, hearing the unfamiliar English words. "Is that who I am, now?"

"So it would seem." He then said to Catalo, "You are not absolved of any of this; I will know what is at work here—only not right now. Right now, I need to lie down."

Isabella hurried to his side to support him. "I can mix the infusion for your aches."

"My aches would appreciate it." Gingerly, he placed an arm around her shoulders, but his head snapped up, as they heard voices approaching from the front of the house, Doña Francesca's uncharacteristically loud as she voiced a protest.

"Such an intrusion! I will not stand for it!"

The Doña then entered the kitchen, accompanied by two soldiers and an officer from the Alcazar, and was met with the sight of Catalo seated at the table, with Isabella standing at the hearth—Raike having ducked out-of-sight behind the door again. The officer regarded them whilst the older woman continued in an outraged voice, "*Madre de Dios*, what was the point of the war, if the soldiers of Spain will harass us in the same manner as the French? If my husband was still alive—"

The officer removed his hat, and with a much-abused handkerchief, dabbed at the perspiration on his bald forehead "My apologies, Doña—the Commander is very unhappy, and wishes me to interview anyone who is lately arrived to the area. I understand your nephew has come for a visit—"

But Isabella interrupted him in a voice rigid with fury. "No more; we are leaving this house of sinners, *immediately.*"

Chapter 28

There was a small silence. "Elena—" said Catalo.

She whirled to face him. "Don't you 'Elena' me; you and your women—"

The big man shrugged. "It was only the maid; you overreact."

Stamping her foot, Isabella noted that the soldiers exchanged amused glances. "She is a trollop, just like all the others, and you were only too eager—"

"Nephew," interjected Doña Francesca, clearly mortified. "Enough, please."

"You *never* liked me!" Isabella threw at the older woman.

Uneasy with his role as witness to this domestic fracas, the officer held up his hands. "I must beg a moment of your time; it will not take long, I promise you."

The back door opened to reveal Valdez, carrying an armload of chopped wood. He paused in surprise, and offered, "I have your wood, Doña."

"By the hearth, if you please," ordered the woman impatiently.

Reinforcements, thought Isabella; *but a gun battle should be avoided at all costs.* "You run an immoral household," she accused the other woman, pointing an angry finger for emphasis. "I will not stay here another *moment.*"

"Now, my dear; please calm yourself—"

"You may arrest my husband, with my blessing," Isabella retorted in the direction of the soldiers, her face aflame. "But I advise you to watch your women."

Just then, Eduardo peered in from the doorway, clearly alarmed by the raised voices. Her heart leaping to her throat, Isabella said to him, "You must go upstairs, my son; I will join you in a moment."

But instead, Eduardo ran toward Catalo, seated at the table, and flung himself into his arms. "Papa—" he sobbed on a hysterical note, "—*please* don't be angry."

"Would it be possible to return at a later time?" asked Doña Francesca, struggling to maintain her dignity whilst the boy wailed into Catalo's chest.

Clearly regretful, the officer spread his hands, and spoke over the din, "Perhaps if I could ask just a few questions of your nephew—"

One of the soldiers who had accompanied him suddenly stepped forward. "Señor," he offered, "I can vouch for this man—we knew each other as boys, here."

"Excellent." The officer dabbed at his forehead again as he tried to speak over Eduardo's wailing.

"We go." He bowed to Doña Francesca. "Forgive us for the intrusion." With a glance at the other men, he silently conveyed his desire to depart before the situation escalated.

As they vacated the room, the one soldier threw them a look over his shoulder, and Isabella smiled her gratitude, then hurriedly closed the door to reveal Raike, leaning heavily against the wall, his pistol at the ready. "Good God; remind me never to be unfaithful to you."

"Come—I will help you to lie down."

He shook his head. "Better to be away as quickly as possible; it will support the tale you told."

With no further delay, the *guerrillas* carefully rolled Raike into a blanket and then loaded him into the back of the wagon, wedged between the other provisions that had mysteriously appeared to help them on their journey.

Hoping to give the impression that she was still angry, Isabella nevertheless said to Doña Francesca in an undertone, "I will never forget you, and your courage. *Gracias*."

"Instead, extend our thanks to *El Halcon*," the woman replied quietly. "And please, let me know that you are safe."

"You will hear from me; my promise on it." Isabella then turned to Ines, who stood beside her. "I am sorry that I slandered you in front of the soldiers, Ines—it was an unkind way to repay your bravery."

The girl dimpled, her eyes alight. "Not at all, *Hermaña;* instead, everyone will know I played a part in *El Halcon's* plan, and I will be famous."

"Then we must find you a husband," the older woman said dryly. "And the sooner, the better."

Señor Tello handed Isabella up to the wagon's seat, and she was careful to sit as for as possible from Catalo, so as to give the impression that she remained angry with her erstwhile husband. With Eduardo seated between them, the big *guerrilla* urged the horses on, and they were underway.

They trundled out along the main road, and as they passed the houses that lined it on each side, Isabella was aware of curtains flicked aside; of covert scrutiny by their silent supporters. Blinking back tears, her throat closed with emotion; the people of Spain had suffered mightily, but their spirit remained indomitable—perhaps because they'd experienced the war on their very doorsteps, and had been asked to join in the battle on a personal level. It was one thing to wait at a distance, to hear what was to come of one's life, and quite another to take up arms to defend it.

She had experienced the same sort of epiphany herself, back at the Monastery, and she would never be the same.

"*El Halcon* is such a hero to them," she observed in a somber tone.

"That is the problem, Excellency," answered Catalo, just as somberly.

Making a slow progress, the wagon rattled away from Santa Luisa, and began the journey toward Aranjuez. Looking ahead, Isabella found that she had mixed emotions; it was in Aranjuez that she had spent much of her childhood, but it was also there that King Charles had been forced to abdicate on that terrible, terrible night, so long ago.

To change the direction of her thoughts, she glanced back at the wagon bed; Raike had not stirred, which was to the good, after his exertions this morning. Valdez and Puente rode unseen and parallel to the road, keeping watch for potential problems, and although they encountered several other travelers as they headed out of town, no one showed any interest in them.

"How long will the journey take?" Isabella asked Catalo. Eduardo's head was beginning to bob, and so she gently pulled him to lie down on her lap, wishing she could lie down herself—the warm sun on her back was making her drowsy.

"Two days, at this speed." There was a small pause. "You are acquainted with *El Halcon*, Excellency?"

"I am," she replied, and added nothing further.

"May I ask if you know—"

Ruthlessly, she cut him off. "I will not discuss this with you, Catalo." Did he think she would be foolish enough to give him any information? *Santos*, the man was lucky Raike hadn't shot him outright, although it seemed to her that some sort of truce had been reached between them, when she had been the source of some unspecified amusement. Truly, men were a different breed altogether.

They had been traveling for perhaps another hour when Isabella felt a covert hand come to rest on her bottom, and she couldn't suppress a smile.

"Where is the water?" asked Raike from where he reclined on the wagon bed. "What is the point of having a wife, if no one brings me water?"

"Let me bring Eduardo to lie down in the back, and I will see to both of you," Isabella suggested. "It might appear strange, otherwise."

"Where are we?" Raike asked Catalo, as the *guerrilla* pulled the horses to a halt, and then climbed down to take the sleeping Eduardo from Isabella's lap.

"About two miles out of Algodor." The *guerrilla* carefully carried Eduardo around to the back, as Isabella scrambled into the wagon bed to receive him.

"Oh? What is our destination?" Raike continued from his prone position.

"Aranjuez," Catalo replied, as he re-mounted the wagon's seat. "We should be there by tomorrow evening."

But Raike could not approve of this plan. "Aranjuez? Why the devil are we headed to Aranjuez, now that we no longer need a witness? We should be heading for the coast with all speed, or even better, to the British garrison in Madrid."

At Catalo's urging, the horses began to walk forward again. "We go to Aranjuez to seize the Spanish royal treasure," explained Isabella in a level voice. "That is why we go to Aranjuez."

Both men assimilated this comment in silence for a moment, and then Raike explained in a patient tone, "Isabella—there is no treasure, and there is no Spanish Mask. It is all just a feint—a piece of propaganda, to send the enemy on a wild goose chase."

Her gaze on the far horizon, she replied, "You are wrong, my friend; I have held Alexander's Mask in my own hands."

Again, she could sense the surprise emanating from the two men. "You *have*?" Raike asked. "Are you certain?"

"Oh, yes," she replied calmly. "There is no mistaking it."

There was a small pause, and she saw that even Catalo gave her a quick glance, from beneath the brim of his hat. In a soft tone, Raike exclaimed, "Son-of-a-*bitch*; it was true all along—you *do* know where the treasure is hidden."

"Yes. And we go to seize it, because it will give me leverage over *El Halcon*."

"I think we should head toward the garrison, first," Raike insisted. "We need reinforcements."

But she shook her head. "We haven't time. *El Halcon* may guess what I am about, and we must get to the Mask first, or he certainly will."

"You said he was there, at the Monastery." Raike squinted, and raised a hand to shade his eyes from the sun.

"*Si*." Isabella debated, then decided she owed her husband more loyalty than she did the miserable *Tio*, who had plotted to kill her husband. "He was the monk who was with us, when we spoke with Maria Lucia."

Raike whistled softly, and then said to Catalo. "You knew this?"

"*Si.*" The *guerrilla* flicked the reins on the horses' backs.

"I didn't know what *El Halcon* had planned," Isabella assured him. "If I'd known, I would have warned you."

"Don't worry, I believe you," said Raike, reaching to lay a reassuring hand on her bottom. "It appears that no one is who they seem in this little drama, save me." He then addressed Catalo. "Have you been in contact with your Prior, since the Monastery?"

Catalo looked into the distance for a moment, as the horses walked along. "No," he finally replied.

"Try to keep it that way. Information has a way of leaking out—especially information like this. We can't put Lady Raike at risk."

"*Si,*" the big man agreed with a nod. "I will take no chances."

"Good man," pronounced Raike, his tone ironic.

Thinking to distract before pistols were drawn yet again, Isabella turned to ask Raike, "What about your people? Should we try to contact them?"

Closing his eyes, he shifted, trying to find a comfortable position. "No—any such attempt may be intercepted. Instead, they will find me."

Her brow knit in concern, Isabella watched the road ahead and warned, "*El Halcon* is likely to find us, first."

"You would be surprised," was all he said, and then grunted in pain, as the wagon hit a particularly deep rut.

"It is time for more of the infusion, it will ease your pains." They stopped again so that she could retreat to the wagon bed, pretending to check on Edward before covertly helping him to drink the mixture. "I can see your eye again; the swelling has lessened."

Gingerly, he lay his head back down again. "The worst of it is the burns; they itch like the devil."

"I'll prepare a salve, when we stop tonight." She thought about it, glancing up at the trees. "There may be elder trees, nearby."

Eyes closed, he managed a smile. "You are a very able wife, orchard-keeper."

Tenderly, she smoothed his hair back from his forehead. "Can you try to sleep again?" Tentatively, she added, "Sween-tart."

"Sweetheart," he corrected. "*Dulce corazon.*"

"Oh—I see. I must learn English."

He squeezed the hand that held his. "Among other things."

She lifted a brow. "What sort of 'things'?"

"We'll talk about it tonight." He shifted, and then turned his head to sleep. "And I hope that I don't re-injure myself, in the process."

Chapter 29

"How much can you tell me?" Raike glanced at Catalo, a two-eyed glance, now that his eye was healing.

"What is it you wish to know?" Catalo replied. They were eating bread, cheese and cold beef, gathered around a makeshift table comprised of a bench with a lantern perched atop. Their long day's journey had been uneventful, and when the shadows began to lengthen, Valdez had scouted ahead to find a farmstead that would take them in for the night; they thought it best to avoid the inns or the religious houses—the fewer who saw them, the better.

As always, a patriotic Spaniard was only too happy to offer his barn with no questions asked, and a generous hamper of food had also been provided. Raike had also asked Valdez to request a bottle of wine from the homesteader, if he had one to spare.

Eduardo was climbing up and down the ladder to the hay loft, brandishing a stick and expending some pent-up energy by pretending to fight an unidentified enemy.

"Valdez," Raike called out. "Can you take that monkey out to Puente? Perhaps he can put him to use gathering wood."

Willingly, Valdez called for Eduardo to jump from the loft into his arms, and Isabella had to stifle her urge to caution them, instead watching as the boy crouched down—hesitating—then launched himself into the air to be caught in Valdez's arms. Bouncing with excitement, Eduardo then left through the barn door, the *guerrilla* listening good-naturedly to the boy's chattering.

Raike took a drink from the bottle of wine, and then handed it to Isabella, as he asked Catalo, "Can you tell me why the Knights of Malta are watching *El Halcon*? What is your Prior's concern?"

Catalo measured his words, his gaze on the lantern. "My Prior is concerned that *El Halcon*'s dealings may be harmful to the Church."

Isabella raised her brows at this; for the Knights of Malta—the Order of San Juan—protecting the Church would be the first priority, and would take precedence over any other considerations, such as allegiance to a particular country. "But I don't understand—*El Halcon* is a good Roman Catholic."

Catalo lowered his gaze, silent, and—gingerly–Raike leaned back against the bench, reasoning slowly, "*El Halcon's* loyalty is to the people, not the monarchy—or even the Church. And now the people have tasted their own power, and they will never go back to the old ways."

But Isabella found this incomprehensible, and looked from one man to the other. "The interests of Spain and the interest of the Church are the same, are they not?"

Carefully, Catalo explained, "The Congress in Vienna—many of the old ways will be changing."

He seemed reluctant to say more, but Isabella remembered what Raike had already told her. "England is in control of the negotiations, and the English hate the Church."

"Absolve me, *España*," Raike corrected her gently. "I do not hate your Church."

"No," she agreed, touching his hand, and struggling with her new role as his wife. "I should not have said— forgive me."

The old ways were indeed changing, and she must not make the mistake of insisting that everything remain the same—it was a lesson the deposed King of Spain didn't wish to learn, and he'd paid dearly for his attitude.

Raike refocused his attention on Catalo, "So; your Order is worried that—to save Spain—*El Halcon* may allow England to weaken the Church." He paused for a moment, thinking this over. "How would it serve his purpose to feed me to the French, though? What was he promised in return?"

Catalo shrugged. "This is what I am trying to discover."

Frowning, Raike bent his head for a moment. "On the other hand, his motive may be the obvious one—it wouldn't be the first time an honest man rises to power, and then discovers greed."

But Isabella protested, "No—no; you do not know him as I do. And *El Halcon* was instrumental in defeating Napoleon; why would he help him, now?"

The two men did not have an immediate answer as the lantern's flickering light reflected off their profiles. "Remember that Napoleon will march again," Raike suggested after a moment. "Perhaps he is hedging his bets."

But Isabella continued to shake her head in disbelief. "He is a very different man from the one I knew, if he is willing to help the *Afrancesados,* and throw an innocent man to the wolves."

"An English heretic," Raike reminded her. "I don't count for much, in his eyes."

"It makes little sense," she insisted stubbornly. "There is something else at play—something we do not understand."

Raike refrained from stating the obvious—that Isabella's insistence didn't match the facts on the ground—and instead he offered the bottle of wine to her again. "How did you meet him?"

She looked up to the two men, who regarded her with barely-concealed curiosity, and decided it would do no harm to tell them; if they were willing to be honest with each other, certainly she could, too—or at least, as honest as she was able. "He was the Royal Gamekeeper at the Palacio."

Catalo frowned, trying to remember. "The man who kept the royal falcons—ah, I see; *El Halcon*."

"Yes. I used to follow him about—asking many questions—and he was very patient with me. On the night the King was forced to flee, he showed me where he'd hidden the royal treasure, in the event he was killed—I promised to tell no one." She stared into the flame, remembering the solemn promise she'd made that night, with all the fervor of a twelve year old girl who—after having had her world turned upside down—was desperate for something to hold on to; something larger than the incomprehensible horror of war.

"And then? How did you come to be at the Convent in the Sierra Moreno?"

She shook off her melancholy, and lifted her gaze. "When I missed the ship, *El Halcon* saw to it that I was smuggled—convent to convent—to the remotest one he could think of." She paused, remembering the perilous journey. "I waited out the war there."

"With Maria Lucia."

"*Si*—with Maria Lucia, to act as my mask, in the event the *Afrancesados* discovered that a Grandee from the royal line still remained in Spain. She would offer herself up in my place, so as to protect me."

Raike leaned forward to tear off another piece of bread. "I am surprised they never made the attempt to smuggle you to Rome, to reunite you with King Charles's court, in exile. Seven years is a long time to be hidden away."

"*El Halcon* did not think it was safe to make the attempt," she explained. "It was not easy to determine who could be trusted, and who could not.

And no one could have foreseen that the war would last so long."

Raike took up the wine bottle, and handed it to her. "A little bit left—perhaps you should finish it."

Willingly, she drank, whilst Raike turned to address Catalo. "And now what will you do? Will you continue in your role with the *guerrillas*, or go and report to your Prior?"

Instead of answering immediately, Catalo looked to Isabella. "You believe *El Halcon* will meet up with us, Excellency?"

"Yes, I do." For a moment, Isabella wondered how she would react when she met up again with the treasonous *Tio*; he had much to answer for.

Catalo replied, "Then I will stay here, and continue to honor my Prior's orders."

"Good," pronounced Raike in a grim tone. "You can hold my coat while I beat the hell out of *El Halcon*."

"And me," added Catalo, without emotion.

Raike did not disagree. "And you—but first we'll have to wait until I no longer need your help."

With a small smile, Catalo bowed his head in agreement, and Isabella again wondered at the incomprehensibility of men.

Chapter 30

"Your bruises are very impressive," Isabella teased. "I have never seen anyone quite so purple." She gently applied the salve to the long, narrow burns that the poker had inflicted on his back, trying not to flinch at the sight of the raw, angry flesh. They had retired for the night into one of the far stalls, where fresh hay had been spread and a blanket laid down. Isabella had been surprised to discover she was not slated to sleep with Eduardo in the loft, but then, on second thought, decided it would be very enjoyable to lie down beside Raike, as she had done when he was in the hidden room. And she was needed to dress his wounds and retie his bandages—she would not trust any of the men to do the task as well as she could.

"Lord, you have a hard head." His voice was slightly slurred, as he lay face down on the blanket.

Smiling, she surveyed his back with a critical eye so as not to have missed a spot. "A 'hard head'—what does this mean?"

"It means the wine does not seem to affect you."

"I suppose not—I am well-used to wine," she agreed. "Let me see the cut by your eye."

Willingly, he turned his head to one side, and eyed her. "On the other hand, it was a mistake to mix the doctor's infusion with the wine; I hope I'll be able to perform my marital obligations."

She applied the salve over the stitches near his eye, and decided it was likely he would have a scar—the cut was quite deep.

She didn't like to think about how it had come about—a knife point, perhaps; she supposed should be thankful they hadn't taken out his eye. "Which obligations are those, Will-i-am?"

Carefully, he raised himself on his elbows, wincing at the effort. "I will worship at your altar—in a manner of speaking—and this question of rival churches shall not arise."

"You are speaking English." She smiled and shook her head. "I do not understand."

He was in a whimsical mood—or more whimsical than his usual; it was very amusing. She ran a gentle hand down his back, assessing. It would be several days before he could expect to be comfortable again, and it would be many years before she would forget what he'd looked like, when she had first seen him at the Alcazar. Truly, it was amazing he did not seem affected by the experience; the English may be heretics, but their courage could not be questioned.

She wiped her hands on a linen whilst he began to sit up with careful movements.

"You are so beautiful," he said in Spanish. "I thought so from the first, Lady Raike." He gently caressed the side of her face with a hand, his dark eyes intent upon hers.

Placing her own hand on his, she turned her face to kiss his palm. "Let me tie your bandages, Will-i-am; it will keep the salve in place." It seemed evident that his mind had turned to kissing, but she would like to avoid having the newly-applied salve rub off on Doña Francesca's dress.

Obligingly he raised his arms, and she reached around to wrap the bandages tightly in place once again, breathing in the masculine scent of him and thinking him a very fine husband, despite a few scars, here and there. "Do your ribs hurt less than this morning?"

"Hmmm. . ." His mouth moved along her temple, and he lowered his hands to pull at the comb that secured her hair atop her head.

"You mustn't—oh, now I cannot see," she laughed, as her hair tumbled around her face. "I think perhaps you are a little drunk, my friend."

"Isabella," he whispered, and gathered her hair in his hands, the weight of it spilling from his fingers. He lifted it aside so as to kiss her neck, his warm mouth sending shivers of delight down her spine.

"I see you are feeling better," she teased, lifting her chin so as to grant him better access. "Let me tuck in the ends of your bandages—can you lie back?"

"Lie back with me," he said in a thick voice, and pulled at her.

Although he spoke in English again, she understood the import, and willingly lay back beside him. More consummation, she thought eagerly, and lifted her chin to place her mouth against his own.

The effect was immediate; he made a soft groaning sound and began to pull at her hips as though he wished her to lay atop him. Despite the impulse to comply, she decided it would not be wise to put pressure on his chest, and gently resisted, disengaging from his mouth to whisper, "Hush, now; you must not hurt yourself—"

He pulled her mouth to his again, and began to slide one of her sleeves off her shoulder, his fingers working the lacings at the back. *He wants us to remove our clothes— like married people do*, she realized, and thought it a rather daunting task, considering his injuries. If it was what he wished, though, she would help to remove his breeches, which were the only article of clothing that he wore.

Lifting her head, she surveyed him, thinking about how to best go about it, when she paused and gasped, her gaze fixed on his groin. "Will-i-am; oh, Will-i-am—you are injured; something is wrong."

He raised his head for a moment, following her horrified gaze, and then lay back, chuckling. "Ouch," he gasped, pressing a hand against his ribs. "Don't make me laugh, it hurts."

Not certain how to handle this development, and a bit alarmed at his casual attitude, she asked, "May I look? Or should I fetch one of the men?"

"In a moment." Taking a long breath, he drew her back into his arms and rested his cheek against her head. "But first I must explain something to you, my sweet innocent."

"You must speak Spanish, Will-i-am—you keep forgetting."

"*Pardon.*" Holding her in his arms, he gently explained the basics of sexual congress between a man and a woman as she listened with growing astonishment.

At its conclusion, she lay in silence for a moment, feeling his breach in her hair. "You are *certain* of this?"

"I am."

She tilted her head to glance up at him, sidelong. "You have *done* such a thing?"

"I have. Never with a wife, though."

She paused, then admitted with some skepticism, "I don't know about this, Will-i-am—"

"That is quite all right," he whispered, drawing her close. "We can wait until you are comfortable."

Relieved, she asked tentatively, "Do you mind if I touch?"

"I wish you would."

Carefully, she did touch, and then—watching his reaction—felt a surge of elation course through her veins—that she could evoke such mindless pleasure was strangely compelling.

Her fingers feather light, she tentatively explored his masculine body; he was Will-i-am, after all, and there was no restraint between them—in truth, there never had been.

Her touches turned into caresses, which in turn became mutual, and more and more heated until she'd wriggled out of her clothes and lay beneath him, trying to find the right balance between bringing him pleasure without causing him too much pain. In the end, it was right, and wonderful, and almost unbearably intimate; and after he'd fallen into an exhausted slumber, she lay in his arms and watched the stars through the small window high on the wall, the scent of her new husband mixing with the scent of the new straw.

Chapter 31

Isabella and Eduardo watched as the horses were hitched to the wagon in preparation for their departure. Raike was standing on his own—although stiffly—and he seemed much recovered from the day before, despite his exertions in their straw bed which, one would think, would have set his recovery back, instead of forward.

As though reading her mind, he looked up, and met her eyes. It is a fine thing to be married, she thought; it is as though we are two halves of the same person—but I think I have felt this way from the first moment he lifted me up in the orchard.

"Catalo snores," Eduardo confided in a low tone, his eyes gleaming with humor. "Not too loud—just a little."

"Did he keep you awake?" This seemed unlikely; the boy slept like the dead.

"No—but I kept waking up, because I thought it was morning."

"That happens to me, too," Isabella commiserated. "It is of all things annoying."

The boy glanced up at her. "He made me promise I wouldn't go in to wake you this morning—he said you needed to rest."

Her color rising, Isabella replied, "That was very kind of him." There was little point in attempting to spare her blushes, though—she had blushed through breakfast with the other three men, each careful not to meet her eye with the exception of Raike, who observed her discomfiture with warm amusement. Ironic, that she who had been so seldom in the company of men now spent every waking moment with a surplus of them.

Carefully, Raike hoisted himself into the wagon bed. "Keep me company back here, Eduardo—I will teach you to sight a pistol."

Nothing loath, Eduardo scrambled up after him, and Raike handed over his pistol. "You must prop it up on whatever is handy; it is too heavy for you, and the recoil will ruin your aim. Bring your head down—no, you are closing the wrong eye." Balancing the weapon on the wagon's side, he showed Eduardo how to sight down the barrel at an unsuspecting cow.

Isabella allowed Catalo to assist her up onto the bench, and then he slapped the reins as they began another day's journey, the horses pulling against the harness as they clattered out of the yard. "You must hide yourself," she leaned back to remind Raike. "Perhaps you can continue the lesson from the floorboards, and shoot at the birds overhead."

"Good idea. I find I am unaccountably tired this morning."

"I kept waking up," Eduardo admitted, as he rather wildly aimed at various objects. "Did you?"

"I did indeed," Raike replied, and Isabella could feel her color rise.

"Can I shoot something, now?"

"Not yet." Raike lay back, and clasped his hands on his chest. "First, let's find something that deserves to be shot."

"We mustn't draw attention, Eduardo," Isabella reminded him. "Once we are safe in Aranjuez, then perhaps you can practice shooting."

Eduardo turned to look at her, shading his eyes with a hand. "Catalo says that you used to live in a palace."

"A long time ago," she agreed. "When I was your age."

"Did you meet the King?" The boy's voice was hushed, and he awaited her answer with avid interest. "Señorita Maria Lucia said you must curtsey to the floor when you meet the King—she showed me."

Isabella surveyed the horizon, and smiled. "I did meet the King—although I don't remember curtseying to the floor."

"Was he wearing a crown?"

Aware of the hoped-for answer, she equivocated, "Sometimes. Mostly, he liked to hunt." She paused, thinking with some bitterness that if Charles had spent less time hunting and more time trying to govern his rapidly fracturing kingdom, he might still be King.

"Catalo says he is not the King anymore."

As this was a sore subject, she could only bring herself to say, "It is true that he no longer lives in Spain, Eduardo."

Responding to her tone, Raike changed the subject. "How do we go about claiming this treasure? Will it be as easy as it was to extract me from the Alcazar?"

"Much easier." She looked back, to smile down at him. "We need only to access the orchards unseen."

"Will the treasure be under guard?" asked Catalo, who was clearly thinking about logistics.

"No," she replied. "It is hidden beneath the trees— we should only be a few minutes."

"After we recover it, we will leave immediately for England."

Raike said it in a tone that brooked no argument, and she could not demur. She hadn't looked beyond securing the treasure so as to gain some leverage to protect Raike, but he was right; they must flee to safety. *El Halcon*'s influence was too powerful, and she couldn't risk staying here in Spain.

It will not be so terrible, she assured herself, and it is necessary; Raike and Eduardo will finally be safe, and the royal treasure—por favor Dios—will not fall into the hands of Ferdinand and the treacherous Afrancesados. I will meet Raike's family, and hope they do not think me too strange—I will have him teach me some English first, so that they do not wonder at his choice.

"Will you go to England, Catalo?" Apparently, Eduardo had his own concerns about the coming journey.

Choosing his words carefully, the *guerrilla* replied, "If I am ordered; we will see."

Gazing out over the plodding horses, Isabella acknowledged that it was a blessing Raike had so many brothers and sisters; Eduardo would need a powerful distraction from the loss of Catalo. If Napoleon was to march again, there seemed little chance that the big *guerrilla* would wind up peacefully abiding in England.

The morning turned to afternoon, and finally they could see Aranjuez ahead of them, the spires and towers rising in the distance, where the two rivers converged. Catalo pulled up to allow the horses to rest under a rare shady tree, and Eduardo stood up on the wagon bed, to lean with his elbows on the seat beside Isabella. "How much longer?"

It was perhaps the dozenth time he'd asked, and Isabella swallowed her impatience and indicated with her hand, "Do you see? We are almost there. Is Señor Raike asleep?"

"*Si*. Can I run beside the wagon for a while?" This idea had been hit upon earlier as a way to allow him to burn off his restlessness; that, and allowing him to sit on one of the horses, as it trudged along in harness.

"Wait until this rider passes," she advised, and they waited whilst a lone horseman approached to pass them on the road, touching the brim of his hat in a friendly salute. As he neared, he made a casual gesture to Catalo. "Señor—I believe you've lost a shoe."

Ingles, thought Isabella, seeing a flash of grey eyes beneath the brim of the man's hat. *Another one; they are everywhere, after the war.*

With a resigned air, Catalo climbed down to take a look. "Which?" he asked the stranger.

Thus invited, the man prodded his horse up beside Isabella and pointed. "The far fore."

Catalo approached the horse, and bent to lift its foreleg. As Isabella watched, she suddenly felt an arm snake around her throat, as the barrel of a pistol was pressed against her temple. "Hold," the man said to Catalo. "Raise your hands where I can see them."

Chapter 32

Slowly, Catalo raised his hands, and turned around, his impassive gaze assessing the situation.

With the pistol barrel pressed against her head, Isabella demanded, "Who are you, and what do you want? You must see we have nothing worth stealing."

His watchful gaze on Catalo, her attacker replied, "I seek an Englishman."

"Then you are a fool; we know of no Englishman," she said coldly. "You will release me immediately."

"Better late than never." Raike's voice came floating from behind them in the wagon. "Give me back my pistol, Eduardo—he's an ally."

The grey-eyed man lowered his weapon, and they turned to observe Raike holding out a hand to Eduardo, who had retreated to brace himself against the back of the wagon, aiming Raike's pistol rather unsteadily at the stranger. As he accepted his weapon, Raike added, "I will give it back to you if he needs to be shot, though—stand ready."

The stranger holstered his own weapon, and assessed Raike with a cynical air. "So; you live. I have heard the most extraordinary rumors."

Raike settled in against the sideboards, and reached to place his hat on his head. "I imagine the majority of them are true. You threaten Lady Raike, by the way."

The man turned his head to contemplate Isabella for a long moment, and she had the impression he was not at all happy to make her acquaintance. She returned his perusal, stare for stare.

"Indeed?" he asked in a dry tone.

"Indeed. You may wish me happy." There was the slightest edge to Raike's voice; he had marked the lack of enthusiasm also, it seemed. Isabella noted that Catalo had put a hand on his pistol, and no doubt Valdez and Puente watched from wherever they were.

The grey-eyed man replied with a trace of malice, "I shall certainly wish you happy, if you first assure me that the lady did not inflict your injuries."

Raike tilted his head, allowing the other to see that he found the suggestion absurd. "No—instead I made the acquaintance of one of Rochon's henchmen."

Startled, the other raised his brows in surprise. "*Rochon* was behind this?"

"Yes—apparently he wanted to know what I knew about our operations." The two men shared a long look, and Isabella was given to understand that this was a disturbing development.

"He dares? With our occupying forces so close at hand?"

Raike nodded. "As you see—they must be more desperate than we think. It was a calculated plot, and they took pains to keep it very quiet."

"Who betrayed you?" The question hung heavy in the air, and Isabella swallowed her annoyance, as it seemed evident he thought her a candidate.

"*El Halcon*, it seems." Raike then jerked his chin toward Catalo. "And this fine gentleman."

Although he betrayed no reaction, the grey-eyed man looked between Raike and Catalo. "I think that perhaps a debriefing is in order—but let us keep moving, if you please."

With a nod to the newcomer, Raike suggested, "Come ride alongside, then, and I will tell you what I know. To begin with, the driver is an agent for the Knights of Malta. He claims he could not go out of cover to protect me."

The grey-eyed man reviewed Catalo dispassionately as the *guerrilla* regained his seat. "And the other two on the perimeter?"

"Not Knights—*guerrillas,* who traveled with *El Halcon.* They are temporarily on loan."

The grey-eyed man prodded his horse into a walk as the wagon began to move forward again. "You think they can be trusted." It was a statement, not a question.

"Yes—if they wanted to betray me, they've had plenty of opportunity; I've been as weak as a kitten."

The newcomer's gaze rested on Isabella briefly. "And I can see there is no question this is the missing Grandee."

"Yes." Raike's tone was amused, and, feeling her color rise, Isabella lifted her chin, and did not deign to look at either of them.

They regained the road, and continued at a moderate pace, the grey-eyed man riding alongside as they headed toward the town in the distance. "Why would *El Halcon* conspire against the British?"

"That," said Raike slowly, "is an excellent question."

The grey-eyed man directed his thoughtful attention to Catalo. "Your Prior is in St. Petersburg?"

His gaze on the road ahead, Catalo hesitated for a moment. "*Si,* Señor."

Still speaking to Catalo, the grey-eyed man referred to Raike with a nod of his head. "Why do you think *El Halcon* wanted to deliver-up this man to Napoleon?"

"I know not."

The other man considered Catalo's profile for a moment. "But your Prior is worried about something, certainly. Otherwise you wouldn't be here."

There was a pause, while Isabella imagined the stranger waited to hear what else Catalo would offer. *Good luck*, she thought; *Catalo is not one to share his insights.* Indeed, she was surprised he had offered as much as he had, considering his role in this tale was not a flattering one.

"I am not at liberty to say," the big man finally offered.

The grey-eyed man walked along in silence for a few paces, and then asked of Raike, "How can you be so certain that *El Halcon* was involved in your capture?"

With a tilt of his head, Raike deferred to Isabella. "Lady Raike knows more about it than I do."

The cool grey eyes rested upon Isabella for a long moment. "I am afraid I must disabuse you. She is not Lady Raike; she is married to another."

Isabella stared at him in abject astonishment, whilst Raike raised a brow. "Is that so? Let me know who's told you such a tale—I'd like a word with him."

"You mustn't spread such lies," Isabella retorted hotly. "I am not married to another—I was only betrothed." She turned to Raike in explanation. "It was the way of it—a marriage was arranged with one of my cousins when I was eleven."

"Poor fellow," observed Raike. "A step too slow."

Apparently, the grey-eyed man did not appreciate Raike's attitude, and continued rather ruthlessly, "I'm afraid my information is solid, and this young lady should not be trusted."

"You lie," Isabella retorted, outraged. "What nonsense is this?"

But Raike only shook his head slightly, as though amused. "Do you think me so gullible, then? It is a wonder you allow me to buckle my boots."

There was a small, tense silence, and aware that he had transgressed, their companion offered in a more conciliatory tone, "Come; you do not know what I know. And it would not be the first time a man in our business has allowed his judgment to be impaired."

But Raike only lifted his head to idly contemplated the countryside for a moment. "Perhaps I should tell you what I know before you tell me what you know. I know I was chained in the bowels of the Alcazar, bloody and beaten and without a ha'penny's chance of survival; my only hope that I would die before I told them too much. And then—lo and behold—my lady comes through the cell door, dressed as a nun, and—without so much as a by-your-leave—coshes the guard and engineers my escape, even though I could barely walk and she'd no other support within the walls."

There was a surprised silence, and then the grey-eyed man turned to regard Isabella. "Holy Christ."

"You mustn't blaspheme," Isabella chided him, only slightly mollified. With a tilt of his head, Raike continued, "So I would venture to guess that she does not work for Rochon." The grey-eyed man nodded, his expression serious. "Certainly not. But then I regret to inform you that the lady was married by proxy, nearly a month ago."

Chapter 33

Puzzled, Isabella looked from one to the other. "It is not true—who has said this?"

But Raike was watching the grey-eyed man, and she could not like the grave expression in her husband's eyes. "Who is your cousin, Isabella?"

"Don Diego. He is related through my mother's side."

Raike looked an inquiry, and the grey-eyed man nodded.

"It cannot be true," Isabella insisted. "I was not made aware of this; surely they must have my consent."

"Don't worry, we will straighten it out." Raike gave her a reassuring smile. "And it seems more than a coincidence that this so-called marriage came about just as everyone was put on notice as to your whereabouts."

Knitting her brow, Isabella had to agree. "Yes, it must all be connected in some way—perhaps an attempt to protect me, once my true identity was revealed."

"Possibly, but it does not make much sense," the grey-eyed man observed. "The French are in a fever to seize the supposed treasure; whether you are married or not is neither here nor there."

But Raike disagreed. "Her bloodline makes her a danger to Ferdinand—that much is inarguable. Therefore, once she is discovered, Ferdinand would be well-advised to marry her to a high-ranking *Afrancesado*."

"Yes, perhaps you have the right of it," the grey-eyed man agreed after a moment's reflection. "This must have been a preventative move, to marry her into the old regime before her identity was revealed."

"Good for Don Diego, then," Raike acknowledged. "I suppose I will have to refrain from beating him senseless."

"I doubt it was Diego's doing," Isabella admitted. "Diego's not someone who would come up with such a plan."

"*El Halcon*?" Raike raised his brows. "But that doesn't make much sense; why would he seek to protect you, and then turn around and put you in danger at the Monastery?"

"I was never in danger," she reminded him. "Only you."

"I will need a debriefing," the grey-eyed man reminded them with some impatience. "And sooner rather than later."

Readily, Raike obliged him. "I suppose the most pertinent point is that Lady Raike insists a hidden treasure does indeed exist."

Isabella gave her husband a swift, admonishing glance, but he spread his hands. "He has to be told, Isabella. We can't allow it to fall into the wrong hands."

But their companion drew his brows together. "My information indicates there is no such treasure, and that the tale was a false flag, meant to send the French on a wild-goose chase."

But Raike cocked his head toward Isabella. "Apparently, this particular goose is golden. Lady Raike assures me the treasure does exist; not only that, but she knows where it is hidden. We travel to Aranjuez to seize it, so as to obtain leverage over *El Halcon*."

"Where is it?" The grey-eyed man demanded of Isabella, his gaze intent.

She lifted her chin. "I am under no obligation to tell you. Your country is a well-known stealer of treasures."

This did not sit well with their companion. "You will tell me, if you please; you are a British subject, now."

"Perhaps, perhaps not—depending on whether my marriage is valid," she reminded him. "But by the grace of almighty God, I am a royal Grandee of Spain. That will never change."

"Pray do not harass Lady Raike," Raike interrupted. "The situation is well in hand, and I will keep you informed."

Frustrated, the grey-eyed man raised his eyes to consider the horizon for a moment. "Then—Your Excellency—at least tell me what you know of *El Halcon*."

Whilst she struggled to overcome her reluctance to tell this annoying *Ingles* anything, he continued, "He is not noble, but worked in some capacity for the royal family, I would imagine."

Impressed despite herself, Isabella warily agreed. "*Si*. He was the Royal Gamekeeper at the Palacio Monteleon, when I lived there."

The man bent his head, processing this information. "I see. And you have spoken to him recently?"

"*Si*—the night before my husband was taken." She used the term with a touch of defiance. "I did not know what was planned, or I would have put a stop to it."

He raised his eyebrows at this. "Could you have put a stop to it?"

"I would have," she insisted. "One way or another. I think he would have listened to me; I know him well."

The other man thought this over, as they made their plodding progress closer to the river, the occasional tree now providing relief from the bright sun. "Do you believe *El Halcon* is allied with the *Afrancesados*?"

Nonplussed, she slowly shook her head. "I have been thinking over what has happened, but despite what I have seen with my own eyes, I cannot imagine it—not for a moment. No matter what Catalo's Prior may think, *El Halcon* would never give aid to Napoleon. It is utterly inconceivable."

After searching her face for a moment, the man looked away. "Then what the devil is he about?"

She insisted, "I know it does not look well, but there must be something here that we do not understand."

The man turned in his saddle to review Raike, seated in the wagon. "I suppose you do not wish to be relieved of duty."

Tilting his head back, Raike squinted up at the sun. "No. I would appreciate anyone you can spare, though—I can't tempt fate by expecting Lady Raike to come to my rescue again; she may think me a sorry fellow, and throw in her lot with Don Diego."

"Who is the boy?" The causal question was asked whilst their visitor surveyed the road ahead.

"A stray, who has transformed before our eyes into a formidable *guerrilla*." Raike ran a hand over Eduardo's head. "If you cross him, you will live to regret it."

At this accolade, Eduardo smiled and ducked his chin.

"By-blow?" the grey-eyed man asked in English, as he gazed into the distance. "Whose?"

Raike responded in the same language. "Unclear if that is the case, but my wife has become attached to him, and there appears to be no one else remotely interested."

"Not the Knight's?"

"No—although it is true they are fond of each other."

"What do you speak of?" Isabella could not like the incomprehensible exchange—she wondered if they were talking about her.

The grey-eyed man turned his horse. "I must return to London—matters are pressing."

"Yes—good luck to you." Raike looked a bit grave.

With a tug on the brim of his hat, the man nodded to Isabella. "Your Excellency."

"Señor." She condescended to nod slightly in return.

"A formidable bride," he commented in English, and then, with an unhurried movement, rode away.

"What did he say? Isabella demanded.

Raike chuckled and leaned his head against the side of the wagon, closing his eyes and pulling his hat over his face to shield the sun. "He said you were the most beautiful woman he has ever seen."

She eyed him suspiciously. "I do not think that is true."

"No," he conceded "But you are a close second."

Chapter 34

"You must hold still, Will-i-am." Isabella smiled as she carefully snipped at the stitches beside his eye with a small pair of sewing scissors. Raike was sitting on a stool before her, ruining her concentration because his hands were wandering all over her torso. "I don't want to poke your eye, now that I can finally see it again."

He leaned forward to plant a soft kiss at the décolletage of her neckline. They were spending the night at a small, out-of-the-way Inn located near the Palacio Monteleon. This establishment had been recommended by the two new members of their group, who had appeared several hours after the grey-eyed man had departed.

The newcomers seemed on friendly terms with Raike, and Isabella noted that when Catalo climbed down from the wagon, both men watched him with their hands on their pistols. *Guards*, she thought; *loyal to Raike, which is a good thing.* El Halcon would no doubt make an appearance, sooner or later, and when he did, she could not be certain about Valdez or Puente. It was best to even the numbers—although surely, now that the British were aware of the plot to seize Raike, even *El Halcon* dared not follow through—retribution would be swift and terrible. Unless—unless the information they wanted from Raike was worth the risk.

Therefore, the new men provided a level of assurance for which she was grateful, despite the fact they hid their curiosity with only moderate success.

If I were two-headed, she thought in annoyance, *I do not think I would evoke any less interest; the tale of the missing Grandee is apparently just as intriguing as the tale of The Spanish Mask.*

In the meantime, she resolved not to think about plots and counterplots, but instead enjoy the luxury of a private evening with Raike in a snug room with—*a Dios gracias*—hot water, and a fire in the grate. Placing a hand under his chin, she pulled his head upright again, and began carefully picking at the clipped thread with her fingernails. "Only two more. Does it hurt?"

"No. Tell me about cousin Diego."

Sighing so that her breath stirred the hair on his brow, she offered, "I think your commander must be mistaken."

"He is very rarely mistaken, unfortunately."

Pausing, she met his eyes. "Will-i-am—"

Reaching up, he held her wrist in a gentle grasp. "Please don't worry, Isabella. We are married. The marriage—I am happy to report—has been thoroughly consummated—"

She laughed and blushed, leaning to swiftly kiss his mouth.

"—and neither Napoleon, *El Halcon,* nor the King of Spain himself is going to convince me otherwise."

"We must obey God," she protested softly.

"Of course we must." His dark eyes were serious upon hers. "But one husband has your consent, and the other does not—I have little doubt which is the true marriage."

"Yes," she agreed, heartened by this practical observation. "I love you."

"And I love you, Lady Raike." He lifted his face to invite another kiss, and in the process pulled her onto his lap.

She nestled into his chest, whilst he held her against him, and ventured in an apologetic tone, "All the same, I don't think we should—that is, perhaps it would be best—"

"Then we won't," he agreed. "Not until it is all straightened out."

She ran a gentle hand across his chest. "I am sorry, *querido*. You will not tell your mother of this problem with Diego?"

"Not your fault—although perhaps you should reconsider; I would like to tell her a tale about how I vanquished a pretender to your hand."

"I think you have no shortage of tales to tell," she replied in a dry tone.

He leaned in to kiss her again. "This is the best one, believe me."

She sat with him, content to be within the comfort of his arms. "I should finish your stitches."

"In a moment—this is nice, isn't it?"

It was; they had so rarely had time alone, during this tumultuous courtship. "I am so happy I met you, Will-i-am." She lifted her face to look at him. "Everything changed—all at once."

He chuckled, his chest reverberating beneath her hand. "Yes—you were dragged into the hills and had to sleep in a hayloft."

"I didn't mind," she said with a smile. "You were there."

"A very fine day." He played with the slender fingers of her hand, his bearded cheek pressed against her head. "I saw you plucking the apples, and I knew how Adam felt upon beholding Eve."

Delighted, she twined her fingers around his. "I didn't know what to do; I liked you so much, but I was a postulant—"

"A betrothed postulant," he corrected her, with an amused cock of his head.

"—and you were *Ingles*."

He chuckled. "I wasn't worried; I caught your eyes on me too often, for all your supposed disinterest."

"I could not stop," she agreed, laughing. "You are so handsome."

"Although now I have an intriguing scar—"

She reached up to gently touch it. "I like it. It makes you look like a pirate."

But he disclaimed with a smile, "I must disagree—I know a very fine pirate, and I cannot hold a candle to him."

She smoothed his eyebrow with her fingertip. "I think your commander does not care for women very much."

He flinched when she took the opportunity to snatch at a thread. "We have a very dangerous situation at home—he can be excused for his ill humor."

"Can you tell me? Or is it a secret?" She slid her fingers in between the placket of his shirt to feel his skin, and then withdrew them quickly—she must not tempt him.

He thought about it for a moment. "I will tell you, if you tell me about Diego—I think you are avoiding the subject."

"*Si*," she agreed.

Tilting his head back for a moment, he thought over what to say. "It costs a great deal of money to mount an army, and fight a war. The last war went on for years—"

"Many years," she agreed sadly.

"And so, there is little money left. Napoleon's people are looking to steal whatever they can lay hands on to finance the next war, and my job is to try to stop them. We've thwarted more than a few plots, but as soon as one is put down, others spring up in its place."

"Yes—like this plot to seize the treasure—"

But he corrected, "Not in this case; we were certain this tale of Spanish treasure was a form of misinformation. Instead, we were hoping to find the missing Grandee, and extract her from Spain before she fouled up the peace negotiations."

"How strange," she observed, frowning. "You—and your commander—were so certain that the treasure did not exist."

"He has very good information, Isabella; it is his job. I believe he made inquiries with those who were in Aranjuez the night the treasure disappeared, and he concluded it was long gone." He dropped a kiss on the top of her head. "He didn't know that *El Halcon* himself was on-site, pulling off a miracle." His arms tightened around her. "You must say nothing of this, right?"

"No," she agreed. "I will honor your confidence."

He leaned his cheek against her temple, so that his voice resonated near her ear. "So—where is cousin Diego, do you know?"

"Yes—we have written to each other, on occasion." Best not mention that *El Halcon* acted as the go-between. "He lives at the Palacio, here in Aranjuez."

She could feel his surprised reaction. "He is not in exile with the others?"

"No. He is here, pretending to be allied with Ferdinand and the *Afrancesados.* In reality, he is feeding information to *El Halcon.*"

With some surprise, he lifted his head. "A fellow spy? I suppose that's another reason I shouldn't beat him senseless."

She smiled at his casual tone. "You have a long list of beatings to perform; I think perhaps you are a violent man."

He brought his head back to hers, his lips on her temple. "I won't beat Diego, but I will definitely bring home the point that he is not fit to touch the hem of your dress."

"You mustn't hurt him, Will-i-am. Indeed, he has every right to be angry with me; we were betrothed, after all."

He squeezed his arms around her. "You are not to defend him, Lady Raike. He must have been a part of this scheme to see you married without your knowledge."

She hadn't thought of this, and it gave her pause. "Oh—I suppose that is true. But it is not as though he thought I would protest, Will-i-am—I am more at fault than he is."

"Our marriage is not to be characterized as a 'fault', Isabella."

"Certainly not," she soothed, and then teased, "Instead, it was a wonderful wedding. I only wish you'd been awake for it."

He chuckled, and happy to change the subject, she rose. "Now, let me finish." She resumed her task, and within a few minutes was daubing the scar with the salve while he sat, a bit more quietly than his usual. "Are you tired, Will-i-am? I think you should lie down."

He took her hand, and raised his eyes to hers. "Would you like me to sleep with Eduardo? Or on the hearth—it is what I am used to, after all."

Pressing her lips to his forehead, she replied, "You will sleep with me on this comfortable bed, my friend. You need to rest."

Feeling very wifely, she then helped him out of his shirt and his boots, inspected his bandages, and then pulled the quilt over him as he sank back into the pillows. "Should I ask for coffee—or something for you to eat?"

"I'd be asleep before it arrives, but send Padilla to fetch something for you, if you'd like."

Padilla was one of the new additions, who now stood guard in the hallway, taking alternate shifts with Santana, the other new man. "No, I am tired too."

Hesitating for a moment, she blew out the candle before undressing to her shift; it was all too new, and she couldn't yet undress before her husband—hopefully Raike was indeed her husband. *Santos*, but it was all very complicated. Carefully, she slid into the bed beside him, and almost without volition, moved to lie against his big body, soaking up his warmth.

"Good night, sweetheart," he whispered in English.

"Say it again." She repeated the English words two or three times, then ran her fingers lightly over the linen bindings on his chest. "Does it still hurt?"

"Not as much; better every day."

She kissed his shoulder, then rubbed her face against it, her hand remaining on his chest.

"Isabella," he warned. "What are you about?"

"Do you think it would be such a terrible sin, Will-i-am—"

"There is no sin; you are my wife."

She pressed up against him, a bit out of breath. "It is the strangest thing; I am so restless—I want nothing more than to have you squash me against the bed."

He chuckled deep in his throat, and carefully propped himself up on his elbows to cradle her head between his hands. "Then prepare to be squashed, Lady Raike."

Chapter 35

"We are monitoring the roads," Padilla reported. "No sign of pursuit."

As the two new men had never been more than five paces away, Isabella was given to understand there were other, unseen members of Raike's contingent who were performing a scouting function.

"Nevertheless, we should go as soon as it is dark," she urged her husband. "Once he realizes I did not return to the Convent, *Tio* will guess what I am about—we know each other very well."

They were planning-out the seizure of the treasure, speaking quietly in the Inn's common room. Isabella had noted that the place seemed to house no other guests, and the Innkeeper showed no interest in any of them— although once she'd caught him watching her, out of the corner of his eye, whilst he was pretending to read his accounts. With an inward sigh, she bore the scrutiny; apparently everyone wanted to give an account of what a living, breathing Grandee looked like; so many were— unfortunately—no longer living or breathing.

"I'll take the two new men, and Catalo, because he's familiar with the protocols." Raike instructed the listening men. Speaking to Catalo, he added, "One false move, and you're a dead man. I'm only looking for an excuse."

"I will not give you one," the *guerrilla* replied.

Valdez, who'd been listening to the plan without comment, leaned to speak in a low tone. "Perhaps I should accompany you to the Palacio. We cannot be certain how many guards will be posted."

Raike nodded. "All right—Puente stays here with Eduardo." He looked at the circle of faces surrounding him. "No one moves except on my order; I am in a mood to shoot first, and ask questions later. Understood?"

As the men nodded, Isabella offered, "It should be simple; we will be there and back within an hour."

"A pleasure trip," Raike agreed, as he rose. "We'll reconvene in the stables as soon as it is dark."

The men rose to leave, and Raike walked with Isabella past the Innkeeper—who did not acknowledge their presence—and called to Eduardo, who'd been lying on the floor, commanding an imaginary army of walnut shells. "Come, bantling; it is dinner time."

"Can I go play outside, after dinner?" The boy was chafing at his forced inactivity; they had stayed indoors all day so as to not attract attention.

"You can, but first I will need you for an important mission."

The boy lifted a hopeful face and scrambled to his feet. "A mission?"

Raike crouched before the boy. "I'd like you to go into the kitchen, and eat with the men. Don't say anything, but listen to what Valdez says to the others, and report back to me later. All right?"

"*Si*," the boy breathed, his little face solemn.

Raike cocked his head. "Don't give it away."

"I won't," Eduardo assured him, and then trotted self-importantly toward the kitchen.

Raike rose, and saw Isabella seated in the small dining area. Watching him, she asked, "What is it? Can you not tell me?"

As he broke off a piece of bread, Raike replied easily, "Eduardo needed something to do."

Isabella nodded. "I thought it a little strange, too—Valdez does not usually make suggestions."

Hesitating, he met her eyes, and so she laid a reassuring hand on his arm. "You don't have to say; I know you are worried that you have told me too much already."

Covering her hand with his, he leaned forward and said sincerely, "I trust you—I do. But I don't want to be in a situation where it is you who winds up in a cell at the Alcazar."

She nodded. "I understand, Will-i-am."

He leaned back in his chair. "That being said, I don't know whether I am more concerned that Valdez has asserted himself, or concerned that he doesn't seem to trust the new men."

Frowning, she thought it over. "He has had many chances to harm you."

"And he hasn't—quite the opposite, in fact. We'll see what Eduardo reports."

But as it turned out, Valdez had reverted back to his normal *persona,* and Eduardo reported that the *guerrilla* had said little during the evening meal. The boy then added with some eagerness, "Puente says he will teach me to throw a knife, tonight."

"Brave man," said Raike, and Isabella laughed.

After darkness fell, the group quietly mounted up in the stables—Raike insisting he could now sit a horse by himself—and then made their way, two by two, out the back; the men silent and alert. For her part, Isabella's hands crept under Raike's coat to linger at his waist. *The pleasures of the flesh*, she thought, her fingers moving to gently press against him. *I never truly understood what was meant; no wonder the nuns shake their heads, and warn the unsuspecting about it.*

"I know what you are thinking." His low voice was amused.

Fondly, she laid her cheek against his back. After they'd made love the night before, she'd ventured to ask a few questions, which he'd answered with warmth and honesty.

One of the more interesting revelations was that now, apparently, she could have a baby. She tried not to think of her Abbess's reaction to such news whilst she was technically married to another—one problem at a time.

The half-moon lit their way as they advanced on the Palacio Monteleon, traveling circumspectly along the fields behind the Inn—Isabella already knew that the *guerrillas* rarely traveled on the roads. *I am almost as familiar with the ways of the guerrillas as I am with the Divine Office of Prayers,* she thought; *I wonder if anyone else can make such a claim. Aside from Catalo, of course.*

They trotted single-file along the trees that lined the perimeter, Isabella directing Raike to the back gate that bordered the expansive royal grounds. Within the gilt-tipped wrought iron fence stood the fruit-bearing orchards, planted in well-ordered rows. In the near distance, the battlements of the Palacio could be seen rising up over the trees, the imposing parapets glinting grey in the moonlight.

Strange, that it was still so familiar to her; as though the seven years since she had last been here—at night, and in panicked flight—had passed in a dream. At the time, hiding the treasure had seemed a temporary necessity—only until the French could be defeated, and the treacherous Ferdinand driven from the throne. How much had changed in the long years between.

The men gathered their horses together in the deep shadows of a tall hedgerow, and held a low-voiced discussion as they considered the guard house which stood beside the gate.

Catalo explained that the guards would change shifts soon, and after that there would be no contact for at least an hour, when an officer of the guards would then ride the perimeter.

"Is an hour long enough?" Raike asked Isabella.

"Yes—we go only a short distance into the orchard; it is not very far."

They waited in the shadows until the guard was changed, and then watched as Catalo and Padilla crept down to the guard house to immobilize the hapless man. Raike then directed Padilla to stay at the post, and signal if anything untoward happened, whilst the others quietly spurred their horses into the orchards.

Without hesitation, Isabella directed Raike to a harvest-cart road that ran between two rows of overarching trees, the dark branches silhouetted against the starry sky. The pungent scent of apricots filled the air, and Isabella felt a pang of nostalgia for the orchard at the convent, and the simplicity of a life spent waiting for others to take action. A simple life, until *El Halcon*—for reasons that were as yet unclear—set a trap for Raike, using herself as bait. *There is nothing like a betrayal*, she thought a bit grimly, *to stir one into action*. "Over one more row," she directed them. "We are almost there."

Chapter 36

"This is it," Isabella announced, and they pulled up before a double-trunked tree, the gnarled anomaly standing unremarked amongst its fellows. They dismounted, and Catalo sparked a flint, and then shielded it with his hand, so that it gave off a faint and ghostly illumination.

Isabella indicated the foot of the tree. "It is buried here—perhaps a foot deep." She indicated a spot between the roots, realizing belatedly that a shovel should have been brought. She needn't have worried, however, since every man produced a wicked-looking knife, and began to dig, their movements quick and efficient, as though this type of activity was a commonplace—which, on reflection, it probably was.

They worked silently, but as they dug deeper, their movements became more and more careful until Raike suddenly said, "Hold." With his knife, he tested the object he'd struck, ascertaining its outline.

"It's not very large," Isabella offered, indicating with her hands.

"Only the one?" asked Raike, as he felt for the edges.

"*Si;* only the one."

As the other men knelt and watched, he dug around the casket until its shape was revealed, and then asked Catalo to pull it up. With a grunt, the big *guerrilla* yanked the wooden casket loose from the dirt, and set it upright on the ground. There was a small pause, whilst they all looked on in silence, the chirping of the night insects the only sound.

"Open it," Isabella said softly, "and behold your heritage."

With careful hands, Catalo and Valdez used their knives to pry the lock, and then opened the casket to reveal several oilskin bags stacked within, each tied tightly at the neck. The first was opened, and a cascade of golden jewelry spilled out onto Catalo's hand. Brooches, diadems and finely-wrought chains poured forth, all set with precious stones, and leaving no doubt as to the value of the cache.

"There are rings and bracelets in this one," Isabella explained as she indicated another large bag. "And this one—this one has The Spanish Mask." Carefully, she pulled out a smaller bag, nestled beneath the others.

She untied the oilcloth, and reached in to withdraw the Mask from its hiding place. Even though she'd seen it before, she caught her breath along with the others, and for a few moments no one made a sound. It was in the shape of a warrior's battle-mask, with openings for eyes and mouth, and fanciful decorations engraved on its surface. It was a dull, burnished gold, liberally sprinkled with all variety of gemstones—rubies, emeralds, sapphires, topazes—all glowing like fire in the flickering light. It was a priceless object, fit for a mighty ruler, and dating back into the mists of antiquity.

"I'll wrap the casket in my coat, and tie it before me on the horse," said Raike quietly. "Everyone stay close to me on the way home. Do not draw attention, and we'll take it back to the Inn." He glanced around at the intent faces, circled around him. "I don't need to tell you that no word of this can leak out—the enemy wouldn't hesitate to kill us all without a second's thought. We should go, now, and quickly. Cover our tracks."

While the others filled in the hole with the loose dirt, Isabella stood to casually pull her tortoiseshell comb from her head, and then quickly slip it into the oilskin bag in the place of The Mask. Turning aside, she then surreptitiously slipped the Mask down the front of her bodice. Perhaps the treasure could be replaced, but The Spanish Mask could not, and Raike's comment about the new men—who were allied with the British—resonated in her mind. She would take this extra precaution, with no one the wiser.

Fortunately—or unfortunately, depending upon how one looked at it—the Mask fit easily over her breast, and nestled against her bodice with no discernable lump. In a strange way, she felt an affinity for the priceless treasure; she'd helped rescue it on the night it was threatened, and she would now keep it near. After all, there was no one, at present, who could rightfully claim it.

"Mount up." Raike instructed, but before they could do so, Catalo said quietly, "To the left."

With a rapid succession of clicks, the men drew their pistols and retreated between the horses. At a small distance away on the moonlit path, they beheld a man, standing exposed between the rows of trees, his hands outspread to show tht he was not armed.

"*Tio*," said Isabella into the silence. "I cannot say that I am surprised."

With several long strides, Raike approached the newcomer, cocked his arm, and struck him full on the chin, knocking him down. He then stood menacingly over the fallen *guerrilla*, one hand clenched into a fist, and the other pressed against his ribs. "Get up, you son of a bitch."

El Halcon shook his head to clear it, and called out, "*Pajarocita*; do they hold you by force?"

"No," she answered. "Instead, you behold my husband."

El Halcon pressed the back of his hand against his bleeding lip for a moment, and assessed Raike, still hovering over him with clenched fists. "I see. That is indeed unfortunate."

"Get up, you bastard," rasped Raike. "You owe me some answers."

"Answers that I cannot give you." Wincing, the *guerrilla* regained his feet, and then stood facing Raike. "But I am afraid I must deliver unwelcome news—"

"We know of Don Diego, already," Isabella interjected, not wishing the others to hear of her bigamy. "That was not well done of you, *Tio*." She stepped forward, because she could see that Raike was barely containing his rage, and she could not be easy with this confrontation; they needed to leave before a brawl broke out between those loyal to *El Halcon* and those loyal to Raike. "Let us agree to meet elsewhere, and discuss these matters."

El Halcon nodded slowly. "Agreed. What of the treasure?"

"I have claimed the treasure, on behalf of Spain," Isabella said coldly. "You have shown you are not worthy of it."

They all paused in alarm, because Puente was whistling an alarm—the guard must be approaching.

"*Familia Santa*," said *El Halcon* quietly. "Tomorrow at nightfall."

"Very well," said Raike. "Bring Diego."

With efficient movements, the *guerrillas* mounted, and then melted into the orchard trees, making their way back to the Inn with quiet speed.

Chapter 37

"All right; we need to stop doing this long enough to have a discussion about the treasure."

Isabella was lying in Raike's arms in their room at the Inn, recovering from the latest session of lovemaking as the morning sunlight streamed in through the window. Last night, she had discovered—with some surprise–that she could barely wait to attain the privacy of their room to slake her lust. There had been something about the danger and the moonlight that had brought on that breathless feeling again, and she'd nearly launched herself upon her husband, much to his amusement.

"You seem to be adjusting well to marriage," he teased, "But we need to rest my ribs for a moment, and discuss what's to be done."

She quirked her mouth. "You are very kind, to pretend that you will entertain my opinion."

He leaned his head back on the pillow, so that he contemplated the low-beamed ceiling for a moment. "I think we have little choice but to hand it over to my people, Isabella. We can't take the chance that Napoleon will get his hands on it."

"Can we trust your people not to send it to England?"

"No." He turned his head to gaze at her. "I imagine that's exactly what will be done. If it all has to be sold so that we can fight Napoleon again, I'll not harbor a single regret. England's treasury is also depleted, after the long war."

Pressing her lips together, she nodded; she'd come to this realization already, and it was one of the reasons she'd secretly taken the Mask, last night.

The treasure was too valuable, and besides, there was literally no one to hand it off to. "I understand, Will-i-am. It may not be the best solution, but it is better than the worst solution."

He soothed, "I imagine every attempt will be made to keep the treasure intact, with the goal of returning it to its rightful owners."

"You are more hopeful than I am, Will-i-am," she replied with a trace of sadness. "There is a good reason *El Halcon* hid it away, rather than trust anyone with it."

In sympathy, he squeezed her slightly. "I am sure there are still honorable people in the world; we just haven't run into any of them, lately."

"Which reminds me that I must rid myself of one husband." Isabella propped herself up on her elbows, trying to lighten his somber mood by bestowing a kiss on his chest. "Show me again why it shouldn't be you."

He closed his eyes and smiled. "Not just yet—I'm knackered."

"Knackered." She repeated the English word slowly, finding the consonants very strange, and then followed up by planting a soft kiss on the hollow of his throat, even though his beard was rough against her skin—he was so very attractive, it was hard to resist.

He bent an elbow behind his head, and idly caught his fingers in the fall of her hair. "You are not to worry about your marriage to Diego; it will be annulled, I promise. Even the *Afrancesados* know better than to cross the British, right now—especially with the Third Division camped less than a day away."

She nodded, and went back to caressing his chest, her fingers lingering on his ribs.

He flinched. "Not quite ready for that, I'm afraid."

She was instantly contrite; it was easy to forget that he was still healing from his horrific experience—he seemed so strong, and steady. "Your poor ribs—I think you reinjured yourself when you hit *Tio*. You must try not to beat the hell out of people."

He laughed aloud. "You mustn't blaspheme."

"That was not blasphemy, my heretic."

With a hand on the back of her head, he pulled her to him for a kiss just as a knock was heard at the door.

"I am to tell you that breakfast is ready, but I am not to go in," Eduardo's voice dutifully reported from the other side of the door.

"We will be right down, *caballero*," Isabella called, and turned to smile down at her husband. "Are you too 'knackered' to be hungry?"

"Definitely not."

"Then go—I will dress."

She watched him go, and then crossed over to the dressing table, only to pause for a moment when she caught sight of the wooden casket that lay on the floor. It was so strange, to think that such an ordinary object could hold such power—that whoever seized it would have a huge advantage in the coming war.

Crouching, she drew a hand along the smooth wood. Raike was right, of course; their lives would be in constant danger if they kept the treasure, and there was—literally— no one else to give it to. She'd entertained an idea of entrusting it to a priest, or even to Catalo's Prior, but Raike had brought up an important consideration; if it must be sold so that the British could defeat Napoleon yet again, that would be the better use for it.

I will keep the Mask, she decided; I can easily keep it hidden, and if nothing else, the most famous treasure of Spain will not be lost. I may not trust the English, but I can certainly trust myself.

She rose to her feet, and contemplated her reflection in the small mirror. There had been no mirrors at the Convent, and she decided that perhaps Raike was not so very mistaken when he had told her last night—several times, and with unmistakable sincerity—how beautiful she was.

She couldn't take credit for it, of course–she had the face given to her by God—but a soft smile tugged at her mouth as she thought of her besotted husband, and his many compliments. *You've had to grow up quickly*, *niña*, she thought, *and now it is time to sort out the future—a future which will take place in a country your family has always regarded with a full measure of scorn.*

She met her own eyes in the mirror. Spain had no reason to look down on any other, just now—and besides, if all Englishmen were like Raike, they must be a very fine race. The road ahead was uncertain, but it was the one she'd chosen willingly—would choose again and again— and the first step was to shed an extra husband. Plaiting her hair because she'd no comb, she checked her bodice to ensure that the Mask was secure, and descended to the dining room.

Raike looked up as she came down the stairs, and she noted that he then glanced at the stoic Innkeeper, who left his post to pass her on his way upstairs. The casket would begin its journey to England, and she could only hope that she'd done the right thing, in allowing the *guerrillas* to dig it up.

"Watch," Eduardo called to her, his eyes bright as he brandished a wicked-looking blade. "Puente taught me how to fight with a knife."

"Show me, *caballero.*" Isabella quashed all qualms, and watched as Eduardo took a stab at Puente, who reacted with a quick movement, securing the boys' wrist in his hand. Eduardo then countered by quickly raising his elbow and thrusting outward with the knife.

"*Bueno.*" Puente gave him an approving nod. "But faster, next time."

Eduardo thrust the knife at an imaginary opponent. "Catalo says I have to be older, before he will teach me how to fight with a sword."

Isabella smiled to herself, thinking of how much the timid boy had changed since they'd hidden on the hill that day, not so very long ago. There was some merit to this wild adventure they'd shared; she had gained a wonderful husband, and Eduardo had gained unbounded confidence—it quite made one think that one should be more inclined to trust God and His mysterious ways.

She teased him, "If you must wait to learn swordplay, perhaps you should learn the Divine Office from Catalo."

"We did the Office already, this morning," the boy informed her importantly. "I am going to be a priest."

This was of interest, and she raised her brows at him. "Are you? Instead of a *guerrilla*?"

"I am going to be a *guerrilla*-priest," he explained patiently, as though she were a bit slow. "Like Catalo."

"A good thing; I imagine there is a shortage."

Raike chuckled, and even Catalo condescended to smile as the *guerrillas* all rose to leave, Eduardo relinquishing Puente's knife only with great reluctance before he came over to join Isabella for breakfast.

She could not resist hugging the boy to her as he lifted her toast to steal a bite. "We have many adventures to speak of, you and I."

But the boy only shrugged as he squirmed from her embrace. "Who would we tell? Everyone we know is here with us."

"The English people," she ventured. "Señor Raike has many brothers and sisters who will wish to hear your stories."

Eduardo licked his fingers, considering this. "I will let them hold my knife," he decided generously. "But then they will have to give it back."

Chapter 38

Isabella was trying to keep up with Raike as they walked toward the chapel area of the *Familia Santa* Convent—the local convent where *El Halcon* had first hidden her, so long ago. Her husband was restless and impatient, and she could not like his uncertain mood. "You must not knock-down *Tio* again; not here at the Convent," she warned.

"I'll make no promises," Raike replied, a bit grimly. "I'm a heretic, after all."

Thoughtfully, Isabella eyed her husband as their footsteps echoed on the tiled floor. The other *guerrillas* had been stationed around the perimeter, politely refusing to comply with the Abbess' request that they relinquish their weapons. As a result, the holy sisters were not much in evidence.

Raike had been adamant that he accompany Isabella when she met with *El Halcon*, but she had argued that she needed to speak to the famous *guerrilla*—and her erstwhile husband, Diego—in private, as they were less likely to be candid in Raike's glowering presence. "Neither will offer any harm to me, I promise. You saw that, last night in the orchard; *Tio* revealed himself—unarmed—out of concern for me."

"You will not be out of my sight," Raike had nonetheless insisted, "or the whole thing is off."

They had finally agreed that he would sit at a distance in the chapel so that he could watch, but not eavesdrop. "Don't allow them to come close enough to seize you," he warned. "If anyone touches you, I start shooting."

"It will be all right," she soothed. "My promise."

They paused on the threshold of the spacious chapel that stretched out before them, the nuns' wooden stations lining the walls. The large altarpiece that covered the back wall was made of marble and gold–as was appropriate for this prestigious convent in the royal town–and the side walls displayed ornate patron's plaques, some dating back to the Middle Ages.

As she reviewed the hushed, sacred space, Isabella's reaction was ambivalent; she had memories of this chapel not as a place of peace, but as a place of heartbreak—it was here that she'd discovered she was an orphan with an uncertain future.

"Look." Raike's hand rested on a large, elaborate marble plaque that adorned the wall, illuminated by a flickering sconce.

Following his gesture, she saw that it was titled, "*In Memoriam*" and marked the names and ages of those who had perished when the royal refugee ship sank, seven years ago. Staring at it, she couldn't find her voice for a moment, and he placed a sympathetic arm across her shoulders, tilting his head so that it rested atop hers.

"It seems so long ago," she whispered. "And then—sometimes—it seems as though it was just yesterday." Her voice trailed off, as she reached up to trace one of the names—her mother's.

"I am so sorry, Isabella."

"I have you, now." Slowly, she ran her fingers along the edge of the plaque. "I could not ask for more."

He covered her hand with his own, pressing it against the marble. "And Spain will recover."

"Yes—although she will never be the same, my poor country."

He lifted his head to consider the list of names. "Which was your father?" And then, when she indicated his name among the others, "What was he like?"

"I rarely saw him," she confessed. "From what I remember, he was rather stern." She turned to him with a tender expression. "I believe your father must have been a good man; you are such a good man—he echoes in you."

Lost in thought, he kept his gaze fixed on the plaque, and said softly, "I did not know he was ill; I was away from home so much, doing my work."

It was the first time she'd heard a trace of self-doubt in his voice, and she laid her hand on his arm, looking up at him with all sincerity. "I am certain he was very proud of you, and of your work, Will-i-am. He would not have wanted to burden you."

"I hope I can be half the father he was."

It seemed very strange, to be speaking of their mutual children—the whole idea was still so new. "We will have excellent children," she ventured.

He smiled at her remark, the somber mood broken, and ran his fingers along the list of names until he came to the last one, set forth at the bottom in larger, more prominent letters. "An infant."

"*Infante,*" she corrected him. "It is the title given to the direct heirs in the royal line."

But his attention was caught, and he turned to rest his thoughtful gaze upon her. "What is it, Isabella?"

"Nothing." She shrugged her shoulders. "Only that it is such a tragedy—to die so young."

He turned back to that last name to trace the words: *The Infante Tomás Alejandro Eduardo de Leandro.* Suddenly, his hand stilled.

"We should move on," she whispered into the silence.

He swore softly in English, which was just as well, as she hadn't the wherewithal to rebuke him for blasphemy. Grasping her arm in a firm grip, he steered her away, walking rapidly outside to the colonnade, and then glancing from side to side in the deserted courtyard area. In an urgent undertone, he asked, "Who knows of this?"

"Will-i-am—" she stammered.

He shook her arm gently in reproach. "You should have told me, Isabella. Ferdinand has no heirs, and he is not known as a pillar of integrity. Good God—Eduardo's life is at risk; we have to smuggle him out of the country immediately."

"No one knows," she whispered, finding it difficult to speak of it, after her long silence. "Only *Tio,* Maria Lucia, and me."

He brought her out into to the center of the courtyard, where no one could approach them unseen, and bent his head to ask in a low tone, "How did it happen? How is it *possible* that no one knows a direct heir is still alive?"

"I am not supposed to say," she whispered, stricken.

He brought his hands up and down her upper arms in a soothing motion. "You can trust me. You know you can— I gave you my promise that I would protect him."

She drew a breath, and whispered, "That night, his nursemaid—she went to fetch a casket of jewels for his mother. There was so much panic and confusion—she handed him to me to hold, but then he started to cry, which made the other children cry, and so I went into the kitchen to seek out the cook, thinking to fashion a teat from cheese cloth. Then we heard gunfire, and the cook pushed us into the pantry and shut the door."

Staring into his chest, she remembered, "I was so afraid he would start crying again, and give us away, but he did not; instead he was silent—looking at me, while I looked back at him—the same as we did seven years later, when the French soldiers searched for us at the Castillo."

Raike reasoned slowly, "That was why you did not go to Rome; Eduardo would not have been safe anywhere, and he is still not safe—not until Ferdinand has his own heir."

She nodded. "*Tio* had a plan. Maria Lucia and I were to act as masks for Tomás, posing as postulants but keeping careful watch over him. If there was trouble, Maria Lucia would hide him at the Castillo—there was a hidden room, somewhere—and then *Tio* would smuggle us all away, pretending to be a family. Unfortunately, that day the soldiers came, I was with him instead of Maria Lucia, and I did not know where the hidden room was. Everything went wrong."

But he could not agree, as he took another careful look around the courtyard. "On the contrary—everything went right. You and Eduardo are now under the protection of the only country left standing, in this mess."

She nodded in resigned agreement. "Yes. We must take him to England, where he will be safe—or at least, safer than if he stayed in Spain."

"For the time being," he agreed. "But he will return to Spain someday—I'll give you my promise on that, also." He made a sound of exasperation. "Another mother who didn't notice that her child wasn't with her—I suppose I shouldn't criticize these royal mothers, because if they weren't so utterly careless, you'd both be dead."

There was a pause. "I will be a better mother," she assured him in a small voice.

He bent his head and started to laugh, drawing her into his arms. "Of course you will, my darling."

"'Darling'," she repeated with a smile. "Like 'sweetheart'."

"Exactly." He kissed the top of her head.

"Forgive me if I interrupt."

Startled, she drew away to see *El Halcon*, standing at a small distance in the shadows of the colonnade—so much for their guards, stationed around the perimeter.

With an apologetic tilt of his head, the *guerrilla* continued, "You must attempt to remember, Señor, that the lady is married to another."

Uncowed, Raike strode over to him. "And you must attempt to remember that I am inclined to report you as a saboteur, acting in defiance of the Congress."

Roughly, he searched the other man for weapons, while *El Halcon* stood with his arms spread. "I hope you do not. We seek the same end, I promise you."

Raike knelt to check the other's boots, and glanced up at him grimly. "I did not have that impression at the Alcazar."

"That was regrettable, but necessary."

Raike rose. "Why?"

"I am afraid I cannot say."

Not liking the way her husband's hands had curled into fists, Isabella decided to interrupt, so as to take the discussion to a less public place. "Allow me to speak with him inside, Will-i-am."

After glancing at her, Raike drew his pistol and made a curt gesture, inviting the *guerrilla* to precede him into the chapel. "Watch the door," he said, and Isabella realized that he spoke to Valdez, who stood in the shadows, watching.

As she followed Raike inside, she overheard her husband say to *El Halcon* in a low voice, "By the end of this evening, we will have an annulment or I will indeed report you as a saboteur, and then there will be no corner in hell for you to hide. Is that understood?"

"Very clearly," the other man replied, and they closed the chapel doors behind them.

Chapter 39

"I will hear your explanation, *Tio*." Isabella sat on a confessional bench next to *El Halcon* as Raike sat at a small distance, watching them closely.

The *guerrilla* bowed his grizzled head and sighed, contemplating the callused hands in his lap. "Our country lies in smoldering ruins, *Pajarocita*. They will put Ferdinand back on the throne, and we have no one at the Congress to defend us; instead the long knives are out—"

"I will hear your explanation," she interrupted in a steely tone. "Sooner, rather than later."

Raising his head, he glanced over at Raike. "Rochon was told the *Ingles* knew important information about the treasure. I would offer him up to them—in secret—in exchange for Rochon's promise that he would not take The Spanish Mask."

"I am ashamed of you, *Tio*," Isabella retorted hotly. "To think you would bargain with such as him—"

But the *guerrilla* held up a hand. "Fah, *Pajarocita;* do you think me such a fool?" The *Ingles* would be sacrificed, it is true. But he would be forced to tell the Frenchman what he knew, and—due to the manner of acquiring this information—Rochon would necessarily believe whatever he said to be true."

Isabella knit her brow, not quite grasping what was meant. "You fed the *Ingles* information that was not true?"

The old *guerrilla* nodded. "The *Ingles* believed there was no Spanish royal treasure, and no Spanish Mask. Instead, that it was only a tale."

Isabella stared at him. "So; you arranged to sacrifice him so as to protect the treasures of Spain."

Her companion nodded. "Yes."

Impatiently, she made a dismissive gesture with her hand. "It matters not, *Tio*; how could you sacrifice an innocent man to die such a death?"

But her companion only continued, "What would be Rochon's reaction, *Pajarocita,* on finding out that I'd fooled him–that I'd fooled him and made him risk so much for nothing?"

Isabella frowned at him. "He would come after you, I suppose."

"He would. He would be justly angry with me, and would search me out—Rochon is a vengeful man. His search, however, would only lead him into an ambush, because I would have alerted the British that Rochon had murdered one of their noblemen."

Slowly, Isabella raised her gaze to the far wall, considering this. "So—your plan was to protect Spain's treasures, and have Rochon charged with murder."

Her companion cocked his head. "Not exactly; if the British made it known that an English lord was murdered by a French operative, such a thing could very well upset the negotiations in Vienna. Instead, the British would see to it that Monsieur Rochon—and his cohorts—simply disappeared." He shrugged. "A fitting end, all around."

But Isabella could not like the satisfaction in his tone, and retorted, "It is so—so *treacherous*. All of it, and on all sides."

The *guerrilla* met her eyes, and would not be moved. "It is war, child, and sacrifices are made for the greater good—and for the survival of Spain. This *Ingles* of yours would have done the same, I can promise you. It is a dirty business."

She lifted her chin. "I think the moment you sacrifice an innocent life, you have lost your war."

He eyed her, unrepentant. "With all respect, *Pajarocita*, you are naïve."

Lowering her voice, she calmed herself with an effort—she didn't want to give Raike the impression they were quarreling. "It is not your place to make decisions that only God should make."

But her companion only spread his hands. "Me, and others like me—your *Ingles*—we work to give God some assistance."

She knew they would not agree on this, and so she changed the subject. "And was I also sacrificed to your schemes, when I was wed to Diego without my knowledge?"

He tilted his head in an apologetic gesture, his boots scraping on the floor beneath him. "I would have to disclose your identity so as to have the French come to find the treasure. I sought to protect you from a forced marriage—surely you can see this? And you were betrothed to Diego, after all—it was not so very strange."

"Instead, I chose my own husband."

The older man chuckled, and the network of wrinkles around his eyes crinkled in delight "Only after you pulled him out of the Alcazar, right under Rochon's nose. They have spoken of nothing else, in Santa Luisa."

But she was not amused. "I had little choice, *Tio*—I could not bear my own role in such a betrayal. He is a decent, brave man; not one who moves people about, as though they were pieces on a chess board. I cannot be sorry for ruining your scheme."

"It was an excellent scheme," he observed with regret. "But never fear; there will be others."

"Not involving the *Ingles*," she warned.

He lifted his head and disclaimed, "No—of course not; how could I have known that you would grow to love him? An *Ingles?*" This last with a trace of incredulity.

She replied honestly, "I don't know if I can ever forgive you, *Tio*—and his scars will always remind me of what you did. But you can redeem yourself when you decouple me from Diego—I would rather not be living a life of sin."

The *guerrilla* tilted his grizzled head toward her, and asked delicately, "Has there been any sinning?"

"Oh, yes," she assured him. "And there will be much, much more."

With a sigh, he confessed, "It is a shame; I thought you and Diego could keep Tomás—at least until this new threat is dealt with. It would have worked out well."

"We will take Tomás to England—the *Ingles* and I— and keep him safe. Do not include him in your scheming; you have done enough harm."

With raised brows, he asked, "You would have him become English?"

But she would not be moved. "I will do what I think best for him; I can no longer trust you to be an honorable man."

The old *guerrilla* grimaced. "You wound me, *Pajarocita*."

"No more than you have wounded me, *Tio*."

The doors at the back of the sanctuary opened, and they looked up to see Valdez enter, his weapon trained upon the man who accompanied him. "This man says you are expecting him, Excellency."

"Don Diego." Isabella rose to her feet with a smile. "It is good to see you." Her cousin was slim and barely taller than she was, with an air of languid elegance; exactly the type of man the *Afrancesados* would not view as a threat.

El Halcon had used this to advantage, posting him at the Palacio to report on the intrigues that abounded there.

"Isabella," the newcomer greeted her with his sweet smile, kissing each cheek. "How wonderful to see you again, cousin; I hear you have experienced quite an adventure."

Raike rose, and approached them, his posture that of a dog guarding a bone, although his words to Diego were conciliatory. "I must beg your pardon, Don Diego. I was not aware my wife had a previous understanding."

"My fault—I did not raise it," Isabella confessed. Not that it would have mattered for an instant, of course, but she didn't wish to hurt Diego's feelings. In the practiced manner of the diplomat, Diego clasped his hands behind his back. "Yes; it is a delicate situation. I have spoken to the bishop who conducted the proxy ceremony and he is—understandably—upset that he bestowed a holy sacrament under false pretenses."

"Tell me how much money will soothe him," asked Raike in an ominous tone.

A bit affronted, Diego raised a brow. "Señor—it is not such a simple matter. A dowry was transferred, and provisions made for children—"

"How much?" Raike repeated, with a hint of steel.

Clearly alarmed by the Englishman's air of suppressed menace, Diego quickly retreated. "Ah—yes; I will speak with the bishop, and arrange for a meeting to resolve these matters. Tomorrow, or perhaps the next day at the latest. He need only hear Isabella's testimony, I imagine."

"Lady Raike," Raike corrected him.

"Lady Raike," the other agreed, with a slight bow.

Chapter 40

Isabella leaned against the post-stile fence as she and Raike watched Eduardo romp with two local boys and a sheepherding dog. Bored to tears and watching out the window, Eduardo had reported with great excitement that a shepherd was marking his sheep on the hillside behind them, and to Isabella's relief, Raike had agreed to investigate this unlooked-for diversion—although the two new men accompanied them, keeping a careful watch.

Leaning on the fence alongside her, Raike idly pulled apart a long blade of grass. "Tell me about Diego—how is he related to you?"

"Diego is my mother's cousin's child—we were often together, when we were children."

The blade of grass having been discarded, Raike now picked up the tail end of her braid, and fingered it absently. "Can he be trusted?"

A bit surprised, she glanced at him. "Why? Do you doubt that he will do as he promised?" This seemed evident—Raike seemed preoccupied, the same as he'd been at the Monastery, the day before he was captured.

He wound her thick braid around his wrist. "I'll admit I am tempted to decamp, and conduct any further negotiations from the safety of England." His gaze met hers, his expression serious.

"You have a good instinct," she agreed. "Better than mine."

He tilted his head in acknowledgment, his long fingers fiddling with her braid. "It is what keeps me alive—except the one time, when I had to rely on my bride to come to my rescue."

She smiled. "That is not quite accurate, Will-i-am; I wasn't your bride at the time—not until later that evening."

"I stand corrected—not that I was aware, either way."

They both smiled at the absurdity of it, but then she sobered, as she turned to watch the boy. "If you wish to leave today, I will do as you ask. I am afraid to trust anyone, anymore—not after what happened to you."

"And to you; your *Tio* served you a trick, marrying you off."

After debating whether or not to tell him, Isabella met his eyes. "When I demanded that *Tio* explain his treachery, he said he wanted the Frenchman to discover information from you—it was false information, but he wanted the Frenchman to believe it to be true."

Raike frowned. "What information?"

"That there was no Spanish royal treasure—that it was merely a tale."

His hands paused, as he looked into the distance to consider this. "I see. A misinformation campaign."

"And there is more—Rochon would be angry when you told him this, and he'd seek revenge from *Tio*, but *Tio* would lead him into an ambush by the British."

Cocking his head, Raike reluctantly admitted, "Not a bad plan. He'd kill two birds with one stone."

Isabella turned back to watch Eduardo. "It does not excuse what he did to you."

But her husband only shrugged. "On the contrary, I'm sure in his mind, he'd do it all over again. I can't say as I'd blame him."

With a sigh, she disclosed, "That is what he said you'd say."

"He's had to be ruthless, and fight against almost insurmountable odds. That kind of war is not for the faint of heart." Raike took up her braid again, to brush the tail against the palm of his hand. "So—do we stay, or do we steal away, before we have the annulment safe in hand?"

Looking up to meet his gaze, she replied steadily, "I will do whatever you ask."

He took her hands in his and kissed them, one at a time. "I have no doubt that we would prevail in the end, but in the meantime, it would eat at you."

Nodding, she dropped her gaze, because as much as she'd tried to hide this from him, it was true; she could not be comfortable with her role as an adulteress, no matter how innocent her part.

The boys began shrieking in the background—they were taking turns trying to ride a sheep, and it was not going well. When it quieted down again, Raike said, "But then we must be away, and as quickly as possible; Eduardo is not safe here, and there is another war coming."

Looking out over the peaceful meadow, she took a long breath. "And you will stay to fight it."

"If I am asked." He placed his warm hand over hers, on the wooden stile.

Lifting her chin, she nodded. She, of all people, understood sacrifice. "I will miss you—and Eduardo will miss Catalo. We will be a sorry pair, when your mother beholds us on her doorstep."

He glanced up to watch the boys—now chasing the sheep—and squeezed her hand. "It can't last long; Napoleon doesn't have the money to fight a proper war."

"I will pass the time learning English." She said it as much to convince herself; if anyone had told her a month ago that she would seek to learn English she would have thought them mad.

Eduardo shouted, "Señora Raike—watch," as he leapt to straddle the sheep, the startled animal bolting away whilst the dog ran alongside–barking madly–until Eduardo landed in an ignominious heap in the tall meadow grass, gasping with laughter. The two other boys tumbled on top of him, and a wrestling match ensued, the dog circling in a barking frenzy whilst the shepherd leaned on his staff and watched.

Raike's ready smile flashed. "I've half a mind to join them. They remind me of my brothers."

Isabella mustered a smile in response, turning her mind away from the coming heartache. "That is to the good, then; Eduardo will be well-entertained in England."

"Carristone. My home is called Carristone." Raike tugged at her braid. "It has a fine orchard."

"Perhaps I will send for some seedlings from the Convent," she mused aloud. "Although the climate will be very different—I shall have to assess."

There was a small pause, whilst he contemplated her, his expression unreadable. "I have met many brave men— and women," he said slowly. "But none braver than you."

She smiled indulgently at this foolishness. "I have only done what had to be done, Will-i-am."

He leaned in to kiss her quickly, even though the boys could see. "Then here's what must be done; we'll go to the Palacio to meet with Diego and the bishop, and we'll get the annulment. Eduardo stays here, though, with my men; I don't trust anyone enough to take him with us."

"*Si.*" She was acutely conscious of the Mask, currently nestled against her breast, and felt a twinge of guilt for conducting her own campaign of misinformation, but it seemed best that no one—save herself—knew where it was.

"I'll be happy to see the last of Diego—how anyone could think such a popinjay deserved someone like you is beyond my comprehension."

"Popinjay." She repeated the strange word with a smile.

"Popinjay," he assured her.

She cautioned, "You must not beat the hell from Diego, either."

"Then he'd best not give me an excuse."

"He won't; he is not a man of action."

With a grin, Raike suggested, "He should marry Maria Lucia, then; she could stray with impunity."

Laughing, she scolded, "You must not say such an unkind thing, Will-i-am; Maria Lucia may like to dally, but she is another who did not hesitate to do what must be done."

He ducked his head in acknowledgement. "True. And for that I am grateful to her."

"But not too grateful," she warned.

Chapter 41

Two mornings later, Raike was giving low-voiced instructions to the men as they assembled in the main room at the Inn.

"I've received information that Rochon is currently searching for us in Madrid; he's followed a false trial laid down by my commander, so there is no immediate threat—although any soldiers in residence at the Palacio are likely to be *Afrancesados,* so we should be wary, nonetheless."

He indicated with a finger. "Catalo, Valdez and Puente come with us to the Palacio. Puente stays on the perimeter, and the others will spread out within earshot. I don't expect any trouble, but if you hear me fire, come to me."

He nodded at the new men, Santana and Padilla. "You will stay here with Eduardo, locked upstairs and out of sight, until we return. Don't allow the boy to plague you into going outside."

And so, once again Isabella found herself mounted behind Raike as they made their way down the road to meet with Don Diego and the bishop. As the horse clip-clopped in a steady rhythm, she leaned to watch the Palacio rise before them and asked, "Tell me more of Carristone, Will-i-am."

He took a quick, assessing glance around them. "It's been in my family for a long time. There are tenants, and farmland—rivers and trees. It was the perfect place to grow up, with lots of room.

We'll have to get a pony for Eduardo."

With a smile, she offered, "I think nothing would make him happier—except perhaps a pistol. He will think England a very fine place."

Turning his chin toward her, he said in a low voice, "He should be well on his way, by now."

Isabella nodded, trying to quell her nerves. The night before, Raike had sought her permission to secretly send the boy away; Raike's men would smuggle him onto a boat traveling down the Tagus River, and then they would all meet up in Portugal to set sail for England. Raike thought it important to take this course of action because he could not be certain that *El Halcon* would not try to prevent the boy from leaving Spain.

Reluctantly, Isabella had seen the wisdom of this. As Aranjuez was in the middle of Spain, the secret journey would take several days, but she was comforted by the fact that by the time anyone realized the boy was gone, he would be safely away, and hopefully untraceable.

Raike's horse approached the Palacio's gates, and because they were expected, the guard indicated they were to proceed up the well-manicured pathway to the portico steps. As the horse's hooves crunched in the coarse gravel, Isabella peered over her husband's shoulder at the imposing edifice that rose before them.

"Does it seem familiar to you, or has it been too long?"

She breathed in the scent of roses as memories came flooding back. "It is very familiar, Will-i-am. I was here most of the time until I was twelve, and I was often bored, so I explored every corner. It seems exactly the same."

"*Pajarocita*," he said with a smile. "Little bird."

She repeated the English translation; she hadn't made much progress learning the language—except for Raike's swear words—but he'd assured her that his mother would hire a tutor to give her a daily lesson. With a mental sigh, she tried not to think about it.

They dismounted, a respectful footman taking their horse, and then she gathered up her skirts and ascended the stairs, her back straight. A servant who had been on the watch for them opened the massive oaken door, and then escorted them down the spacious hallway to the receiving room, his heels clicking faintly on the marble-tiled floor.

The hall seemed strangely silent; through the perceptions of a child, she remembered it as constantly busy, with voices echoing off the high stone ceilings as the members of the royal entourage jockeyed for favors—the women dressed in figured silks and the men self-important in swallowtail coats and glossy boots.

There was no one in residence at present, which was not unusual—the main Palacio was located in Madrid—but the lack was also due to the unfortunate fact that at the present time, Spain had no official king.

It was just as well—Isabella could not be certain of her reaction were she to be confronted with the despicable Ferdinand, flush with renewed power after having betrayed his own father, all those years ago.

It was different in England, Raike had told her; the people's allegiance was to their country over their king, and undoubtedly such a sentiment came from having held a revolution. France had held its own revolution, too, but then had fallen into the quarreling factions that had allowed a tyrant like Napoleon to rise in the place of a king. Unfortunately, it seemed that *bella España* was headed for the same kind of upheaval, with her own quarrelling factions making her weaker rather than stronger.

Unwilling to pursue this discouraging line of thought, she turned to look out a diamond-paned window toward the expansive gardens in the back, where she had wandered for many a happy hour. A curious child—and longing to be outdoors—she'd been drawn to the kindly and clever gamekeeper, who'd allowed her to follow him about whilst he conducted his chores. A happy time, until the world had come crashing down in the course of one terrible night.

The servant opened the door to the formal reception room and then bowed as they walked past him to enter. Near the ornate fireplace, Diego stood in quiet conversation with his companion, the Bishop of Aranjuez, who was easily identified by his garb. Both men turned to greet them. "Your Excellency; Señor Raike."

"Your Eminence." Isabella knelt to kiss the bishop's ring, and noted that his hand felt clammy in hers. As unobtrusively as possible, she wiped her hand on her skirt.

"Come—let us be comfortable." Diego began to pull out a chair for her, only to be supplanted by Raike, who moved to see that she was seated. She cast him a look, to remind him that there were to be no beatings, and declined the tea that was offered by the servant.

The bishop rendered a small smile but made no comment, and Isabella noted that his forehead was beaded with perspiration, as he fingered the heavy cross around his neck.

"Shall we begin?" asked Raike, with a hint of impatience.

"Of course," Diego agreed smoothly. "You will not be disappointed, Señor; we have already discussed the matter, and His Eminence—" here he nodded toward the bishop, "understands the necessity of clearing up this unfortunate matter as quickly and as discreetly as possible."

Raike shifted in his seat, and Isabella knew he wanted to take exception to this characterization of their marriage, but managed to refrain. This was to the good; as long as it could be settled quickly, they shouldn't quibble about the details. Truly, it was no one's fault the problem had arisen; Diego could not have known she would break their betrothal in such a dramatic fashion, and the bishop could not hold it against her, either.

"I have taken the liberty of having the documents drawn up," Diego continued. "You may review them, of course–"

"How much is this going to cost?" Raike bluntly asked the bishop.

Flushing, the clergyman turned to Diego, and Diego replied, "As to that, I am given to understand that a donation to the diocese would be much appreciated."

"Much appreciated," echoed the bishop with a nod.

Isabella, however, had suddenly realized something very strange; the bishop was not behaving like any bishop of her acquaintance—he was allowing Diego to take the lead. He is very much afraid, she realized; and a fearful bishop was a contradiction in terms.

With a smile, Isabella addressed him. "I am so pleased to see you again, Your Eminence. You may not recall, but we met years ago, when I was a child. You were attached to the papal legate in Ciudad Real."

There was a small, silent pause. "Ah, yes," the man nodded. "I remember it well."

Isabella turned to meet Raike's eyes. "Son of a bitch," she said in English. There was no papal envoy at Cuidad Real, and there never had been.

Raike reacted immediately by leaping to his feet and drawing his pistol to hold it on the other men. "No one moves," he commanded, and moved away to stand by the window, glancing out and assessing. "Stand away, Isabella."

Responding to his command, she stood and stepped back and away from the table, only to gasp as she was seized from behind—she had forgotten the servant, standing silently by the door.

Holding her against him like a shield, the man pressed a knife against her throat. "Put down your weapon, or I'll cut her throat."

But Isabella had learned a lesson from the *guerrillas* that it is important, in such a situation, to react quickly. Therefore, with a swift movement she tried to imitate the defensive move that Puente had demonstrated with Eduardo, forcing the knife down and away. The man staggered slightly, and immediately the discharge from Raike's pistol echoed in the chamber as her assailant was struck in the chest, and collapsed to the ground.

"How many others?" Raike barked at Diego, as he crossed the room to shove a heavy chair against the door. "Speak—it would solve a lot of problems if I just kill you now, so don't tempt me."

"Perhaps twenty soldiers—a few French," Diego confessed, pressing his handkerchief to his lips, as he bent his head in shame. "They threatened us—our families—" Miserably, the false bishop nodded in agreement.

The sound of alarmed voices and running footsteps could be heard from beyond the door, so Raike took Isabella's arm, and pulled her with him toward the window.

Wielding the butt of his pistol, he smashed it out, standing back to allow the glass to clatter, and then breaking out the remaining sharp edges around the frame with a few quick movements. "Let's go—quickly." He then vaulted out the window onto the garden bed below.

"I am so sorry, Isabella," Diego pleaded as she lifted her skirts, and stepped up on the sill, "We had no choice."

Without deigning to reply, she leapt out the window into Raike's arms.

Chapter 42

"Stay close beside me." Raike set her down and began walking swiftly toward the rear of the grounds, pulling her by the hand as he held his pistol at the ready.

"Careful—the soldiers' barracks are that way," she cautioned. He immediately reversed course, moving toward the outbuildings with long strides as his gaze raked the battlements that surrounded the perimeter of the Palacio. Keeping her head down, she hurried beside him, hoping at any moment to be joined by the other *guerrillas*, who surely must have heard the shot.

"Where is the gate into the orchards? We would have plenty of cover, there."

"This way." She directed him behind the smokehouse, and around a corner. "I thought Rochon was in Madrid—" Panting, she trotted to keep up with him, and noted that he held a hand against his sore ribs.

Grimly, he picked up his pace. "Misinformation. Unless this is *El Halcon*'s handiwork."

"No," she said with certainty, "it must be Rochon." Tamping down a sense of panic, she added, "Which means it is you they want—not me. They don't know that you've spoken with your commander, and they're trying to keep you from reporting what happened to you."

"They won't get me." Seeing a Spanish guard walking toward them, Raike pulled her inside a recessed doorway, and they waited in tense silence until the man passed by.

"Keep walking," he instructed her, as they resumed their tense progress. "We may have to separate in the orchards, to confuse the pursuit."

"No, we won't," she said firmly. "I stay with you."

But her husband directed, "No; if they take me, you are to accompany my men away from here and get help."

"I won't leave you," she retorted, annoyed. "Stop asking."

Before he could respond, a shout rang out, and a group of soldiers began to run toward them from the far side of the outbuildings, cutting off their route. Grasping her hand, Raike began to run in the other direction, pulling her along with him.

Isabella ran as best she could in her skirts, wondering how long Raike could keep up his pace and trying to fight her fear—it did seem an impossible situation, if they were to be trapped within the Palacio grounds with all escape cut off.

He ran directly toward one of the four towers that marked the corners of the perimeter walls, and–as the pursuing soldiers closed in behind them—he pulled her through the tower's entry door, whirling around to lower the stout oaken bar from the inside.

"We'll barricade ourselves in here," he directed, his hand once more pressing against his ribs. "We need to make a stand, and hold them off until my people in Madrid realize they've been misled." He glanced around the interior, as the frustrated soldiers began to pound on the heavy door. "Is there another access to this tower at the top?"

"Yes," Isabella panted, trying to catch her breath. "There is a door at the top of the stairs. It opens out onto the tower roof, and then onto a walkway that connects the four towers."

"Good—we'll get to the roof; it will be easy to defend." Grasping her hand again, he ran up the narrow stone stairway that spiraled up two floors to the top of the tower, and then, when they'd reached the door, he flung it open and they emerged into daylight.

The tower's flat roof was edged by a stone parapet, with one side open to allow access to the elevated walkway that connected the battlements. Of immediate concern was a solider who was advancing along this walkway toward them, holding his musket at the ready and looking very much surprised. "Halt," he commanded. As there was no one with him, it seemed evident he'd been posted there on guard duty.

After ducking behind the shelter of the parapet, Raike drew his weapon on the approaching man. Involuntarily, Isabella gasped in dismay, and after a slight hesitation, Raike directed the soldier, "Throw down your weapon and retreat, or I will fire."

The two men stood in a tense standoff for a moment, the soldier standing his ground despite his exposure to Raike's weapon.

"You may shoot him," Isabella said quietly. "I am being foolish."

Raike made a threatening gesture with his pistol, and the man reluctantly bent to place his own musket on the stone walkway, and raise his hands. "You may as well surrender; you won't get far." This, said with a touch of bravado to make up for his capitulation.

Raike didn't respond, but instead gave a sharp whistle, and Isabella was immensely relieved to see that the other *guerrillas* were crouched on the opposite tower roof, at the other end of the walkway.

"Can you shoot a pistol?" asked Raike of her, as he glanced down at the soldiers who were gathering on the flagstones below.

"No, but I can learn." Another failing; truly, she was not of much help, in situations such as these.

"Stay back." He leaned forward between the pillars on the stone parapet and began to fire on the soldiers gathered below whilst the *guerrillas* ran along the battlement walkway toward their tower, firing their own weapons.

The soldiers in the courtyard scattered to take cover behind fountains or columns, and then began to return fire upon the racing men, who managed to dive next to Raike unscathed whilst Isabella flattened against the parapet wall so as to stay out of the way.

"It was a trap," announced Raike to the panting *guerrillas,* as they reloaded their weapons. "We'll make a stand here, until reinforcements arrive."

"What do we do with him?" asked Valdez, referring to the surrendered soldier.

"We send him back." Turning to him, Raike addressed the man. "I am a British lord, and if I am taken by the Frenchman, the repercussions will be swift and terrible. Spain may lose any gains she has made at the Congress, so let's not make this worse than it already is."

But the man, aware that his life was to be spared, was unrepentant. "You shout into the wind, *Ingles.* Napoleon comes, and he will defeat the British, this time. I will be well-rewarded."

Furious, Isabella could not contain herself, and addressed the man with biting scorn. "How *dare* you—*how* can you call yourself a Spaniard? You will bring our great country to its knees out of nothing more than greed and spite."

With an equal measure of scorn, the soldier sneered, "There is no 'great country' any more, or haven't you noticed?"

With a mighty crack, Isabella slapped the man across his face, and in a voice of cold fury informed him, "I am Isabella Maria Teresa Eugenia de Léon; royal Grandee of Spain, and *no one* tells me my country is no longer great. Away, you sniveling *Afrancesado;* I hope you wear your chains lightly."

"Get him out of here," said Raike to the others, and they grasped the man's arms to throw him back out onto the walkway.

Chapter 43

"I am sorry," Isabella apologized again to Raike, as they sat in the tower, leaning back against the stone parapet. "If you wished to shoot him, I should not have interfered."

But Raike shrugged. "No—it is better that he tell them the British will avenge me—let them mull that over; Napoleon is still a prisoner on Elba, after all."

"We will need more ammunition," Catalo noted, peering out through a notch in the parapet so as to survey the courtyard below.

Raike smiled in satisfaction. "Fortunately there is plenty—the first floor of this tower holds an armory. If we guard the door below, and this walkway above, we should be able to hold them off indefinitely—and the door below looks solid."

"They may try to batter it—or burn it," Valdez warned.

Raike nodded. "Good point; let's bring the ammunition up here. Then—even if they break through the door—it will be easy to guard the stairwell; they can only pass one man at a time, and it would be suicide to make the attempt."

Valdez and Catalo disappeared down the stairwell to fetch ammunition and additional weapons, while Raike watched the battlement walkway, Isabella by his side.

It was quiet—almost peaceful, compared to the chaos of the past hour, and she wondered if perhaps Raike was right; the enemy was having second thoughts about the wisdom of pursuing him, now that their evil plans were exposed.

He broke the silence. "Well, I can't say much about your taste in second husbands."

"I think that you are the second husband," she pointed out fairly, drawing up her knees to hug them. "But I am very disappointed in Diego—he has been around the Palacio and its intrigues for too long, I think."

Raike watched the men pile the extra ammunition in the corner of the tower's roof. "I should have known—it was too quiet."

"You did know—your instinct was right, again. It is all my fault; my nonsense about wanting the annulment."

He placed a hand on hers, atop her knees. "It is not nonsense, and I will move heaven and earth to straighten this out, Isabella. We've plenty more arrows in the quiver, believe me."

She ventured, "It does seem that your people owe you a favor, after all that has happened to you." Diplomatically, she did not mention that most of his misfortune could be traced directly back to her.

He brushed a thumb over the back of her hand. "If I have to stand with my foot on Napoleon's throat, it will be done."

With a smile at this professed determination, she pointed out, "I think it would be more helpful to stand with your foot on the bishop's throat, and I will gladly assist."

He made a derisive sound in his throat. "That fellow was such a paltry imposter that even I was beginning to be suspicious. Can you be certain *El Halcon* was not behind it? Perhaps he meant to turn me over to the *Afrancesados*—again—and allow Diego to carry off the prize; two problems solved."

Frowning, she shook her head. "No—but it is difficult to explain why I know this. Now that he knows you are dear to me, he would never do such a thing."

He did not make a reply, but she could sense that he was skeptical—as he had every right to be. The other men had taken up their positions again, armed to the hilt, and Catalo asked, "It is quiet—do you think they mean to parlay?"

Without taking his gaze from the battlement walkway, Raike replied, "It would not surprise me. The *Afrancesados* may have followed their orders up until now, but now that they are aware they risk England's wrath, they may reconsider. I haven't seen any French as yet; perhaps they pulled out, when things went awry."

But this was not to be the case; after an interval of time when there was no further activity, a voice suddenly rang out from the courtyard below. "Monseigneur Raike; *je voulais parlez.*"

"Monsieur Rochon," Raike shouted in return, "*J'ai rien dire.*"

Rochon? thought Isabella in alarm. It seemed the French had not withdrawn, after all.

The conversation continued in French. "I was amused by your subterfuge about The Spanish Mask—a clever gambit."

"I am a clever man," Raike replied in the same language.

"I am grateful for the gift of the comb—I know just the woman who will do it justice."

"What does he say?" Isabella whispered, unable to follow.

Raike shrugged. "He makes little sense; he speaks of The Spanish Mask, but says it is a comb."

In growing horror, Isabella stared at him. "*Madre de Dios—*"

Raike watched her reaction in surprise. "What is it?"

Her mouth dry from panic, she stammered, "He—he has seized the treasure; I was afraid to leave the Mask behind and so I substituted my comb—"

With grave alarm, his eyes met hers, and she could see he was thinking the same thing she was; if they had seized the Mask—

Rochon's voice drifted up. "I have someone here that may be of interest to you."

Without conscious thought, Isabella tried to leap to her feet, but Raike and Valdez grasped her arms and hauled her back down again. "Isabella," Raike said urgently, his face close to hers. "You must say nothing—nothing. Do you understand?" He turned to Valdez and Catalo. "Keep her quiet."

Stricken, she watched him rise to his feet, and address the Frenchman in a loud tone. "The French wage war against children, now?" He'd switched from French to Spanish.

"These are desperate times," the other replied. "Is the boy your bastard, or hers?"

"The boy is a Spaniard, nothing less," shouted Raike.

Struggling to control her horror, Isabella realized Raike was trying to create dissension in the ranks of the Spanish soldiers, and indeed, a low murmuring could be heard, rising up from the courtyard.

"The boy will come to no harm," Rochon assured him loudly in Spanish, aware of the other's tactic. "I only seek to parlay with you. You have information, I have the boy. Come, we are reasonable men."

There was a pause. "I will need assurances for his safety," Raike called out in Spanish, for the benefit of the listening soldiers.

Rochon's tone hardened. "I have little time, *très malheureusement*. You must come down, or I cannot answer for the consequences."

"Have a rope handy," Raike said in a low voice to Catalo, as he tucked an extra pistol in the back of his waistband. "Everyone, be ready for an extraction—Puente, you come to cover my back."

In acute misery, Isabella watched him prepare to go down—an impossible choice between the man she loved and her cousin, the *Infante*—and once again, she was responsible for leading her husband into mortal danger. It did not help matters that he was already in a weakened state, and she must have made an involuntary sound, because Valdez laid a hand on her shoulder. "Be easy—he is not a fool. They will bring the boy back."

She saw Raike meet Valdez's gaze for a silent moment, and then shift his eyes to her by which she was given to understand that Valdez had standing instructions about what was to be done with her, if things did not work out well.

We shall see, she thought, suddenly filled with a cold fury; a pox on all high-handed men, English or otherwise—there is not a soul among them who is a match for me; me, who has a thousand generations of Spanish arrogance at my back.

Raike directed Catalo, "Keep Lady Raike away from the wall. Come along, Puente; we'll be back with Eduardo—be ready." He then opened the door, and entered the tower to descend.

Leaping to her feet, Isabella stayed Puente with a hand on his arm. "Do not go; instead close the door and lock the *Ingles* in the tower."

"*Que*?" the man asked, startled.

"Lock the door—it is I who am going to parlay, instead of the *Ingles*." As they all stared at her in surprise, she stamped a foot, and commanded, "You will obey me, and *immediately.*"

After the barest hesitation, Puente obediently swung the heavy door shut with a clang, and secured it as Raike's startled exclamation could be heard at this unexpected turn of events. Lifting her chin, Isabella then turned to stride out onto the battlements walkway.

Chapter 44

Her face aflame, Isabella strode out onto the elevated walkway and turned to face the surprised, upturned faces of the soldiers who were assembled in the courtyard below. It was a simple thing to recognize Rochon—he was the only man not in uniform. Beside him, a French soldier held Eduardo by the shoulders, and even from this distance she could see the boy's pale, frightened face lifted toward her. There seemed little question that Raike's men were no longer alive, and she tamped down her outrage that this despicable enemy would subject a child to such brutality.

"*Frances,*" she shouted out to Rochon, her voice rigid with contempt as it echoed off the walls. "You have caused me a great deal of inconvenience."

"*Pardon,*" Rochon responded with great irony.

"That's her—that's the Grandee." Isabella heard a hushed voice, and thought she recognized the guard she'd slapped; apparently, she'd penetrated his insolence, after all.

There were perhaps twenty Spanish soldiers—*Afrancesados*—stationed behind the columns and fountains in the courtyard with their weapons at the ready, while only a handful of French soldiers surrounded Rochon and Eduardo toward the back—good.

With an expression of outrage, she surveyed the assembled men below her. "Men of Spain!" she shouted. "What has happened to our poor country, that we serve a Frenchman in his quest to capture an Englishman?"

"Sit, woman—you are at risk," Rochon called out impatiently.

Raike had opened the face plate in the tower door, and was now shouting through it, "Pull her back—Catalo, you son of a bitch, I will shoot you where you stand—"

Ignoring the ruckus behind her, Isabella continued to address the *Afrancesados*. "We may disagree about our future, my countrymen, but we are as one mind about our ancestors—those who fought to retake our country from the Moors; King Leovigild the Conqueror and—by the grace of almighty God—the allegiance forged by Ferdinand of Aragon, and Isabella of Castile. An allegiance that built a mighty empire out of a mighty people; a mighty empire that once used France as its footstool, and England, too."

"Isabella—" shouted Raike, pounding on the tower door. "Enough; someone pull her back—"

But no one moved, as the assembled men watched her in profound silence.

"We are Spaniards," she insisted, gazing upon the soldiers who silently stared up at her. "We do not take up arms against our own. We do not harm children."

"Away, or the boy will suffer." Rochon's tone held an edge of wariness; he had noted—as had Isabella—that the Spanish soldiers were now exchanging glances, their hesitation palpable.

She turned to shout at Rochon with open scorn, "Do you think *you* have the ordering of *me*, *Frances*? I, who carry the bloodline of Isabella of Castile?" With an impatient gesture, she addressed the Spanish soldiers again. "Send this Frenchman on his way, and let us not add to our country's misery."

Two things happened almost simultaneously; a shot rang out, and she was knocked backward so that she fell heavily against the battlement wall. She could hear Raike shouting in a hoarse voice as Valdez ran to help her up, and—gasping for breath— she realized she'd been shot.

Her immediately reaction was outrage, and scrambling to her feet, she shook off Valdez and glared at the men below. "Who *dares*?"

The soldiers backed away, murmuring among themselves, and several making the Sign of the Cross.

"Seize her!" shouted Rochon.

"No!" she shouted in fury as she pointed at the Frenchman. "Seize *him*!"

Immediately, a melee broke out as the soldiers began to fight amongst themselves whilst Isabella shouted her encouragement, until an arm came around her waist to lift her behind the tower's parapet—Raike had been released.

He and Valdez pulled her down onto the tower roof as Raike's hands quickly moved over her torso, assessing. "Breathe slowly, sweetheart—let me have a look." Staying his hands, she looked up into his face, which was drawn and pale. "I am not hurt," she assured him. "The ball hit the Mask."

The circle of faces above her stared in silence for a moment. Lifting her hand, she knocked on her left breast, as though she were knocking on a door. "The Spanish Mask."

"Holy *Christ*," breathed Raike, dropping his chin in profound relief.

"You mustn't blaspheme, Will-i-am."

"I will blaspheme as much as I like—I deserve it. Where the hell is Catalo?"

It soon became apparent what had happened to Catalo; the reason he'd opened the tower door for Raike was so that he could descend into the courtyard, hoping to seize Eduardo in the general confusion.

Seeing his aim, the *guerrillas* knelt along the parapet and drew their weapons so as to give him cover, and they watched as Catalo felled the French soldier who held Eduardo with one mighty blow. Then—tucking the boy under an arm—the big *guerrilla* turned to race back toward the tower.

Another French soldier pursued him, and managed to tackle him around the waist, but Catalo was not an easy man to bring down and kept his feet, dragging the man along with him as he struggled to break free.

With a quick movement, Eduardo reached to pull the French soldier's pistol from his belt and fire point blank into the man's chest.

With a cry, the man dropped to the ground, and Catalo was once again running toward the tower, Eduardo under his arm.

While the *Afrancesados* were more interested in their own insurrection than in re-capturing Eduardo, the French were another matter, and Rochon leapt onto a bench in an attempt to locate the boy, furiously shouting at his men.

Taking careful aim, Raike fired at Rochon, and the man recoiled, a hand to his shoulder as he retreated back beneath the cover of the balcony.

"Stand by the door below to let him in, then bar it, once they come through," Raike directed, but it was too late; several of the French soldiers had managed to cut off Catalo's escape route to the tower.

"Stop him!" shouted Rochon. "But do not hurt the boy—bring him to me."

"Lower the rope on the other side of the walkway, and give him cover," Raike commanded the *guerrillas*.

Valdez and Puente ran, crouching, across the walkway, then threw a rope down by the far tower whilst Padilla and Raike waited, pistols drawn, for an opportunity to pick off the French as they exposed themselves to crossfire.

Carrying Eduardo, the big *guerrilla* raced to the rope, but one of the French soldiers knelt behind a fountain, took careful aim, and fired, staggering Catalo.

"Eduardo—grab the rope," Raike shouted, firing to keep the soldier pinned behind the fountain.

But the boy knelt beside Catalo, who had collapsed to the ground. "Catalo!" he called frantically. "Get up!"

"Finish him!" shouted Rochon.

"Do not! He is a priest!" shouted Isabella.

At this, even the French soldiers lowered their weapons, although one ran forward to pull Eduardo away from Catalo. Furiously weeping, the boy struggled against the man's grasp, repeatedly beating at the soldier's face with a closed fist.

"Bring him to me—quickly," Rochon called from the recesses of the columns.

Carefully propping his pistol against the stone parapet, Raike aimed, then fired at the grappling pair. The soldier dropped to the ground, dead.

"To the rope, Eduardo," Raike called out in an urgent voice. "Follow orders—now!"

But instead, Eduardo returned to Catalo, who was now attempting to stand, and helped him rise to his feet. It was an eerie sight; the soldiers—French and Spanish—watched the struggling pair in silence, as Rochon shouted futile commands from the back—he dared not expose himself to the *guerrillas'* fire again.

With a labored motion, Catalo hoisted the boy onto his back, and then—with Eduardo clinging like a monkey—climbed the rope, hand over hand, until he heaved himself over the top of the walkway, Valdez and Puente pulling on his arms to assist him. Between the boy and the men, they supported the stumbling Catalo back to the parapet, where he collapsed onto the tower roof. The men then quickly surrounded him, unbuttoning his coat to assess the damage.

Isabella fell to her knees beside the big *guerrilla*, her jaw clenching as she noted the spreading bloodstain on his chest. Pressing his hand in hers, she asked, "Do you ask almighty God to forgive you your sins, Catalo?"

"*Si*," the fallen man responded in a whisper.

"Catalo!" Eduardo knelt, and frantically grasped the man's bloody shirt with both hands "No!"

Struggling to keep her composure, Isabella looked into Catalo's unfocused eyes and told him, "Eduardo is the *Infante* Tomás, Catalo—the one they thought was drowned as a baby. You have saved his life. *Deo Gratias.*"

There was a small pause. "*Deo Gratias*," the wounded man whispered.

"May the Lord who frees you from sin save you and raise you up," she recited in Latin, whilst Eduardo dropped his head on the big man's chest, weeping in anguish.

Raike had been assessing Catalo's wounds with probing fingers, and now stood to pull her away. "I'm sorry to interrupt, sweetheart, but no one is going to die, here—help me get him below."

Leaving Puente to guard the walkway, the others carried Catalo down the spiral staircase—no easy task—and then laid him out on the wooden table in the armory room. Quickly, Raike took his knife and began to cut the man's shirt away. "Is anyone familiar with field surgery?"

"I am," said Valdez, who began rolling up his sleeves.

"Tell me what needs to be done, and I will do it," Isabella offered, afraid to hope that Catalo would not perish before Eduardo's eyes.

Raike glanced up at the cupboards and shelves in the room. "There should be a medical kit here somewhere— find it." To Padilla he said, "Whiskey—or any type of spirits—there must be some close to hand."

Frantically opening the cupboards, Isabella came across a leather satchel. "This?"

"Good. Bring it over, with any luck there is some laudanum, but we can't wait very long—he has lost a lot of blood."

Catalo groaned, and Raike addressed the unconscious man as he rolled up his shirtsleeves. "You are one lucky bastard; it looks like they missed your lung."

Taking the proffered bottle of whiskey from Padilla, Raike liberally washed the table down with it, and then washed Catalo's torso, pausing to take a long pull from the bottle, himself. "Light a fire; we'll need to cauterize the wound." He took several sharp looking implements from the satchel, and splashed the whiskey on them. "Another bottle," he directed.

"Should we take the boy out?" asked Valdez.

Raike glanced up at Eduardo from under his brows. "You can stay, but you can't touch anything, and if you're sick, no one is going to help you."

"Your Highness," added Padilla respectfully.

"I am not a king," Eduardo responded in confusion.

"Given what has already happened in this miserable country, you never know," replied Raike. "Let's cut."

Chapter 45

Isabella was not certain if she should watch the procedure—she did not want to faint, and distract Raike from his task—but she found that she was needed to wash whiskey into the wound and soak up blood with a roll of lint, so that she didn't have the opportunity to think about how gruesome it all was. Eduardo stood silently in the corner, his face pale, and his eyes wide.

They had propped up Catalo's head to give him whiskey mixed with laudanum, but nevertheless it took two men to hold his arms down when Raike began to probe for the ball with an instrument; the patient groaning and trying to move, even though he was not conscious.

"Two, I think," said Valdez, who held the separated skin and muscle apart with another instrument, whilst Raike probed. "One in the side of his chest, and one near the shoulder."

"Not gut shot," agreed Raike, as he continued his endeavors. "He's lucky they were trying to avoid shooting Eduardo. We'll need you to thread a needle, Isabella."

"Oh," she replied, setting down the whiskey bottle. "How much thread?"

"About a foot."

She pulled the needle and thread from the surgery kit, and tried not to reveal her inexperience as she completed this task, her fingers trembling slightly.

"There," said Raike with satisfaction, as he dropped a musket ball on the table with a click. "Shake the basilicum powder in the wound please, Isabella."

Valdez then applied the hot poker, and Isabella fought dizziness, as the smell of burning flesh brought back memories of Raike in the Alcazar.

Valdez gently took the needle and thread from her hand. "Do you need to sit?"

"No—I am fine." Righting herself with an effort, she manned the whiskey bottle, as they stitched up the wound.

"It is quiet," Valdez commented.

Raike began to probe for the second ball. "I doubt the French would dare to rely on any further support from the *Afrancesados,* here; hopefully, they have departed with all speed. And Rochon was wounded; there is that." He glanced up at Isabella. "We are fortunate that Lady Raike knows how to stir up a riot."

The others chuckled, and Isabella lifted her chin and did not deign to reply. With deliberate movements, Raike once again began to probe for the musket ball, and the laudanum must have been working, because the patient no longer reacted as strongly.

"Near the bone—do you see?" asked Valdez, indicating with his head.

"*Si—gracias*. Where have you done this before?"

As she leaned to blot the blood, Isabella stole a look at her husband; the question seemed casual, but she had the impression it was not.

"Saragossa," Valdez answered easily. "I was injured, and made myself useful while I recuperated."

Raike grimaced. "A bloodbath."

"There was plenty of work in the surgery, unfortunately."

Even Isabella, locked away in the remote convent, had heard of the months-long siege at the Spanish city, where the inhabitants had fought the French hand-to-hand in the streets, with nearly sixty thousand dead.

The second ball hit the table with a click. "More basilicum, Isabella."

Isabella sprinkled the powder over the wound and then averted her eyes, as she heard the sound of sizzling flesh.

"Is he going to be all right?" asked Eduardo in a small voice.

"He's a tough bastard," Raike answered as he began to stitch up the wound. "Only the good die young."

Isabella glanced over at him. "Are you injured, *caballero*?" It was hard to tell; Eduardo was smeared with blood.

"No—my hand hurts a little."

"Here, let me see." Valdez led the boy over to the lantern and examined his hand; the web of skin between his thumb and forefinger was blackened. "From the pistol's discharge," the man explained. "It will sting for a while; it was a good shot."

"Better than mine," said Raike in a grim tone. "I wish I'd killed that bastard."

Valdez tilted his head in commiseration. "A little souvenir, instead—he'll not soon forget you."

"No—in fact, I hope he looks under his bed every night, expecting to see me." Raike leaned in to bite the thread off with his teeth. "Someday, he will."

"He shot you, Señorita." Eduardo's wide gaze slid to Isabella. "He shot you; I tried to stop him."

"Did him precious little good," noted Raike, and the others chuckled again.

Raike splashed more whiskey over the inert man's chest, before they began bandaging him—carefully rolling Catalo from side to side to complete this task. "Can you give me a report from Puente, Isabella? We should try to gauge the mood, outside."

Nodding, she thought about enlisting Eduardo to accompany her, but saw that the boy's gaze was anxiously fixed on Catalo, and so she left him to his vigil.

After climbing the spiral steps, Isabella paused to lift her arms to stretch out her back, before emerging into the sunlight—*santos*, she was weary, and the day was not yet over. Stepping out onto the tower roof, she saw Puente, seated with his back against the parapet as he watched the silent courtyard, a musket across his lap. Upon her approach, he rose respectfully. "How does he, Excellency?"

"I am not certain," she replied honestly. "They found two musket balls, and he yet lives; I think they don't want to say too much in front of Eduardo."

"Eduardo—Eduardo is the *Infante.*" He met her eyes in wonder. "My mind is full of this. You are certain, Excellency?"

Belatedly, Isabella realized that perhaps she had been less than circumspect. "Promise me you will say nothing of this, Puente; his life is at risk."

Fervently, he nodded in agreement. "I will say nothing, Excellency—but it is like a miracle."

Upon reflection, she decided she couldn't disagree. "It is quiet, then? Raike wishes a report."

"*Si*—they have all cleared out." He gestured with the musket toward the grounds. "No one." Turning, he stilled suddenly, then pulled on her arm. "Down, quickly."

With a gasp, she followed his instruction and crouched beside him, as he peered out one of the notches in the battlements. On the far horizon, a large body of horsemen could be seen, approaching steadily.

Madre de Dios, she thought, closing her eyes briefly— no more, I beg of you. "French, or *Afrancesados*?" she asked in a whisper, her mouth dry.

The man squinted, assessing, as the figures came closer. "British," he replied with some surprise. "They are British soldiers."

"Oh—" She turned to the man, unable to control her wide smile, and clapped her hands on his shoulders. "Oh, *Puente*—it is the *British*—I must tell Raike."

Nearly giddy with relief, she descended the stairs two at a time. "Will-i-am," she called. "The British army is coming."

The men in the armory looked up in surprise at her announcement. "The devil!" exclaimed Raike, wiping his bloody hands on a rag. "Are you certain?"

"Puente says so—it is a large group of horsemen."

"Let me see, then."

They all assembled on the parapet—save Eduardo, who stayed with Catalo—and watched the arrival of the group, now close enough to be easily identified. Raike nodded in satisfaction, leaning with his palms against the stone. "Not a moment too soon." He turned to Puente. "Let's go down below. I can't imagine there will be any trouble, but stay here with Catalo and Lady Raike until I return with the all-clear."

"I will stay, instead," offered Valdez to Puente. "You go."

"What if the *Afrancesados* resist the British?" Isabella was unable to believe that their troubles were so easily over. "What then?"

"They won't," Raike assured her, grimacing slightly as he shrugged into his coat. "They may have been willing to support Rochon behind the scenes, but they don't dare attempt an open rebellion—at least not until Napoleon is free, and not against such numbers." Gesturing with his head, he indicated Padilla was to unbar the door.

"Nevertheless, take no chances," she urged.

Chuckling, he pulled his hat brim down, and stepped out into the courtyard. "Now, that is rich, coming from you."

Chapter 46

After re-barring the door, Isabella ran her hand over Eduardo's curls as she walked over to the foot of the spiral stairs. Sinking down, she settled in to wait where she could watch the tower's door, even though she knew it would be a while before Raike returned. Eduardo stayed on his stool beside Catalo, his head leaning against the edge of the table, and his small hand tucked under the unconscious man's arm. Even from the stairs, she could hear Catalo's breathing and thought, Eduardo is right; Catalo snores.

After a moment, Valdez strode over, and sat on the step below hers, stretching out his legs to cross his boots. "Was it your husband, who betrayed us?"

A bit surprised that he addressed her without being asked, she turned a cold gaze upon him. "My husband is Señor Raike. To whom do you refer?"

Caught out, the man ducked his chin in acknowledgment. "Your pardon—I have been listening to private conversations."

She sighed without umbrage. "Privacy is a luxury, I suppose. I would ask that you do not repeat the story of the proxy marriage—I would not like Señor Raike's family in England to hear of it."

"No—of course not. It is an unfortunate turn of events."

Quirking her mouth, she could appreciate the understatement. "One of many, it seems."

He nodded. "Do you travel to England, Excellency?"

There seemed little harm in admitting it. "Yes—at least until Napoleon sorts himself out."

Although she tried to keep her tone neutral, she must not have succeeded, because her companion glanced up to assure her, "Napoleon will not prevail."

She nodded, trying to convince herself, more than anything else. "That is what Señor Raike says, too."

"I would believe anything Señor Raike says about it; he is in a position to know."

Thinking she should probably turn the subject away from Raike's mysterious work, she asked, "Have you ever been to England, Valdez?"

He tilted his head. "I have not. But I understand the beefsteak there is very good."

She smiled. "There is that."

Slowly, he continued, "I sought out this opportunity to speak with you privately; I must tell you something that I think will give your heart ease."

She met his eyes in surprise; he was not one to seek out a personal conversation, and especially not one with her.

After glancing up at Eduardo for a moment, he continued in a low tone, "Because the King did not approve your marriage to Diego, it does not exist. You are a royal Grandee; the King must give his permission for any marriage, and he did not."

Knitting her brow, she stared at him, considering. "This is true?"

He nodded. "It is."

It was such a simple answer, she could only stare at him in bemusement. "*Santos,* but that is good news, Valdez." Suddenly struck, she added with some dismay, "But then—by the same account—I had no permission to marry Señor Raike, either."

"You will be given permission—my promise on it." He lifted his gaze to meet hers, a small smile playing around his mouth.

She could not be more astonished, and stared at him. "How is this? You have the ear of King Charles?"

He shook his head slightly. "No; King Ferdinand, instead."

Dumbfounded, she stared at him. "You—you are a spy for—for *Ferdinand*?" It was such a distasteful charge, she could hardly say the words.

"You must not say," he admonished her gently. "I will keep your secrets, and you must keep mine; I tell you only because I don't want you to worry about your marriage—I will see to it."

She shook her head slowly, and decided she was utterly incapable of being shocked anymore. "How–how *extraordinary*. You, Catalo, me—no one was who they said they were; we were all masks."

He shrugged. "These are extraordinary times, Excellency."

"I suppose that is inarguable." She looked at him, curious. "Why does Ferdinand wish you to spy on Raike? Does he also seek to discover what the British know?"

"Not Raike," he corrected. "You."

She lifted her brows in surprise. "Me? Does Ferdinand seek the treasure, too?"

Her companion brushed a trace of basilicum powder from his trouser leg. "No. I was asked to see if you were who you were rumored to be. The King—"

"Ferdinand is *not* the true king," she flashed, unable to contain her annoyance.

But he insisted with a small smile, "*King* Ferdinand is naturally concerned.

The Congress will place him on the throne, but there will be a large faction who refuse to recognize him as the true King. And so Ferdinand wanted to ensure you were no threat to his power, if it was true that you were the missing Grandee."

Staring at him with dawning horror, she struggled with the realization that all along, Eduardo's true enemy was right here, in their midst. If Ferdinand saw her as a threat—she, who was merely a grand-niece—Eduardo could not be allowed to survive; after all, Ferdinand had no heirs. Indeed, few even knew of Eduardo's very existence, therefore it would be a simple matter to eliminate him—

"Señor Valdez," she began humbly, then struggled with how best to beg—she who had never begged for anything in her life. "Please—oh please; Eduardo—"

"What of him?" The man's dark eyes were guileless as they met hers. "Poor fatherless boy; perhaps you will take him to England for a time, until all danger has passed."

After a moment, she managed to breathe, "*Si*." She found that her throat had closed, and her lower lip trembled so that she could not speak. As though it was entirely natural, the *guerrilla* drew the Grandee into his arms whilst she wept on his shoulder, relief mixed with reaction to this thoroughly miserable day.

"Hush, now, Isabella. You have nothing to fear from me."

She was surprised that he addressed her by name, but then discovered this was the least of the surprises as he lifted his head to gently kiss her mouth. Placing a hand along the side of her face, he brushed a tear aside with his thumb, the expression in his eyes a mixture of tenderness and regret.

Not wanting to encourage him, but on the other hand, not wanting to antagonize him, she said sincerely, "I will never forget you, Señor Valdez. *Mille de gracias.*"

He withdrew to a more respectful distance. "We must hope the next few years are easier for the country we both admire so much."

She nodded, recovering, and wiped her eyes with her palms. "I meant no insult, but I cannot think of Ferdinand with kindness."

"No," her companion agreed. "He is not a kind man, but he is my King."

Suddenly struck, she said, "May I ask another boon?"

"Whatever you wish."

"In Santa Luisa, I stayed with Doña Francesca, do you remember?"

"I do."

"When her husband fell at Cadiz, he was wearing his *Medalla de Valor*; could you ask Ferdinand to replace it—with my compliments?"

"I will do it," he agreed. "It is a very thoughtful gesture."

"She said it meant so much to him—it was a symbol of so much—" Here she suddenly paused, and lifted her gaze.

The *guerrilla* agreed, "It is in times such as these that the symbols are very important. Many have sacrificed so much that there is little else left."

Slowly she turned her face to him. "The English have an expression, 'a dog in the manger'. Do you know it?"

Bemused, he conceded, "I do not."

Reaching into her bodice, she wriggled The Spanish Mask from its hiding place, and held it for a moment in her hands. "I have something for you—for you to give to Ferdinand."

She watched the gems glimmer in the dim light, and felt the full weight of the Mask's significance. Softly, she said, "It belongs to the King of Spain."

"It belongs to Spain," he corrected her. "But I shall give it to the King, for safekeeping."

"That is what I meant," she reasoned slowly, handing it over to him. "The English have it right, I think; a country is more than its King."

"*Gracias.*" He carefully placed the Mask within his shirt, and then rose. "*Vaya con Dios*, Isabella. You will be a good wife for him, I think. But if you are not, you must send word, and I will come running."

She smiled at his insolence, and made no response.

"Keep me in your prayers, *por favor*." He then left up the stairway, without looking back.

Chapter 47

Isabella heard voices approaching, and–with a great deal of pent-up anticipation–leapt up to stand beside the door, listening.

"Open up, Isabella, the cavalry has arrived."

With a happy smile, she heaved at the heavy wooden bar, and then blinked in the bright sunlight for a moment; Raike stood with a British officer beside him, and several soldiers lined up behind them. "Allow me to introduce Captain Billings. My wife, Lady Raike."

Isabella bowed her head. "Good night," she said in careful English.

After the barest hesitation, the man bowed in response. "Good night, my lady."

I got it wrong, she thought, annoyed; I always mix it up.

"The wounded man is on the table," Raike directed the others, and they moved past her into the room; she could see that one was a capable-looking older man who carried a medical kit.

Isabella laid a gentle hand on the boy who sat next to the table. "Eduardo, come aside, and let these men see to Catalo."

"I believe, my lady—" the Captain ventured with no little astonishment, "that perhaps you have need of some assistance, yourself. I believe you have been shot."

Isabella glanced at her bodice, which sported a ragged hole over her heart. "Oh," she said. "It was nothing."

"Where is Valdez?" asked Raike, glancing around the room.

She thought about her answer for a moment. "He went upstairs."

He gave her a glance, and then took her elbow in his hand. "Shall we go back to the Palacio? The Captain would like us to sit for a debriefing."

Hesitating, she couldn't help but ask, "We are certain it is safe?"

He nodded and squeezed her arm in reassurance. "The *Afrancesados* have cleared out—as I suspected they would—and only the servants remain. I thought we'd stay here tonight, and then beg for an escort to the coast."

"I am at your service," the Captain offered in his rudimentary Spanish.

"Thank you," Isabella said in English, and felt slightly better.

"And who are you?" the surgeon asked Eduardo in a friendly fashion. The boy was hovering at the edge of the table, anxiously watching as the man examined Catalo.

Glancing up through his blood-matted hair, the boy replied, "I am Eduardo, although I think I am also Tomás."

"You are Eduardo," said Isabella firmly.

"He is with us." Raike held out his hand to the boy. "Come along, Eduardo."

But the boy didn't move, his expression mulish. "I want to stay with Catalo."

Isabella moved to crouch down before him, and hold his arms in her hands. "Only long enough so that we may clean you up, *caballero*, my promise." She smiled. "Look at us—we are as dirty as we were in the rabbit burrow. And once again, we have outwitted the enemy."

With his own smile of remembrance, the boy ducked his head. "The enemy are fools."

Gently, she urged, "Come; they will put Catalo in a soft bed, and you can sleep in his room tonight—my hand on my heart."

"I am hungry," he admitted, sliding a glance at Catalo.

She stood to take his hand. "I am not surprised, we have had a very busy day."

They began to walk across the courtyard, and she was relieved to see that all corpses had been discreetly removed, the occasional bloodstain the only evidence of the fierce battle that had waged. "Valdez?" Raike asked her in an undertone.

Gathering her thoughts, she summarized, "He is a spy for Ferdinand, and has left. He will not cause trouble. I gave him the Mask, to give over to Ferdinand."

To his credit, Raike didn't break stride, and Isabella decided he was indeed very good at his job. "I can't turn my back on you for a moment, can I?"

"No one was more surprised than I," she defended. "But if he wanted to harm Eduardo, he had every opportunity. Instead, he will say nothing, as long as we take the boy to England."

A bit grimly, Raike said, "Then we will, and as soon as possible. One thing I have learned in this business is that no one is more paranoid than heads of state."

The Captain turned to address them, as they crossed the flagstones toward the main building. "The injured man—he is one of yours?"

"No," said Raike shortly. "He's a traitorous son of a bitch."

"He is a priest," offered Isabella.

"He saved me," Eduardo added.

"Ah," the Captain said, and asked no further questions.

As they approached the entry doors, Isabella inquired of Raike, "Is Diego still here?" She wasn't certain she could bear to be in the same room with her erstwhile husband.

"No," Raike replied in an even tone, as he strode along.

She eyed him. "Did you beat the hell out of him, Will-i-am?"

"Just choked him a little—I didn't want to scar his pretty face."

With a small smile, she chided, "I will not say he did not deserve it, but you must have more compassion for those not as courageous as you, my friend."

But he was unrepentant. "I don't know if it was cowardice, as much as he hoped to rid himself of a rival without dirtying his hands."

Reminded, she glanced at the Captain to be certain he couldn't overhear, and told Raike in a low voice, "Valdez told me that the marriage to Diego is a nullity because I did not have the King's permission—and he tells me he will acquire the King's permission for our marriage, instead."

With raised brows, Raike held the entry door for her. "Excellent—a simple solution to all problems. I'd guessed that Valdez was an agent, but I was inclined to believe he worked for the Russians."

"The Russians have spies, too?"

"Everyone has spies here, my sweet innocent—and it seems as though we have encountered at least half of them." He glanced at her. "Is that why you gave Valdez the Mask—in return for permission to marry?"

With a sigh, she stepped into the cool foyer. "No—I decided all on my own. The ground is shifting beneath my feet, and I am not so arrogant that I cannot feel it."

Reacting to her tone, he paused to lay a hand against her cheek, his expression sympathetic. "I'm sorry, Isabella. It seems such a shame, after all you have sacrificed—all these years, protecting Eduardo, and waiting to be restored to your rightful places."

Tenderly, she clasped his hand against her face. "It wasn't so difficult—truly. I only needed to be reminded that Spain is greater than the person who happens to rule her."

"I love you, Lady Raike." He bent to kiss her, and Eduardo made a strangled sound of embarrassment.

The Captain cleared his throat. "If you wouldn't mind—it will just take a moment." He indicated the reception room, and ushered them within. "I've asked the servants to turn out your rooms." Apologetically, he indicated a workman, putting up a board over the window. "Unfortunately, the window seems to have been broken."

With a graceful hand, Isabella gestured to a waiting servant. "Tea, please. And the boy is hungry."

"Yes, Your Excellency." Sketching a respectful bow, the man hurried away.

With raised brows, the Captain cast a curious glance at Raike.

"My wife is a royal Grandee," Raike explained. "Rather like a royal duchess, in England."

"Oh," said the Captain in surprise, and then, on reflection, shook his head in disapproval. "I must say, Lady Raike, that the English would never treat a duchess in such a way—unconscionable."

"It is a strange and sorry tale," Raike offered, unwilling to elaborate. "But tell me how you came here; I thought that your Company was at least a day's march away."

"I hesitate to tell you, it is such a fanciful tale." The Captain accepted tea from the servant and then disclosed, "We were warned by a monk in the dead of night."

With a mighty effort, Isabella refrained from looking at her husband.

"A monk?" asked Raike.

"Yes—the fellow said an attack was planned, and that we'd been fed false information. He was so adamant that the sentries woke me up, and I decided I may as well believe him—a man of the cloth, and all."

There was a moment's silence. "He'd better not kill Rochon before I do," remarked Raike in an ominous tone.

"You know this monk?" asked the Captain, raising his brows.

Raike let out a long breath. "Another traitorous son of a bitch. One who has redeemed himself, it seems." He glanced at Isabella, who'd managed to snatch a tart before Eduardo ate the last one. "I will fill you in—as much as I am able—but in the meantime, I think we'd all like to get cleaned up."

Captain stood and gestured to the servant. "Of course—of course; I imagine your rooms are now ready, and we can speak again later."

"I have to go to the chapel, first," Eduardo announced importantly. "I have to pray for the man I killed, and ask for forgiveness. Catalo told me that is what should be done, when the enemy is killed."

Once again, the Captain met Raike's eyes in surprise, but Raike only tilted his head. "That sounds fair."

"Then I will take you," offered Isabella, thinking that such concerns should be encouraged.

"Allow me." Raike took the boy's hand, and the two then left to do their contrition, Eduardo importantly explaining the prayers that needed to be said as the door closed behind them.

As the servant opened the door to escort her to her rooms, Isabella wearily gathered up her skirts, and glided past the Captain. "Good morning, señor."

"Good morning, my lady," he replied, and bowed.

Chapter 48

With rhythmic strokes, the maidservant brushed out Isabella's hair as she sat on a tufted stool by the fire, allowing it to dry. She had bathed and eaten, and found she felt strangely bereft, no longer surrounded by the men with whom she'd traveled, day in and day out, for so many days. On the other hand, it was a fine thing to have a maidservant again—it had been a long, long time since someone else had brushed her hair.

Mesmerized by the fire, her thoughts were interrupted when Raike's voice could be heard from the doorway, "Lady Raike; you are a sight."

The maidservant paused in her ministrations as Isabella lifted her head to smile at him. "Eduardo?"

"He's with Catalo, and Puente and Padilla are with them—they'll all stay in the same room, tonight. Everyone is secure—not to worry." He tossed his hat onto the sumptuous bed. "I give you fair warning; Carristone is a nice place, but it is nothing like this." They'd been assigned to the suite of rooms usually reserved for visiting royals, the lofty canopy threaded in gold, and the appointments lavish and elaborate.

"You mustn't put your hat on the bed, Will-i-am," she chided him. "It is bad luck."

With mock concern, he retrieved the hat to hang it on a chair back. "Is that so? I'd hate to court bad luck."

Unable to help it, she started to laugh, and he laughed in turn, and soon they were both laughing heartily as he strode over to hold her face in both hands and kiss her soundly, taking the brush from the maidservant's hand.

"I'll finish this; you may go."

With a smile, the woman rose and discreetly shut the door behind her.

"You must never cut your hair." He ran the brush through it with one hand, and smoothed it afterward with the other. "That is an order."

"As you wish." She ran her hand lightly along his forearm and—thus prompted— he leaned in, the brush forgotten as he slowly kissed her neck, his breath warm on her skin.

Pausing, he lifted the edge of her robe to glance down at her left breast, which sported an impressive bruise. Using unfamiliar English words, he swore softly.

She stroked him in a soothing fashion. "Better than a wound, surely."

"I am going to hunt him down, and take great joy in cutting that bastard's throat."

"Oh," she said breathlessly, her hands stroking his chest.

With a chuckle, he held her hands in his and pulled, so that she stood. "You'll have to make your own way to the bed, my darling; I don't think I should lift you—not just yet."

"No—we must protect your ribs." She stood on tiptoe to plant kisses on his throat, and impatiently pulled his shirttail from his breeches. "Hurry, Will-i-am—"

A short and very satisfying time later, they lay entwined and exhausted on the sumptuous bed, the bedclothes in a tangle on the floor. "If you can wait a minute," he said, "I should take off my boots."

She chuckled, and he chuckled, and soon they were laughing again. "Everything seems so very amusing, now," she observed, running her hands down his back. "I suppose it is because the danger has passed."

"It's what happens after battle—the men get a little giddy." Carefully lifting himself from her, he sat up to take his boots off. "And everyone wants a woman."

"I can understand this," she said earnestly. "It is the danger, I think—it makes the blood pound in your veins."

He lay back down beside her, and drew her into his arms. "I think I may have to disagree, sweetheart. You wouldn't recognize danger if he walked up and introduced himself."

She shook her head. "No—that is unfair; I dug a rabbit burrow for Eduardo because I saw danger coming—and from a long way off."

"I suppose that's true. So—more correctly—you do recognize danger, but he's the one who should be frightened, not you."

They lay in drowsy contentment for a few minutes, until he asked, "So; what do we do about Catalo?"

With a sigh, she rubbed her face on the side of his chest. "Would you mind, Will-i-am, if he came with Eduardo and me, to recover at Carristone?"

"I could see this coming." His tone was grim as he stared at the elaborate canopy stretched above them. "As I pulled the musket balls out of that son of a bitch, I *knew* he was going to survive, just to foul up my life."

"Eduardo loves him so," she ventured, her fingers moving gently on his abdomen. "And it would be nice to have a priest at hand." Sensing that he was softening, she nuzzled his arm. "He speaks English—or some, at least."

Reminded, Raike said, "There is an English girl who is traveling with the army, here in Spain. Her father was a Colonel in the Third Division—he was killed, recently. She speaks Spanish passably well, and I'll see if I can enlist her to come to Carristone as your interpreter. I feel a bit sorry for her—I don't think she has anywhere else to go."

"I speak English," Isabella insisted. "Good morning. Please. Thanks you. Good eving."

He kissed her temple. "Almost—'Good evening'."

"Mmm." She nuzzled him some more; his skin tasted a little salty from their brief but very satisfactory lovemaking session—truly, when one was raised by nuns, one had *no* idea.

He crooked an elbow behind his head, still making plans. "If Catalo's going with you, I'll have to hire someone to tend to him. Perhaps a physician, or a field medic—there are probably some around here, after the war."

"Catalo is a tough bastard." She nibbled at his earlobe.

Chuckling, he drew her to him. "You do know your English."

"Oh, I know my *Ingles*," she agreed, her hand wandering down his abdomen.

He tilted his head toward her with a soft sound, because he liked what she was doing. "We'll let the Home Office know about Eduardo—or Tomás—which is it to be?"

She paused, thinking it over. "I will ask him—he is old enough to decide."

He teased, "Will you have to curtsey to the floor, now that his identity is no longer a secret?"

Smiling at his ignorance, she replied, "Of course not, Will-i-am; not until he is sixteen. I am a royal Grandee, after all."

Her caresses were having an effect, and gingerly, he rolled atop her, and began to kiss her neck. "And a wife, lest we forget. You are much better at being a wife that a postulant, vixen."

"*Que es* 'vixen'?"

"*Zorra*," he murmured into her throat. "Don't tell my mother I said."

Laughing, she gently ran her hands down his back. "Poor woman—not only will she discover she has a Spanish daughter-in-law, she will be presented with a small boy and a wounded *guerrilla*."

"She will take it in stride, I promise."

"I will miss you," she said softly, her hands stilling.

"And I you." He paused, also. "God willing, the next war won't last very long."

"Do you think—" she ventured, "Do you think we will come back to Spain, soon?"

"As soon as it is safe," he promised. "And as often as you like—I should have made that clear from the first; perhaps we'll buy our own yacht, to go back and forth."

Intrigued with the picture thus presented, she confessed, "That sounds wonderful, Will-i-am; I have never sailed on a boat."

"No, you missed the refugee boat, thank God." He bent to kiss her, gently.

She drew him close. "I'm sorry I spoiled the 'giddy', Will-i-am."

"No matter; I will get it back."

He began to kiss her throat again, and so she sank back into the luxurious bed and sighed with delight; she'd learned that there was no point in trying to gainsay him, when his mind was made up.

Chapter 49

Isabella stood with Eduardo on the docks of Lisbon, watching the many activities that went into preparing a vessel for voyage. They had stayed at the Palacio until Catalo was well enough to travel, and then had been escorted by a contingent of British soldiers to Portugal. The journey down the river was achieved without incident, but with each passing hour Isabella knew that the moment was fast approaching when she would leave her country and her husband behind, and strike out on an unfamiliar new life.

She knew that the journey was necessary—indeed, she had undertaken a similar one when she was twelve years old—but as she watched the routine preparations for the sea voyage, it was easy to believe that they were overreacting; that Napoleon was firmly contained on Elba, and that no one—surely—would threaten a little boy for no better reason than the blood that ran in his veins.

With an inward sigh, she reminded herself that it was this sort of complacent thinking that had led to the fall of King Charles–the unwillingness to recognize the trouble that was brewing, because it was so very inconvenient.

Raike was standing near the gangway, holding a low-voiced conversation with the ship's Captain whilst porters hoisted the cargo aboard the ship.

It turned out that the Colonel's daughter had already left for England, and so Raike had hired Lisabetta, a pretty Portuguese girl who was to act as translator and maid servant. The girl was friendly with Eduardo and seemed genuinely enthusiastic about the journey to England; she'd never been, she said.

Adding to the general noise and confusion, hawkers called from the docks, selling their wares and souvenirs to the passengers as they arrived or departed. As she idly watched the busy scene, Isabella heard one voice in particular, raised a little louder than the others, and– after considering for a moment–took Eduardo's hand, and walked along the docks to come to a halt before a hawker in a hooded tunic. The man was selling wooden bird whistles, laid out in rows upon a mat.

Isabella leaned down to Eduardo, and said near his ear, "I must tell you a secret, *caballero*."

"*Si*?" The boy's gaze strayed to the wooden whistles.

"This man before you is *El Halcon*, the great hero of Spain."

Eyes wide, Eduardo stared at the vendor, who crouched down before him, the man's gaze warm on the boy's face. There was a long, poignant moment, and Isabella felt her throat close with emotion.

"Highness," the man said gruffly. "It has been a long time."

"I am going to be a *guerrilla,* too," Eduardo informed him importantly. "And a priest." He paused for a moment. "And a surgeon."

For a moment, the man could only look upon the boy, the deep creases around his eyes softening. "I am glad to hear it. Would you like a bird whistle?"

While Eduardo eagerly bent to examine the offerings, the man asked, "What is to become of him, *Pajarocita*?"

"He will stay with me until it is safe for him to return— and then the Knights of Malta have offered to foster him."

"The Knights?" The man lifted his brows, and his gaze rested, for a moment, on Catalo, where he stood on the ship's deck, leaning heavily on a cane. "I suppose that would answer."

Isabella decided she should not be surprised that *El Halcon* had penetrated Catalo's deception—the wily old *guerrilla* was a master at misinformation, himself.

"I am told the Knight risked his life, to save the *Infante.*"

Gently, she corrected, "No, *Tio*—he risked his life to save Eduardo. He did not know Eduardo was the *Infante* at the time."

El Halcon nodded thoughtfully. "Perhaps some of Wellington's gold will find its way to these two Knights, instead of to Rochon, who sails for London and hopes to seize it for himself."

Thoroughly alarmed by this statement, Isabella warned, "You must say nothing that I cannot tell my husband, *Tio*."

The old *guerrilla* bowed his head. "I understand; you are a good wife."

They watched Eduardo as the boy came to a decision, and then blew on the whistle, testing it out. The old *guerrilla* then crouched and began to fold up the corners of his mat, gathering in his merchandise, as Isabella took Eduardo's hand. "Be careful, *Tio;* I will remember you in my prayers."

"*Hasta la vista,* Señor." Eduardo said politely. "I am glad to have met you."

"And I you, Highness." With a final, lingering glance at the boy, the *guerrilla* tucked his mat under his arm, and disappeared into the crowd.

"There you are, Isabella," Raike called out. "Come; I'll introduce you to the Captain."

This proved to be a large, affable man with a ginger beard. "Welcome aboard the *Sophia*, my lady," he bowed, an appreciative gleam in his eye.

"And you too, young sir. Perhaps you will join me for dinner tonight; I have need to brush up on my Spanish, and I have stowed some excellent Madeira."

Isabella bowed her head. "With pleasure, Captain."

She could sense her husband's irritation, and as they moved away, Raike leaned in to say, "Best to avoid him; Englishmen are notoriously vulnerable to Spanish eyes."

"I do not think he is *Ingles*," she replied in an even tone, her hand on his arm.

"You don't think he is English?" Raike glanced back at the Captain in surprise. "Then what?"

"I think he is aligned with Catalo—with the Knights of Malta."

Frowning, he considered her. "How do you know this?"

"*El Halcon* was on the docks just now, posing as a vendor; I think he wished a better parting than the one we'd had." She paused. "He knew that Catalo and the Captain were Knights, and he said that Rochon sails for England, seeking Wellington's gold."

Raike stopped in his tracks to stare at her. "Is that so?"

She nodded. "That is what he said, just now."

With an excited exclamation, Eduardo ran ahead of them to Catalo, and as he began demonstrating the bird whistle it occurred to Isabella that someone should probably hide it, for the remainder of the journey

"I'm coming with you," her husband said abruptly.

It was Isabella's turn to be surprised. "Truly?"

"Yes. I'll need to convey this information with all speed."

Unable to help it, she smiled broadly. "It feels very strange to be grateful to Rochon, but I must thank him, it seems."

And Tio, she added silently; *who must have anticipated exactly this reaction when he gave me this information.*

With a quickened step, Raike steered her up the gangplank. "It's just as well; I wasn't certain I'd be able to see you off, when the moment was actually upon me. Thank God I won't face that test."

"And thank God you will be present, to introduce me to your mother."

With a smile, he cautioned, "Don't tell her about the Alcazar."

"I am not so foolish; I will not add to her burdens."

He lifted her hand, to kiss it. "On the contrary, she'll be the only hostess in the shire with a royal Grandee in residence, and no doubt will enjoy it hugely. Although you should try to avoid staring down the local squire; he's a bit puffed-up, and wouldn't handle it well."

With an answering smile, she offered, "I will stay to the orchards, then. As long as there are songbirds—and no hidden treasures—I will be quite content."

As Raike signaled to the Captain, he said, "Speak for yourself, *España;* I have fond memories of finding a hidden treasure in an orchard."

Laughing, she replied, "You are tedious, *Ingles.*"

Made in the USA
Coppell, TX
23 May 2020

26266576R10180